TEMPTING FATE

A KIMBELL TEXAS SWEET ROMANCE

ANGEL S. VANE

BONZAIMOON BOOKS

BONZAI
MOON

BonzaiMoon Books LLC
Houston, Texas
www.bonzaimoonbooks.com

This is a work of fiction. Names, characters, places and incidents either are the product of the authors' imaginations or are used fictitiously, and any resemblance to actual persons, living or dead, business establishments, events, or locales is entirely coincidental.

Your FREE Book is Waiting

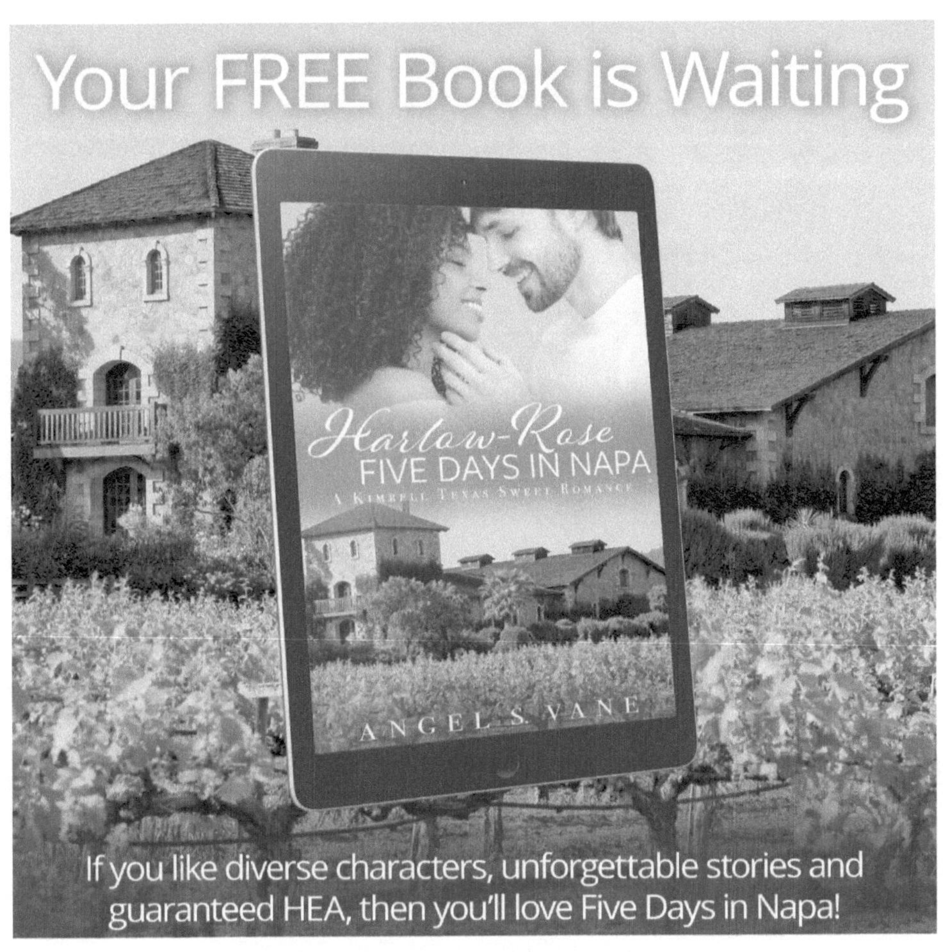

GET MY FREE BOOK NOW

https://BookHip.com/PLWQZRK

CHAPTER 1

S ANTOS

~

It was too late to turn back now.

I run a finger along the neck of my cotton button-down shirt, trying to ease the strangulation of the tie I'm not used to wearing. It only seemed appropriate to dress up after I got the text to meet Victoria Landers at one of the most expensive steakhouses in The Woodlands. My pace quickens as I walk along the sidewalk crowded with happy couples and families meandering under the darkening sky.

To be carefree like them still feels out of reach.

But maybe tonight will be the breakthrough I've been hoping for.

Why would Victoria ask to meet me if she didn't have good news?

Life-changing news.

Pausing as a raucous group of drunk businessmen stumble through the doorway, I grab the heavy wooden door and walk inside the cool air-conditioning of the restaurant. It reeks of money and prestige. The kind of place I don't belong.

"Wow, you clean up well." Victoria's voice floats from behind me.

I turn slowly and size her up in one quick glance. The red mini-dress hangs off her thin, bony frame, and she teeters on stiletto heels. Her face is overdone with dark red lipstick and smoky shadow on her eyes. She's not unattractive, per se, just not my type. At all. Yet, I get the sense she's trying to be, which is disturbing.

I'm not here for a date.

I want to know if she can get me the loan I need.

Victoria runs a hand through her limp, brown tresses and steps toward me.

I lean over and give her a half hug. "Thanks. I was surprised to get your text to meet you here." I raise an eyebrow as I glance around the mahogany walls of the entrance to the restaurant.

"Hopefully, the place gave you a hint that there could be something to celebrate." Victoria gives me a wide grin then loops her arm in mine.

We step forward to the hostess desk and then are whisked through the restaurant to a prominent table in the back that overlooks the rippling waters of the lake outside.

Settling into my seat, I rub my now sweating palms against my slacks and wonder how long she will drag out the suspense. She has to know I'm about to lose it, wondering if I'm getting the loan.

Victoria rests her elbows on the table and leans toward me. "How was the drive? Not too bad, I hope."

"No big deal," I say, running a hand absently through my unruly curls. After being turned down by dozens of banks, I'd gotten a referral to Creek Forest Bank by Luke and Ronan, two buddies of mine working at the Kimbell Fire Station. They both thought that going with a small, family-owned bank might be the way to get the relief I needed. Large banks only focus on the numbers and statistics, which I fail spectacularly. Smaller banks have significant resources and care about their clients. They will listen to the story behind the need and factor that into their decision to give a loan.

"Good." She winks at me. "I actually live here and commute up to Creek Forest, so that's one of the reasons I suggested this place."

"And the other?" I hold my breath. Two days ago, I'd sat across from Victoria, the Vice President of Loan Operations, and completely bared my soul. I hoped that hearing my story would convince her I was worth taking a chance on despite my lack of assets and credit score in the toilet. She'd been non-committal, giving me appropriate sympathy but not offering any help … until the text today.

"To celebrate. It took some heavy wrangling, given your credit situation, but we will be able to provide a loan to meet your needs."

My mouth drops open, but no words come out.

Did I hear her correctly?

"So, you'll loan me part of—"

"Not part." Her smile turns slightly seductive. "I can loan you the full amount, but there will be some … unique conditions."

My attention is drawn to the feel of her bare foot stroking slowly up my calf to my knee, then settling against my inner thigh. A spike of rage courses through my veins. I force myself not to glare at her. To keep my expression neutral.

"What kind of conditions?" I ask, managing to smile. I watch as she almost melts in front of me, excitement filling her dull, blue eyes.

"Excuse me." The waiter, who'd been lingering back from the table for several minutes, approaches.

Victoria shrieks, her foot falling to the floor as she glances over at the man dressed in the all-white uniform. She looks like a kid who's been caught with her hand in the cookie jar.

The waiter hands a wine list to Victoria and me, then asks, "Would you like a recommendation?"

Victoria looks nervous, her eyes downcast as she responds. "Yes, please. I prefer reds, something robust."

I lay the wine list onto the table, not bothering to look it over. My mind races through my options. I know exactly the unique conditions Victoria is attaching to the loan. Just another example of the rich using their influence and power to take what they want from the poor and desperate.

Forget ethics and morals.

She's attracted to me. A fact I guess I knew from the moment I stepped into her office. I wanted a fair shot at a loan. I was upfront and forthcoming about my predicament and how I ended up drowning in debt that was about to bankrupt me. Not once did it cross my mind to manipulate her using charm and my looks.

Now it's clear that Victoria has different plans. She sees the loan as a bargaining chip to get what she really wants. She thinks I'll do anything to get the loan.

No doubt, I need the money.

Bad.

But am I willing to sleep with her for cash?

That's a hard no.

I suck in a sharp breath as Victoria rambles on about the type of wine she'd like. Devastation slowly replaces my anger. To be this close and yet feel forced to turn down the cash sours my stomach.

"I think I have something that you'll adore," the waiter says, his eyes lighting up. "We have a limited quantity of one of the most sought-after wines this year. It is an international multi-award winning Cabernet Sauvignon from Harlow Rose Winery out of the—"

"Harlow … Rose?" I stammer, now completely focused on the conversation between the waiter and Victoria. A flutter of excitement shoots through my heart that I don't bother to ignore. I haven't heard her name spoken in almost two years other than in my thoughts.

"Yes, sir. It is divine."

"Have you heard of the winery? Is it any good?" Victoria asks.

I nod my head, not trusting myself to speak.

"Would you like a taste?" The waiter asks.

"Please," I say, my mouth suddenly dry.

"It's been selling fast. Let me see if we have any left." The waiter dashes away from the table.

Instinctively, I rub a hand along my upper bicep, where the tattoo is hidden by my sleeve. It could be a coincidence, but I know that isn't likely. Still, I want to see the bottle to be sure.

Every ounce of my strength funnels to keeping the onslaught of memories of Harlow Rose from dominating my thoughts. There's still the matter of Victoria, the loan, and her indecent proposal. But I can't deal with that now.

Not until I see the label of the wine bottle.

Questions linger in my heart about the week I spent with Harlow. If she remembered me after I was long gone. If those days had meant as much to her as they had to me. If she wanted to keep a part of what we shared alive in some tangible way, just as I did.

I'd know soon enough.

For better, or worse.

The thought settles within me like a heavy weight.

"I never imagined you'd be a wine drinker," Victoria says, twirling strands of her hair between her fingers. Her head tilts to the side as she stares at me.

"I'm not," I mutter, then pause. Except for that one week with Harlow. The one time when exploring the various types of wine had been the only thing I wanted to do with her by my side. I clarify, "I'm not a regular wine drinker, but I do enjoy a cab every once in a while."

Cabernet Sauvignon is Harlow's favorite. I could never forget that.

Victoria says, "Me too. Looks like we have that in common. I have quite the collection in my wine cellar at home. Maybe we could try some together—"

"This is our last bottle," the waiter interrupts, stepping toward the end of the cloth-covered table. He turns the bottle toward us.

In an instant, all the air is forced from my lungs. I'm sucker punched as I stare at the label, a dark red rectangle on the black bottle. Inside the rectangle is the letter H hovering near the bottom. The outer line of the letter extends upward into the shape of an abstract rose, all emblazoned in gold.

My hand involuntarily flexes, and I'm transported right back to the restaurant in Napa Valley, leaning over the table to shrink the distance between myself and Harlow. The frustration furrowing her brows had been too cute for me to resist. All I wanted was to solve the problem she'd been dealing with.

Grabbing a broken pencil from the pocket of my jeans, I sketched my vision for her winery logo onto a crinkled napkin. My fingers moved quickly as if on auto-pilot, pouring emotions I didn't want to categorize into the lines. After a few minutes, I was done. I turned the paper to face her.

"It's … " Harlow traced the design with the tip of her fingernail, then gazed up at me with her intensely beautiful dark brown eyes. "Perfect."

No, you are perfect. Everything you make me feel is perfect, I thought but stopped myself from saying the words. Instead, I pretended that her reaction hadn't meant the world to me.

"I'm thinking you invert the colors from what you were planning," I said, tapping on the drawing. "Everybody expects the rose to be red. What about gold and make the background red. It'll be more eye-catching that way."

She reached across the table and grabbed my hands, lacing her fingers within mine.

"Santos," Harlow whispered.

"Yeah?"

"It's like you read my mind, my heart, and my passion for the winery. I'm stunned."

I leaned forward, brushing my lips against the back of her hands in a gentle kiss. Her exhale sent a shiver down my spine. I knew exactly what she was thinking. What she was feeling. But knew better than to say it out loud for fear of losing it.

"I have to pay you for this," Harlow said, breaking the electricity charging between us.

"It's yours. I don't need your money," I said, even though that wasn't the truth.

But she didn't know that.

The man she thought I was didn't have a financial care in the world. I was her equal in every way—education, money, experiences. I wasn't going to do anything to make her think otherwise. To ruin the connection that intoxicated me every time we were together. She'd brought me back from the brink of darkness, showing me that light and hope still existed in the world. That it was worth getting my act together to be worthy of a woman like her, even if I could never have her.

Crossing my arms over my chest, I gave her a sly grin. "Who knows if you'll actually use it. I'm sure the companies you're meeting with this afternoon will come up with something better."

Harlow raised an eyebrow but didn't respond.

The fog of memories dissipates as my eyes travel from the waiter to the bottle in his hand.

I reach for it and rub a finger over the label, unable to control the deep sense of longing bubbling within me to see Harlow again.

"The logo is stunning," Victoria says, then takes a sip. "But it's nothing compared to the wine. This is amazing. It has a fruity sweetness and no hard edges. Very smooth palate. Hints of vanilla, spicy oak, and a tinge of sweet tobacco. I'm beyond impressed."

The waiter looks pleased, then turns toward me. "Sir?"

"The lady's recommendation is enough for me," I say.

Victoria adds, "We'll take the last bottle."

"Very good," the waiter says, then pours wine into both of our glasses. "Would you like to hear our specials?"

"Can we get some bread and a few minutes before ordering?" Impatience creeps into Victoria's voice as she tries to usher the waiter away.

"Of course."

Her eyes settle onto mine as she reaches into her purse and pulls out a set of documents. She places them on the table. "Now, where were we?"

"The loan and the unique conditions," I say, unable to hide the edge in my tone. I wonder how many times had she manipulated some poor guy into a relationship with her influence at the bank.

"Don't look so serious." She laughs then takes another sip of the wine.

Harlow's wine.

Harlow is just as rich and privileged as Victoria, but I can't imagine that Harlow would ever do something this despicable. Her sweetness and optimism were infectious. Harlow was about uplifting people to be their best, not exploiting weaknesses for her own gain like Victoria.

"I promise, you'll find the conditions to be easy and enjoyable."

My cell phone vibrates in my pocket as a series of shrill beeps fill the air.

"What's that? Is everything okay?"

I grab the phone and glance at the name on the screen—Byron Magee. Getting a call from the Deputy Chief of the Lasso County Fire Marshal's Office only means one thing.

"I'm sorry. I have to go." I push back from the table. "It's work. We'll have to finish this some other time."

I rush through the restaurant toward the entrance as I press the answer button on my phone.

"What's going on?"

"Two-alarm fire at the Elm Street Brewery," Byron barks in my ear. "Lots of suspicious items noted already. Looks like arson. I need you to get over there now."

"In Kimbell?"

"Look, I know you'd rather not step foot back in that place, but I need you to do your job. It's an order."

I sigh, knowing Byron is right. "I'm on my way."

CHAPTER 2

H*ARLOW-ROSE*

~

RESTING MY HANDS ON THE NEW WROUGHT IRON GATE,
I finally allow myself to smile with pride.

I stifle a squeal.

Is this really my life?

I hold my arm out toward Mr. Ruiz as he checks the lock.

"Oh, now you want me to pinch you?" He chuckles, then slaps
my hand away. "I'm guessing you're pleased with the results."

"It's stunning." I walk toward the gate and run a finger along
the outline of the "H" painted gold. It sparkles under the bright
headlights of Mr. Ruiz's truck. I slide my finger along the edges of
the logo, working up the side of the "H" to the stem of the rose.

"Thanks for working late to get it done," I say, surprised by the emotion welling in my voice. "Opening the winery to the public for the first time tomorrow is huge for me. I want everything to be perfect."

"And it will be, Ms. Robinson," Mr. Ruiz gives me a warm smile. "You deserve all this success. Your hard work and dedication paid off big time."

Hard work is an understatement.

Since I moved from Napa Valley two years ago, my personal life has been on pause. Every waking moment, I live and breathe the vineyards, the winery, and the production of seven varieties of wine. When I released my inaugural production a year ago, I had no clue what was in store for me. I wanted the world to take notice, but what happened shattered even my wildest dreams. Instantly, I became the newest overnight winery success. In reality, this moment was seven years in the making, but the articles on my small Texas Hill Country winery gloss over that fact every time.

A giggle escapes my lips as I press my forehead against the logo.

"Mark my words, that logo will be a tourist photo op in no time. That rose is special. It's simple and sweet, yet complex and abstract, kinda like its owner. Whoever designed it did a fine job," Mr. Ruiz says, giving my arm a gentle squeeze. "I'm going to check out a few things before I head home. You want to head on up to the house? I can lock up out here."

"Thanks," I say, then make a mental note to send an extra tip to Mr. Ruiz and his team. Pressing the keypad on the gate, I watch as the latch slowly opens. I walk along the crushed gravel of the parking lot toward my home away from home.

The modern mission-style architecture crafted in limestone is illuminated in soft, warm light, paying homage to my family's brewery in Kimbell. It has a quintessential Texas flare that perfectly captures my winery's essence. Stepping under the covered portico, I open the wooden doors purchased from an abandoned 19th-century monastery in Mexico and enter the space.

Glancing around, I rifle through a mental checklist and confirm everything is ready for tomorrow. The vineyard and winery tours sold out months ago. I have ample bottles for hundreds of tastings. A partnership with a local restaurant in downtown Fredericksburg will supply the charcuterie and chocolates until I can get the onsite restaurant up and running. There's nothing left for me to do but wait the twelve hours until we open.

I lock the doors behind me then take the stone stairs up to the second floor to my living quarters. I step into the open space of my living room. To the left is a small kitchenette, an office nook, and next to it, a door leads to the bathroom. To the right, another door leads to the bedroom. It's simple and cozy and lacks my normal luxurious creature-comforts, but it works for what I need. A place with minimal distractions to allow me to focus all my attention on making this winery a success.

Slipping out of my shoes, I toss my purse onto the couch and head into the bedroom. The anticipation about tomorrow is exhilarating and exhausting.

Collapsing onto the bed, I close my eyes and take a deep breath.

Before I have a moment to relax, the soft melodic cellphone ringtone fills the air. Groaning, I force myself off the comfortable mattress and grab the phone from my purse.

"Hey you," I say.

"So, how do you feel?" Zaire asks, a hint of excitement in her voice. If there's anyone who knows how big of a moment this is for me, it's one of my oldest and dearest friends. Zaire is no stranger to launching a successful company. Her real estate and interior design services have been the top in Lasso County for years.

"Nervous." I curl my legs under me as I plop back down on the bed.

"Good answer. If you weren't, then something would be terribly wrong," Zaire says, then exhales softly. "You've come a long way. I hope you're as proud of yourself as we all are of you."

The journey was long but well worth all of the ups and downs. Purchasing an abandoned winery in a fire sale right after college had seemed like a risky move. Doubling down to get my masters in viticulture and enology helped me focus on what it would take to be a successful winemaker, but I knew it wouldn't be easy.

"Sometimes I feel like I was more lucky than good," I admit. "Landing that apprenticeship in Napa Valley was such a long shot, but I was the one selected out of the hundreds that applied."

"Because you are smarter and more ambitious than you ever give yourself credit for, Harlow-Rose. You deserved every break you got. Not just working those three years under one of the top retired winemakers in the world, but then to land another year-long mentorship with the current winemaker at Robert Mondavi takes a lot more than luck. You are talented and passionate about wines, and everyone can see that."

"You're great for my ego," I tease, then lean back onto the bed. "Seriously, though. I learned everything I needed to know about vineyards in Napa, but how to run a successful business I learned from you."

"We women business owners have to stick together," Zaire says.

She was never one to flaunt her own corporate prowess and

excellence, but I had seen first hand what a shrewd businesswoman Zaire could be. It was Zaire who'd helped me buy this property for a fraction of the value when it had gone into foreclosure all those years ago. I literally owed my success to her.

"Did you get the wine I shipped to you?"

"I'm drinking a glass of the international award-winning cab right now. Care to join me?"

Leaning over, I grab my own bottle underneath the bedside table and pop the cork. "Don't mind if I do." I pour the dark liquid into a wine glass and take a sip. A warmth oozes through me, and I feel giddy. This wine was my creation, and now it is being enjoyed by thousands of people worldwide.

"Despite your reservations, I'm glad Napa Guy convinced you to focus on the winery and stop worrying about working at your dad's brewery."

I almost choke on the wine going down my throat, sputtering as I manage to sit the glass back on the bedside table. As if on cue, thoughts of the handsome man fill my mind. The dark unruly curls that I stroked my fingers through. The honey eyes that bore into mine with an intense and undeniable longing. The strong arms that wrapped around me, making me feel like the most beautiful woman in the world. Why did she have to mention Napa Guy? The last thing I need is to be reminded of him.

Zaire laughs out loud. "You alright over there?"

"I'm good," I manage to get out between a few more coughs.

"When was the last time you thought of him?"

"Who?"

"Girl, please. Napa Guy."

I glance at the clock and count. Five hours ago, as Mr. Ruiz and his crew were finishing up the gate, I allowed myself to get lost in the memories of the first time I met him.

The President of Mexico and his family were on vacation in California and had secured a private, two-day event at the Mondavi winery. On the last night, they celebrated with a large party complete with the most expensive wines, a catered dinner, and a live performance by Ariana Grande.

I worked the room providing private wine tasting of vintage bottles of Mondavi wines for hours. Midnight approached, and the family showed no signs of winding down, but I was exhausted. Steeling away from the crowd, I walked toward one of the smaller courtyards and noticed a man standing alone along the edge, staring out toward the rolling hills. The dark night sky twinkled with stars, and the moonlight cast an intriguing glow upon him.

I recognized him immediately.

One of the bartenders pointed him out earlier as the nephew of the President. A man most in the family believed would follow in his uncle's footsteps to become a political powerhouse and ultimately make his own run for the presidency in the next couple of decades. His wine preferences had been noted on the cards provided to me. I quickly slipped them out of my purse and looked through them until I found the one with his name on it.

S. Briceño Alvarez - prefers robust reds, private tasting recommendation is the 2018 Reserve Cabernet Sauvignon

Without taking my eyes off of him, I slipped behind the outdoor bar and grabbed the prestigious wine, two wine glasses, and headed his way.

He stared at the moon in deep concentration. His face was ruggedly handsome and unforgettable. The kind of handsome that sears into your memory and makes you do a double or triple take to convince yourself that what you saw is real. Yet, there was a relaxed and down-to-earth vibe that I hadn't detected from the President's other family members. The combination was wickedly attractive, and I gave myself permission to stare at the full length of him.

Sexy, unruly mahogany curls framed deep tanned skin. His broad, muscular physique was impossible to be ignored under his tailored, expensive suit.

Before I knew it, he was staring at me, staring at him.

A playful hint in those intoxicating honey eyes had me reeling. My legs turned to jelly. I was at a loss of what to do next.

"Hola." His deep voice was like a soft caress floating on the wind across my skin. I felt dizzy being so close to him.

I kicked myself for taking French instead of Spanish at Excelsior Prep. I'd grown up in Texas, for God's sake. Why hadn't I learned a language that would be a lot more useful to me? Sure, the French had come in handy as I toured wineries in France during the summers, but it wasn't doing anything to help me right now. Nothing that would impress a future Mexican dignitary.

Responding as I had over the past two days and fully expecting that his answer would be 'yes,' I asked, "Habla usted Inglés?"

"Si, hablo Inglés muy bien."

I laughed. "You do, but you're choosing not to with me, is that it?"

He gave me the sexiest grin that was my undoing, then pointed to the bottle in my hand. "What do you have there?"

"The only wine worth tasting … Mondavi's Reserve Cabernet Sauvignon."

"Is it your favorite?" He asked, a challenge in his gaze.

"For now," I said. One day, I wanted my own wine to be my favorite and the world's. But I kept that little nugget to myself.

I poured the wine into one of the glasses, then pressed it toward him. He eased the glass from my hand. His touch left a blazing trail of heat across my skin.

"Won't you join me?"

"I really shouldn't." I took a quick glance behind me. We were all alone, tucked away in this small corner as if it had been specifically reserved for us.

"You would really rob me of the chance to enjoy an amazing wine with a breathtakingly beautiful woman? That's cruel," he said with a wink.

Breathtakingly beautiful?

He could not be talking about me. Could he? I mean, I'm no troll, and I'm pretty cute most days. But, breathtaking? Beautiful?

How could a man who looks like him think that about me?

"I'm not a cruel person," I said, glancing behind me again.

"Prove it." He slipped the bottle of wine from my hand and poured the empty glass full. Resting the bottle on the table, he lifted the glass and extended it toward me.

Careful not to brush his hand, I grabbed the glass from his and asked, "What should we drink to?"

"Breathtakingly beautiful women … of course."

I laughed.

"That smile is devastating. Are you doing this on purpose?"

"Doing what?"

The intensity of his stare lured me. My gaze dropped to his lips as the urge to kiss him became overwhelming. I'd never felt such an immediate and powerful attraction to a man in my life. I looked away, trying to break the trance I found myself in.

"Making me want to spend more time with you," he said.

"Well, that's not possible since you'll be heading to Lake Tahoe tomorrow for the next part of the vacation, right?"

"I guess that leaves tonight … Ms.?"

"Harlow-Rose."

"Lovely name." He took a sip of wine, his eyes never leaving mine, then added, "I'm Santos. Care to spend this last night in paradise with me?"

Zaire clears her throat. "Let me guess, you zoned out into a Napa Guy fantasy."

"No, I did not," I lie, my voice hitting a higher octave than normal. I could never tell Zaire the truth about this. She'd launch into another lecture on how I need to call up the President of Mexico's office and find a way to get in touch with his nephew. Throw caution to the wind and try to reconnect with the man who'd given me one of the most thrilling, romantic, and intense weeks of my life. But, I know me. It's not something that I'd ever do. My life is in Texas with this winery, and his is building a political career in Mexico. "To answer your question, it's been a while. I have been busy getting ready to open up this place for tours and tastings."

"Yeah, right. Tell that to someone who doesn't know you as well as I do."

A sharp beep comes from my phone, signaling another incoming call. I glance at the screen and see Mom's face staring back at me. Why am I not surprised that she's checking in … again … to make sure I'm ready for the grand opening tomorrow. I'd spent most of the morning and early afternoon going through a myriad of final to-dos with my perfectionist mother. As annoyed as I pretended to be, I feel more confident and ready for everything because of Mom's relentless attention to detail.

Thankful for the interruption, I say, "Hey, my mom is calling. I'll check back with you tomorrow after we close."

"Alrighty. Tell your mom I said hi."

"Will do." Swiping the screen, I disconnect from Zaire and answer the incoming call. "Hey, what did I forget?"

"Harlow-Rose." Mom's voice is tense and measured, sending ice slithering through my veins.

"What's wrong, Mom?"

"There's no easy way to say this," Mom says, then exhales heavily. "And I will tell you, but Harlow-Rose, you must promise me that you will go through with your grand opening tomorrow. Nothing that I tell you tonight should change your plans."

"Are you trying to freak me out?" My heart pounds in my chest as every worst-case scenario shuffles through my brain.

"No, but I have bad news. The brewery is on fire."

There it is with no preamble, no sugar coating, no warning.

I grip the phone tighter in my hand. "Our brewery?" A sob catches in my throat, but I know better than to let my voice show any emotion. "Elm Street Brewery?"

"Yes, Harlow-Rose," Mom says, a tinge of annoyance in her tone. "The firefighters have been trying to put it out for over an hour now, but it is still burning."

"Oh God," My hands tremble as I struggle to process what I'm hearing. Through the phone, I hear the low wail of sirens and the crackling sounds of the blaze. "Are you there now? Is everyone safe? I can get on the road in about thirty minutes—"

"You will do no such thing. There's nothing you can do by coming tonight. No one was hurt in the fire. Your father is getting regular updates from the firefighters, and we'll know more once they put the fire out."

"But I need to be there with y'all."

"Your father and I both agree that your grand opening can't be ruined by this. You will come tomorrow night after you've wrapped up the events at the winery. I'll have your room ready for you."

"Are you sure?" I ask.

"Of course, I'm sure," Mom says as if she's insulted. "Now get in the bed and get some rest. You'll need it for all the guests arriving tomorrow."

"Okay."

"And Harlow-Rose?"

"Yeah."

"Be amazing. We're proud of you."

CHAPTER 3

S *ANTOS*

~

T HE AUTOMATIC SLIDING DOORS CLOSE BEHIND ME with a resounding click, causing my muscles to tense. Rooted to the spot inside the emergency room, my eyes dart back and forth, taking in the sight that is still too familiar to me.

The place is nearly empty, but a frenetic energy and sense of urgency still permeate the air. Patients move slowly along the intersecting hallways, some with bandaged body parts and others limping, favoring whatever ache or pain brought them in.

The low murmur of dozens of conversations bounces off the walls as nurses wearing pale blue scrubs stationed at a central circular desk answer questions and direct people to different areas of the hospital. St. Elizabeth's Medical Center is the largest hospital in Lasso County and serves several neighboring counties between Houston and Austin. It's where the worst of the worse cases are brought to receive top-notch medical care to most.

Just not to the one that mattered most to me.

"Hey, you okay?"

I jump, then close my eyes for a moment, trying to force the anger away.

Turning, I stare into the concerned green eyes of Luke Diamond. "Yeah, I'm fine."

My words don't convince him or me.

"I'm surprised to see you here," Luke says, running a hand through his blonde hair. "Is this the first time you've been back since—"

"It is. Byron got it in his head that I'm the best choice to investigate the suspicious fire at the brewery, so here I am."

"How nice of him." Luke sighs, then beckons for me to follow him into a sitting area behind the nurses' station. We pass a woman reading a Harry Potter book to a child in a low, animated tone and ease behind a family near tears, huddled in a circle praying.

Luke plops down on a beat-up recliner in the corner of the open space. "So, Ronan thinks this could be arson?"

I nod my head, ignoring the dark coffee stains on the armrests and the worn seat cushion, and sit down across from him. "They aren't close to putting the fire out yet, though. So, I thought I'd head over here and get a jump start on the interviews. You alright?"

"This was unnecessary. I should be back at the brewery fighting the blaze with the guys, but you know Ronan."

I do know Ronan O'Reilly all too well. Long before he became the A-Shift Captain at the Kimbell Fire Station, we were college roommates for four years at the University of Texas at San Antonio. He's like a brother to me. "Better to be safe than sorry. I take it the docs here cleared you."

"Yeah, I spent some time getting oxygen, then they said I could go."

"But you're still hanging around?"

"Nate's still here."

"Asthma?"

"He always pulls through, but it was bad back there. I'm not leaving until I know he's out of the woods."

"I don't know Nate that well, but I'm guessing he's going to give you hell for sticking around and worrying about him."

"I can take it. We both have formidable best friends from college, don't we?" Luke manages a chuckle as he leans back in the recliner chair.

"Tell me about it," I say, remembering the tirade I'd heard from Ronan as I drove to Kimbell. He was more pissed than I am that Byron assigned me to this case, but part of me realizes it's time to find a way to put the past behind me. I have a job to do, and it's no secret that I run the more complex arson cases for Lasso County. Why should that change because of what happened in Kimbell two years ago?

We fall into a comfortable silence, and I'm content to hang in the waiting room with Luke until he gets news about Nate. I'm not in the right headspace to interview the three people rescued from the burning building anyway. I focus my attention on the television in the corner as Luke texts on his cell phone.

A replay of the Channel 4 breaking news covering the brewery fire comes on the screen.

"What the ... is that you Luke?" I ask, watching as the firefighter appears on the screen next to reporter Ciara Thompson, a native of Kimbell. It's no surprise that the station sent her down to cover the story.

A flush of red blazes across Luke's cheeks then disappears quickly. He squeezes the bridge of his nose and looks away from the television. As the interview progresses, I can see why. When it's over, I turn to him. "You and Ciara got something going on?"

"No!" Luke barks, shaking his head. "It was a standard interview. Nothing more."

I raise an eyebrow. "That's not what it looked like to me. Some major sparks were going off between the two of you."

"I don't even know her. I mean, it was the first time I'd met her in person."

"But you want to get to know her better."

"I didn't say that. She ambushed me, and I did the interview to be nice. It lasted a few minutes, and then I was off in the ambulance with Nate to come here," Luke says.

He's rambling, which tells me one thing. Luke is very interested in Ciara Thompson, and I can definitely see why. The camera loves her. She's more than a little pretty and has a great body with a dynamite personality to match. I could see them making a love connection if Luke got out of his own way, but I don't tell him that.

If anyone knows how it feels to fight feelings for someone out of reach, it's me. Memories of Harlow float through my mind. Every part of me wants to whip out my cell phone and do a quick internet search on her winery. I want to find out everything about her now that I know she'd made her business a success.

Who am I kidding?

I want to know if she's still single.

Not that I have a chance with her now any more than I had two years ago.

But a guy can dream a bit, especially when I'm back in the place that she helped me escape. Even if it was only for one week. Memories of the time I shared with Harlow were the only thing that kept me uplifted over the next devastating year of my life.

I push the thoughts away and focus on Luke, who is still trying to convince himself that he doesn't have a thing for Ciara.

"Wait, did you say she covered the firefighter calendar, too?"

"She did," Luke says. "And before you jump on the bandwagon that Wiley is driving, it doesn't matter one bit that she showed my month during her segment."

I laugh out loud thinking about what the jokester, Wiley Alexander, would do with information about Luke having an interest in Ciara Thompson.

Luke continues, "That was a coincidence. I'm sure if you'd done the calendar like the committee has been begging you to, she would've focused on your month instead."

"I'm not pimping myself for a calendar. I don't care how many years they try to convince me to do it," I say, shaking my head.

"It's for a good cause. The Kimbell Community Center fund could get up to fifty thousand dollars in proceeds because of me being in that calendar."

"Why would I want to do anything to help Kimbell?"

"Of course, it wouldn't be the one I picked, but whatever charity of your choosing."

"I'm not that charitable. I've spent most of my life being the charity case." Tension claws along my neck. I'm still a charity case, begging a bank Vice President for a loan to get myself out of mountains of debt only to realize what she'd want in return. "That hasn't changed."

"What happened with Creek Forest Bank?" Luke asks, raising up to face me.

"I can get the loan if I sleep with Victoria," I mutter.

"You're lying."

"I wish I was."

"Well, that ain't happening. I'm sure we can figure out another way to get you a loan. Just need to put our heads together," Luke says.

"And until then, you want to give your statement about the fire?" I ask, ready to be done with discussing my dismal life.

"Let's do it."

CHAPTER 4

S *ANTOS*

~

Locals meander through the westside of downtown Kimbell to pay their respects to the loss of a long-time, historic landmark—Elm Street Brewery. The success of the many beers produced here had put the town on the map.

Now it was gone.

From what I can see, it's a total loss.

"You miss it?" Ronan asks as he steps around a burnt and charred remnant of one of the back walls of the brewery that toppled to the ground during the fire.

I tear my eyes away from the crowd lingering outside the chain-link fence surrounding the brewery and pause, considering the question. I'd spent years being on the front line, fighting fires as part of the San Antonio Fire Department before making the switch to become an arson investigator.

Life had forced me to make the change.

"No," I finally answer. "But I do have to work harder to keep my sexy physique."

Ronan rolls his eyes and makes a gagging motion.

I chuckle. "That's a small price to pay for the work. It's interesting and challenging. I'm surprised you didn't make the change, you know after …"

I stop the words before they come out. I don't want to remind Ronan of the worst moment of his life like I don't want anyone reminding me of mine.

"I thought about it, but this is in my blood," Ronan says, seemingly not fussed about my faux pas. "I can't imagine doing anything else. Plus, the schedule actually works for raising my boys. One day on, two days off limits how much I have to juggle getting daycare and babysitters."

"How are your little hellions?" I ask, thinking of the O'Reilly twins, Finnegan and Declan, who unfortunately look exactly like their deadbeat mom. I couldn't imagine how hard it is for Ronan to look into two little faces that remind him of the woman who ripped his heart to shreds.

Pride swells in Ronan's face. "Well, they were pretty upset that Daddy didn't come and pick them up this morning because he had to spend the day working with Uncle Santos."

"You threw me under the bus?" I glare at him, stunned.

"I wasn't taking the hit for that. I'm their hero, remember."

"Alright, well, let's wrap this up so you can get on home to them," I say, then glance down at the notes I'd taken with my team as we launched our investigation. Eight hours on-site, and there was more than enough cause for concern that the fire wasn't simply an unfortunate accident.

"Did you review Gary's notes on what I told him?"

"A few times," I say, then point to an area of rubble cluttered on the grass between the brewery and the corporate building. "So that was a covered walkway that led to the production areas?"

"Yes. It housed air ducts that would've connected the entire complex. Not just the corporate offices, but to the beer garden and restaurant too."

"We saw signs of a faulty or broken silo in the brewery," I say, surveying the war zone that was once Elm Street Brewery. "Not sure yet if it contained grains or malt, but it doesn't really matter. Either could let out enough flammable dust clouds to cause a chain reaction of explosions."

"The employees had been offsite at their annual corporate retreat. No one was inside the brewery to detect the situation and stop it from destroying everything," Ronan says, crossing his arms over his chest. "Every 9-1-1 call mentioned sounds like bombs going off at the brewery, then seeing the fire balls shooting up into the sky."

Everything Ronan is telling me lines up with my interviews at the hospital last night. The three individuals rescued from the fire basically gave the same statement. They'd returned to take care of some work that each felt couldn't wait until the next day, although none of it seemed time-sensitive to me.

"Fire was called in by several local businesses?"

Ronan nods and gives me the approximate times of the calls. "I gave the names to Gary, so y'all can interview them."

"What can you tell me about the owners?" I ask, then scan my notes for their names. Usually, in these cases, the owners have hit a rough patch and decide to torch their business to get out of financial trouble. "Scott and Qingyang Robinson. Any reason why they would've set their business on fire?"

"No, they're good people."

I glance up at Ronan, giving him my best skeptical look. "Are they rich?"

"Very."

"Then my money is on them being behind this some kind of way," I say. Experience has taught me that rich people pull every lever within their disposal to manipulate situations to their advantage. Arson is one of their favorites.

Ronan shakes his head. "This place was Scott's whole life. I can't imagine he'd ever do anything to destroy it, even if he was in some kind of trouble. Plus, he and Old Man Bell are thick as thieves. Bell wouldn't let him suffer financially."

"What about someone who has it out for him? Any chance of that?"

"My money is on Joe Little," Ronan says, squatting down to pluck a dainty white flower that survived the fire. "He was the former CFO of the brewery and a real bad actor. His wife left him a month ago after years of emotional abuse. Then a week later, he was fired from the brewery after working side by side with Scott for over twenty-five years."

"Timing is interesting, but that doesn't necessarily turn someone into a fire starter."

"After Joe was fired, he stalked Scott to Thorn Restaurant over on Lake Lasso and started a big argument. Several witnesses heard Joe tell Scott that he would make him regret firing him. He would blow his whole world up."

"Blow his world up? He used those exact words?"

"It's in the police report filed by Scott when he sought a

restraining order to keep Joe away from his family and his business."

"Where is Joe Little now?"

"That's just it. No one has seen him since the argument at Thorn."

Small town drama and intrigue never ceases to amaze me. At least this gives me a lead to start on.

"Need me for anything else?" Ronan asks, rubbing his fingers across his bloodshot eyes.

"No, man. Go get your boys and go on home. You look like crap."

"Trust me, I feel worse." Ronan slaps a hand on my back. "Let's grab dinner before my next shift. I know being back here is hard for you."

"Sounds like a plan." I take a deep breath, then let it out slowly as Ronan walks across the singed lawn. There's no point in dredging up the past. No reason for me to make this town the villain because of what happened to my father.

I got what I wanted.

Justice had been served.

I need to let it go.

Turning back toward the corporate offices, I approach the one area that was most disturbing in the whole scene. The spot that had triggered the request for me to be here in the first place.

The blaze pattern in this office defied all logic if the dust explosion had spread the fire from the brewery through the air ducts to the other buildings on the property. This office that once had been Joe Little's. The burn pattern was definitively from the bottom up and toward the air duct, not down from it.

Gary had gathered hundreds of samples from the area to send to the lab. If an accelerant had been used to spark the blaze in the office, we'd find out. But if Joe Little was behind this, why would he be so careless to start the fire in his old office? It doesn't make sense, but revenge could push people to do stupid things.

Slipping my tablet back into my backpack, I decide to call it a day. I'd sent Gary and our assistant back to the hotel an hour ago. There was no point in me staying longer. We had a lot of evidence to get through, and the case wouldn't get solved in a day.

I walk away from the charred wreckage and exit the chain-linked gate, securing the lock closed. Goosebumps pepper my skin as an unusually chilled breeze whips through the trees. It only lasts for a moment, but it's enough to make the hairs on my neck stand on end. I glance behind me, senses acutely attuned to the surroundings, but see no one suspicious there.

I got to get it together.

Turning the corner from Elm Street to Main Street, I stroll past the glass windows of various businesses—a car repair shop, beauty salon, a florist, a woman's clothing store. On the opposite side, wooden benches line the wide sidewalk. Next to them are large kiln-fired clay pots emblazoned with the town crest and overflowing with Texas wildflowers.

As the sun sets, the lights from the antique street lamps come on, and the area bustles with more people. Restaurants come alive with a good number of customers already packed inside. Turning my head, I watch the cars driving down the street as I walk by the ever-popular Salsa Warehouse and then Baker Bros, where live conversations pour through the open windows of the barbecue restaurant.

I'm staying on the opposite end of Main Street at Crockett Manor, a bed and breakfast housed in one of the oldest mansions in Kimbell. This morning, I walked over to the brewery when the town was still asleep. Now, as I navigate back through the crowds alone, I regret that foolish decision.

I have no desire to mingle with the people in this town. No desire for any of them to recognize me. Some would ask how I'm doing, looking at me with pity in their eyes. Others would glare at me or go further and demand to know how I could think about coming back. Neither option is one I look forward to experiencing.

Stopping at Peach Street, I wait for the light to change then pick up my pace. Only a few more blocks, but I can't stop myself from getting distracted by Elevation Cupcake Shop. Known more for the outstanding variety of unique desserts and less for the dry and uninspired cupcakes, I slow down to peer through the glass window at the decadent desserts. The menu changes daily at the owner's whim to keep patrons coming back frequently.

I'm a sucker for chocolate in any form. I resign myself to grab a treat, then run it off later tonight after the crowds leave downtown. My gaze rakes over the pastries, truffles, and cakes until I see what I was hoping for—mini-chocolate tarts piled on a glittering platter near the far end.

I glance up from the display case and grow rigid.

A rush of adrenaline floods my body, and my heart pounds in my chest. My eyes lock on a woman inside the shop. I stare straight into her beautiful, dark brown eyes. Her thick hair has grown, the curly ends reaching the top of her shoulders. The strands are tucked behind her ears, revealing a stunning heart-shaped face, cute, flared nose, and thick, luscious lips.

I drink in the sight of her as she stares back at me.

Deja vu hits me like a freight train.

Only the glass window separates us.

It's definitely her.

Harlow Rose.

CHAPTER 5

ARLOW-ROSE

"SANTOS?"

I stare out the window at the man perusing the pastry display.

His chocolate brown, unruly curls are shorter than I remember. A hint of a beard covers his chiseled jaw. The broad, muscular chest and massive arms trigger memories of how it felt to be enveloped in his embrace. This man is gorgeous.

But there's no way he could be Santos.

Could he?

He glances up, and our eyes meet.

My breath catches in my throat.

Those eyes, the color of the sweetest, natural honey, stare back at me.

Panic races through my veins. I look down at the box of mooncakes trembling in my grasp.

Am I seeing things?

Santos has no reason to be on Main Street in Kimbell, Texas, of all places.

There's nothing here that would lure the nephew of the President of Mexico for a visit.

But he is here.

Looking into his gorgeous eyes proves that I'm not hallucinating.

Santos is in Kimbell.

My mind is a jumbled mess of confused thoughts.

What am I supposed to do?

Should I go outside and say something to him?

Pretend like I don't recognize him?

Let him go about his business and not bother him?

When he left Napa Valley, we knew we'd never see each other again.

He lives in Mexico City.

He thought my life was in California.

I hadn't bothered to clarify that the foreclosed winery I'd purchased was actually back home in Texas. None of that had mattered at the time. We were both leaving Napa and going back to our real lives. The fantasy, the fairytale, had come to an end.

After returning home, I was riddled with regret for not suggesting that we keep in touch. I'm no fan of long-distance relationships because they'd never worked for me in the past. Yet, somewhere deep inside, I'd wondered if it would be different with Santos.

We could've tried to make it work, flying to see each other every few weeks. Expensive but not impossible. We both had enough money to make it work. That wasn't what stopped me.

I was worried about what would happen as we grew closer.

Moving to Mexico City wasn't an option.

My home, my family, and my winery are here in Texas. It's the only place I want to be.

Santos wouldn't have walked away from his political aspirations in Mexico. We didn't need to talk about it for me to know that was true. Something important was calling him back to his home, distracting him during the amazing time we were sharing together. There was nothing I could've said or done to stop him. Nor would I have wanted to stand in the way of what was important to him.

If we'd tried to forge ahead with some kind of relationship, it would've been a disaster. Over time, an unavoidable strain would've festered, killing the spark, the intense chemistry, and the deep connection that existed between us. Even worse, we would've shattered each other's hearts when we realized that a life together wasn't possible.

What was the use of setting ourselves up for heartbreak?

We both knew it.

That's why neither of us discussed a future beyond that one unforgettable week.

It had been the right thing to do.

Question is, what's the right thing to do now that Santos is standing on Main Street in my hometown?

There's no way I can ignore him.

I have too many questions.

And an insatiable desire to be near him again.

I take a deep breath and glance up.

Santos is gone.

Whipping around, I slam into a strong, imposing, muscular body. The box of mooncakes with assorted fillings of lotus paste, green tea, and cream cheese skitter across the mosaic tile floor.

Strong arms brace me from toppling over.

I hear the familiar sound of a deep, cocky baritone.

"Whoa, slow down there."

"Nathan," I say, shocked to see him. I clench his rock-hard arms to steady myself.

"Good to see you, Harlow-Rose. Even though I wish it was under better circumstances," Nathan "Nate" Bell says, flashing me a smile that would make girls around the world fan themselves.

I hesitate, looking beyond him toward the glass doors of the shop. Hoping that Santos has come inside to see me. To talk to me. A steady stream of people, couples and families, roam outside, but there is no sign of him.

He vanished.

Stifling my disappointment, I turn my attention back to Nate. "Me too. Sorry for running into you."

"It's okay. I'm sure you're in a hurry to see your folks," Nate reaches down to grab a couple of the mooncakes that rest near his feet and tosses them in the trash. He turns toward the counter and calls out to the worker behind the counter. "Can you get another dozen mooncakes and put it on my card?"

She gives a quick nod and a smile, then disappears into the back.

"You don't have to do that."

"I want to," Nate says, squeezing my hand. The generosity and support touch me, and I smile up at him. "Plus, I like getting extra points with your mom. Never know when it could come in handy."

"As if you need them. She loves you to death," I say, moaning under my breath. Mom never misses an opportunity to push me to rekindle my relationship with Nate. Doesn't matter that it's been years since we were a couple all throughout high school. In her mind, she is rooting for a Robinson-Bell union. Since Nate and I have been single for a while, it only makes sense for us to reconnect.

"I love your family, too. That'll never change."

"Were you there last night? At the brewery?" I ask. For some reason that no one in the town understands, Nate has doubled down on his commitment to be a volunteer firefighter in Kimbell, working his shift while holding down the corporate job his family expects of him. I wonder if he could give me some details on what happened.

"I was initially. It was a tough blaze to get under control. Two alarms. We called in crews from all the neighboring towns for help," Nate says, then drags a hand down his face. "Few people were trapped inside—"

I gasp. "Please tell me they got out okay."

"Luke and I went in and rescued them before the whole roof collapsed in the main building."

"You went into the burning building? Nate, you can't do that. Your asthma."

"Tell me about it, but I wasn't letting Luke go in there alone. I spent the night in the E.R. for my good deed."

"I'm glad everyone got out okay, especially you and Luke," I say. Hearing the seriousness of the blaze is sobering. With my grand opening earlier in the day, I had an excuse to avoid all the news reports about the fire. The thought of seeing the brewery that I'd grown up in burned and destroyed was something I wasn't ready for.

"My parents were there last night, right? Did you see them?"

"No, but I heard from Wiley and Darren this morning that your dad was really torn up, especially once he found out it could be arson."

"Arson?"

The young woman interrupts, holding a fresh box of mooncakes out toward me. "Here you go. It's on the house."

"Thanks," I mutter and grab the box. I lower my voice and lean closer toward Nate. "Are you saying that someone set our brewery on fire on purpose?"

"Ronan picked up on quite a few suspicious areas as soon as we arrived. He called the Lasso County Fire Marshal's Office to get an arson investigator out here as soon as possible. I'm not sure what exactly tipped him off, but he was concerned enough to make the call pretty fast."

"Who would do that to us? Destroy my family's business. It's cruel."

Nate places his hand on my elbow and steers me toward a table away from the door as a family with three raucous kids burst inside. I ease down onto the stool.

"Rumors are flying around town that it was Joe Little," Nate says, then sits down across from me.

"That's ridiculous. Joe has been Dad's CFO for over twenty-five years. They're friends. He'd never betray Dad like that."

Nate looks away.

"What is it? What don't I know?"

"Your dad fired Joe Little a few weeks ago. It was within weeks from when Joe's wife left him, too."

"What?" I screech. The family and the three kids pause in their antics to look our way. I lower my voice, embarrassed by my outburst. "I didn't know that. Why wouldn't Dad have told me?"

Nate rests his hands on top of mine. "Come on, you can't be surprised that he kept this from you. If the fire hadn't been all over the news, I doubt your folks would've told you about it either."

"What are you talking about? My parents and I have a great relationship. They don't hide things from me."

"You're their princess."

"Don't start with the beer princess crap."

Nate scrunches his face, then smiles. "You're kinda the queen of wines now."

"Seriously?"

He nods his head and tries to stop laughing. "You were promoted."

"I can't believe this." I roll my eyes.

"Harlow, you know your parents adore you. You're their pride and joy. They've sheltered you from bad things your whole life. I don't blame them. When we were together, I did the same thing. You always see the good in every person and every situation, so we don't want you to see or experience the bad."

"I can handle bad news. I'm not fragile. I won't break." I say, annoyed by the pity that crosses Nate's face.

"When have you ever had to deal with a major life challenge or obstacle? Tell me."

"How about the run-down vineyard that I bought, then found out the soil needed to be completely recultivated if I ever had a hope of getting grapes to grow in it."

"You mean the vineyard you bought after graduating from Stanford with passive income from the dot com you invested your college fund money in since you'd secured a full scholarship to Stanford. That vineyard?"

My mouth gapes open.

"And when that little challenge popped up, you hired a slew of soil experts to do the job while you traipsed off to grad school. The land was ready for planting around the same time you got your masters. Perfect timing, too, since you were about to kick off a highly sought after three-year apprenticeship with a renowned winemaker in Napa."

"Nate!"

"I'm not done," he says with a laugh.

"Yes, you are." My skin flushes with heat, and I chew on my bottom lip. Was Nate, right? Had I lived a sheltered and privileged life without the stresses that most people faced?

Nate strokes a finger along my cheek and rests it under my chin. "I'm sorry. Didn't mean to call you out like that."

"This coming from the heir of the family that founded this town and has billions of dollars," I counter. "How many times have you had to deal with real disappointment?"

"More than you'll ever know," Nate says, a seriousness infecting him.

I pause, staring at him. My mind races to know what he isn't saying. What hurt he could be hiding that I missed all these years. He doesn't say another word. In seconds, the melancholy is gone, and he's back to his cocky self.

"You're too hot to walk these streets alone after dark. Want me to escort you? I'll beat up any guy who tries to hit on you along the way."

I laugh out loud. "That won't be necessary. My car is parked across the street." I stand and reach for the box of mooncakes. "Good seeing you, Nate."

Nate slips a hand around my wrist, stopping me from walking away. "If this thing with the fire gets bad, promise you'll call me. I'll do whatever it takes to help you."

"Thanks," I say, as fear creeps through me for the first time. Something tells me I will be taking Nate up on that offer.

45

CHAPTER 6

Gasping for breath, I collapse onto the porch steps that lead to the front of Crockett Manor. Sweat drips along my hairline, down my face, and plops onto the wooden planks. My heart pounds from the exertion. The mad dash sprint of over a mile.

What is wrong with me?

Did I really run away from Elevation Cupcake Shop like the devil was after me?

And for what?

Because I'd seen Harlow.

God, I'd seen Harlow.

For the first time in two years, I'd been mere feet from her.

She wasn't in my dreams. She was really here. I wanted to burst through the doors of the cupcake shop and slip my arms around her. Hold her close to me. Recapture the feel of her curves against my body. Kiss the lips I'd missed kissing for two years.

She was more beautiful than I remembered.

Her thick, tight curly hair rose like a halo around her exquisite face. She'd dyed it a subtle shade of copper that complemented her warm, brown skin. Her eyes had locked onto mine, paralyzing me. Her lashes fluttered as she seemed to struggle with comprehending that it really was me standing outside the cupcake shop.

When she looked down, I took off running before realizing what I was doing. Weaving through the crowds arriving on Main Street for dinner, I pressed to put distance between Harlow and me.

The more I thought of her, the faster I pushed myself. The streets passed in a blur until I recognized Poplar Street. Dodging and darting through the cars at the stop light, I kept my pace and headed straight to the bed and breakfast.

"Santos, dios mío, what happened? Is someone after you? Are you hurt?" Alma drops to her chubby knees to check me for injuries. Her hands press against my arms and chest efficiently. "Speak to me! Are you shot?"

"No," I say, stopping her roaming hands. "Nothing is wrong with me."

Alma's eyes are wide, full of fear and distrust.

It wasn't exactly the truth, but I didn't feel like explaining why I'd taken the coward's route. Why I'd run away from Harlow when for the past two years, all I'd wanted was to run back to her.

"Then why were you running so fast in your work clothes?

You'll get blisters all over your feet in those shoes. Tell me, what's going on?"

"Just trying to get back here to see you," I say, flashing her my best smile as my breathing finally returns to normal.

Alma glares at me. Her large chest heaving as she gives me a look that means she's not buying what I'm selling. "The adorable smile of yours isn't reaching your eyes. I know something is wrong. But I won't push you to tell me before you're ready."

She stands and holds out a hand toward me.

I place my hand in hers and stand.

I tower over her. Leaning down, I wrap my arms around her in a big bear hug. She returns my embrace with fierceness.

"You don't know how happy I was to hear that you'd be back in town. I canceled a couple of reservations to make sure you and your team could have rooms here with me for the next couple of weeks," Alma says. "I was worried when they came back without you, but they said you were catching up with Ronan."

"We'd put in more than a full day, so they deserved to take off early. Tomorrow will be another long day." I loop my arm in hers and help her ascend the three wide wooden steps, freshly painted a glossy white.

"I'm hoping that the investigation won't take long," I say.

"The quicker you find Joe Little, the quicker you'll be able to arrest him for burning up our brewery," Alma says, shaking her head. "That man has some nerve to be so petty and vindictive. Mr. Robinson didn't deserve that after everything he'd done for Joe Little. But I'm hoping he hides out, so you'll stick around for a bit. Have you gone to see your father recently?"

Alma opens the door to Crockett Manor and walks inside. I step over the threshold and pause to admire the grandeur of the old house built over a hundred years ago. I say, "Not since last year."

"You should go. I was there a couple of weekends ago. They do a beautiful job up keeping the grounds, and they placed lilies in the vase on the headstone," Alma says as she leads me through the parlor past two flowered sofas arranged in front of the fireplace. "I paid my respects to your mother, too. Looks like she got the man in the end, but I still cherish the amount of time I got to share with Tito."

When Papi had first been diagnosed, he was referred to St. Elizabeth's in Lasso County for treatment. It hadn't taken the man very long to stumble across Alma in Bell Park and fall head over heels in love. Papi was a natural flirt and swept Alma off her feet. I was happy that he'd had someone he cared for deeply to support him in what would be the last years of his life. It had made all the difference in the world until the one day it hadn't.

"After the investigation, I'll drive down, and you can come with me," I say, hoping she'll take me up on the offer. The last time I'd gone to San Antonio to visit Papi's grave, it had been much harder than I thought. Wrecked me for weeks as I struggled with the simmering anger that still hadn't completely gone away. With Alma by my side, she could help me focus on the good times and not how Papi's life ended.

"It's a date," Alma says and squeezes my hand.

We pass through another sitting area filled with landscape paintings of iconic parts of Kimbell hanging on the dark mahogany walls. Walls the same color as Harlow's stunning eyes. We pass by the dining room where Gary and the assistant are having dinner— lasagna, baked ziti, and Caesar salad. I give them a quick wave but don't linger. The music room is on the opposite side, filled with a grand piano and a harp settled in opposite corners. Alma makes several more turns then leads me into the massive kitchen.

"Have a seat."

I do as I'm told, then ask, "I heard mean, old Mrs. Crockett has been put into Oakbrook. What does that mean for you?"

Papi and Alma had both worked for the widowed millionaire in exchange for room and board and a salary that was embarrassing.

"Don't call her mean. She was always good to Tito and me. Don't ever forget that." Alma pokes a finger against my chest. "This place earns too much money for the family. They aren't going to sell it, even though none of her kids want it. The lawyers have hired a management company to run the place now. Mrs. Crockett left specific instructions that I could continue to stay here and work as the cook and housekeeper for as long as I want."

"I guess that was nice of her," I mumble under my breath.

"Get this. When it all transitioned, the fancy lawyers from Houston came down and gave me a raise. Something about fair compensation, non-discrimination, and ranges of salaries for positions at other bed and breakfasts across the state," Alma explains. "I didn't really understand what all that meant, but when I saw my new salary, I knew it was very good news."

"I hate that Papi worked nonstop to keep the landscaping to her impossible standards and didn't live long enough to receive fair compensation. All he got was a chance to live in a raggedy rundown shack in the woods by the lake." Why he was so proud of that place, I'll never understand.

"What would you like for dinner, mijo?" Alma says, ignoring my venting. She has an uncanny way of diffusing my anger before it festers and distracts me for hours. "I know Italian food is not your favorite."

"Tamales?" I ask, noticing the smell of the dish in the air. I hope she's made a special batch for me like she used to after Papi died.

"Good choice," Alma says, then turns to open the upper oven. She pulls out a pan filled with fresh tamales. "Speaking of Tito's house. Why haven't you gone out there to pack up his things? Don't you think it's about time?"

"Was kinda hoping you'd do it for me."

"If I haven't done it in two years, you should've taken the hint and gone out there yourself," Alma chides.

It's one more thing I've avoided since Papi's funeral. I can't bring myself to go back to the place Papi had called home. I don't want to be reminded again of losing the only family I have left in the world. "Can't be much out there anyway. I can hire a company to clean it out if the Crockett family wants to use it again."

"They aren't interested in that land or the house, even though they should be. Zaire Kincaid's fancy real estate business is buying up a bunch of property around the lake to have luxury lake houses built. They could make a lot of money from that land."

Alma heaps a plate full of tamales then pours gravy on them. Dipping her fingers in a bucket of shredded cheese, she sprinkles a bit on the tamales then places the food in front of me.

My mouth waters, and I quickly dig my fork in. The spices and flavors erupt in my mouth, instantly comforting me.

"Is good?"

"Muy bueno," I respond. Alma grabs a Topo Chico and places it next to my plate. I'd much rather my father's favorite vodka, but I keep that to myself. Alma wouldn't let me indulge anyway.

"So, tell me about the girl."

I nearly spit the food out of my mouth, shocked by Alma's abrupt change in topic. "What ... girl?"

"The one who had you running like a bat out of hell back to

Crockett Manor," Alma says, a knowing look on her face. "Who is she?"

"Doesn't matter."

"What happened between the two of you?"

I stuff my mouth with more tamales to buy some time. Alma has an annoying ability to read me, figure out what I'm thinking, and force me to talk about it, whether I want to or not. Some days, I'm grateful for her skills. Other days, like today, I wish she would mind her own business.

I grab the mineral water and take a long gulp.

Alma is patient with a pleasant look on her face that says, "I fed you a special meal. Now you owe me information."

I place my hand on the table, lean back in the chair, and give in. "Do you remember the trip I took to California a couple of years ago?"

"Of course. You were so lost after your father's funeral. When you told me you were going away to clear your head, I knew that was the best move for you," Alma says. "But I was amazed at how much you'd changed when you got back. It was like something had revived you. You were finally able to push past your grief and try to live again."

"Not something. Someone."

"Interesting. Tell me more."

"It's a long story, but I met her the first day I got to Napa Valley. We clicked, connected on a level that I'd never connected with anyone before. I spent the entire week with her, and it was amazing."

"What happened after you got back home?"

"Nothing," I say. "We went back to our lives before we knew each other."

"You didn't keep in touch?"

"No."

"That's crazy. The two of you could have at least tried."

"I think about that all the time, but it would never have worked."

"Why?"

"Because I lied to her. When I got to Napa, I didn't want to be Santos Estrada anymore. I wanted the loneliness and the sadness to go away, even if for a short time. So, I pretended to be someone I wasn't, and it snowballed. By the end of the week, I couldn't get out of the lies. It was easier to walk away. If she knew who I really was, she wouldn't have wanted to try a long-distance relationship with me. It was better this way."

"You should give yourself more credit. The Santos Estrada I know is worth his weight in gold. Any woman should be honored to have you in her life."

"You're biased."

"So, what. Now tell me what happened today. Did she call you out of the blue?"

"I saw her … here … in Kimbell."

"No!"

"Yes."

"No!"

"Yes."

"No!" Alma bangs on the table. "Santos, it's a sign. Your job forces you to come back to this place that's been a source of pain for you for so long, and when you get here, you see the one woman who brought you joy in the midst of your grief. It's fate."

"It is not fate. I have to figure out what she's doing in a small Texas town, though. It's strange."

"You didn't say anything to her when you saw her?"

"No. She was inside Elevation Cupcake Shop, and I was outside looking at the desserts through the window."

"Well, you need to go back there. See if she's still hanging around Main Street and speak to her."

"I can't. I'm not who she thinks I am. She doesn't know the real me."

"Are you sure about that?"

"Yes," I insist. "What would be the point? I'm not going to set myself up to be disappointed because of my own lies. Better to not say anything to her at all."

"But what if you're meant to see her again? Be with her again? Isn't it worth a try?" Alma presses. "I'm sure if you explain to her everything you were going through and why you misrepresented yourself, she might understand. She might want a chance to spend more time with you."

"Trust me, we're from different worlds. It's better this way."

An alarm sounds on the timer.

"Tiramisu is ready. I need to put this out for the other guests," Alma says. She takes a massive tray filled with the decadent dessert from the refrigerator. "I'll be back in a few. Finish your tamales. I have a piece of tres leches with your name on it."

I smile then watch her walk out of the kitchen.

All this talk about Harlow has me anxious to discover what she could be doing in Kimbell. There weren't any wineries in Lasso County or any reasons I could think of for her to make a trip to this town. It shouldn't be on her radar.

Slipping my cell phone from my back pocket, I access the internet and type in "Harlow Rose Winery." In less than a second, the website for her business appears as the first link in the search results.

A short description is on the page beneath the link.

Harlow-Rose Winery founded seven years ago in Fredericksburg, Texas. Come enjoy our award-winning wines, now open for tours and tastings.

I curse under my breath and slam the phone down.

She's been here this whole time, and I never knew it.

CHAPTER 7

 ARLOW-ROSE

"WHY DID YOU BUY MORE MOONCAKES?" MOM GLARES AT me as I pass by, without trying to hide her exasperation. She is adorable in her 'Kiss the Cook' apron and her bone-straight black hair pulled into a low ponytail secured with a chopstick.

"Because Dad texted me and told me he'd finished off the last dozen you bought, and I thought it might lift his spirits," I say, then lean over to give her a quick kiss on the head before placing the box in front of my beaming father.

Mom can't fault me for indulging him.

From the food spread across the kitchen table, she is doing the same thing. A platter overflows with Northern Chinese comfort food—spicy lamb skewers, pork dumplings, and barbecue beef buns. Mom stirs the contents of an oversized pot resting on the back burner of the industrial stove. From the smell, I know without a doubt it's her lamb noodle soup. My stomach churns in anticipation of devouring it once it's ready.

Food has always brought comfort to my family.

There's no greater time when we all need to be comforted than now.

Dad stands and walks toward me. He's wearing a red polo shirt that fits snug around his beer belly and Dockers. I meet him halfway as he pulls me into a tight hug. It's only been a couple of weeks since I last saw him at my winery, but he's aged ten years. He looks weathered and worn, the lines etched in his face deeper than I remember. I'm thankful to still see a hint of the spark in his blue eyes as he smiles at me. Despite everything that's happened, my dad is resilient. I know this.

"I'm so glad you're here," he whispers into my hair. "How was the drive?" He asks, a bit louder where Mom can hear. We walk back to the table.

I shrug, then ease down into a chair next to his. "Fine."

"What took you so long?" Mom asks, giving me a steely gaze. "And don't tell me you were late getting here because of those mooncakes from Elevation."

"Well, that is the reason," I say, grabbing one of the fluffy, soft buns. I take a bite and moan with satisfaction from the amazing flavors. "I would've been here earlier if I hadn't run into your favorite person."

Mom turns around with a bright smile. Out of the corner of my eye, I see Dad frown. They couldn't be further apart on their views of Nate Bell.

"How is my darling, Nate?"

"He's good," I say, although I'm not entirely sure. Our entire conversation was about the brewery fire, but I got the sense something heavier was weighing on Nate. "We caught up, and he told me he was working last night. He helped save some employees from the fire."

Dad rubs a hand over his receding hairline. "I'm thankful no one got hurt. It's devastating to see what's left of my brewery … or rather how little that's left."

I reach out and squeeze his hand. "We're going to get through this. I can help out to make sure production can start back up as soon as possible."

"Rosie, I don't need your money."

"Dad, I want to help." Everything I have now, I owe to him and Mom. If they hadn't adopted me, I'm not sure what kind of life I would have. But I doubt it would've been as good as the one they gave me.

"I'm serious, Rosie. That's what insurance is for. All I need is you, right here. Having you around for support means more than anything."

"Well, operations at the vineyard are doing good, and I can stay here during the week. I do want to go back on the weekends since we're kicking off our tours and tastings, though."

"How was it today? I heard a news crew from Austin came down for it," Mom says.

I fill them in on the grand opening, number of visitors, sales figures, and the free publicity I got from a reporter that loves my wine. "Tours are sold out for the next two months. I want to expand and open up more days, but I really want to wait until I get the restaurant going."

"Don't rush it. People like scarcity, and it's going to make them want your wines even more," Dad says, beaming with pride.

"That's going to work for you, too, Dad. People are already buying out Elm Beer in the stores since the fire. As soon as production starts back up, you'll get a boost in sales and get back everything you're losing now during the shutdown."

Dad grows quiet and picks at a skewer of meat before popping a piece into his mouth. Maybe it's too soon to start talking about rebuilding the brewery, especially with the arson investigation looming. I'm not sure if I should bring it up since my parents seem to be determined to keep me in the dark, at least for now. What I can't understand is why? They must know I'll find out sooner rather than later. The insurance money that Dad needs won't be released until the investigation is complete, and that could take weeks or months. I really want to do more to help, but he doesn't seem open to it at all.

"I can't think about that until the investigation is over," Dad finally says, then glances up at Mom. She gives him a reassuring nod then turns her focus back to her soup.

He says, "They think it was … arson."

"Yeah, that's what Nate told me," I admit.

Dad looks relieved that someone else has broken the news to me.

"He says they suspect Joe Little did it," I say, then pause.

"Joe and I parted ways a couple of weeks ago, and it wasn't amicable," Dad says, rubbing a hand down his jaw. "Still, I've known that man for most of my life. I can't see him doing anything like this to me. I don't care how upset he is."

"What happened? Why did you fire him?" I ask, curiosity getting the better of me.

"Joe was beginning to forget that the brewery is my company, not his. At the end of the day, I decide on the direction we should take. I thought that was clear, but I found out otherwise. So it was time for us to part ways," Dad says with a finality that made it clear that was all he was going to say about the situation.

"Scott has his interview with the arson investigator on Tuesday morning. Harlow-Rose, you can drive us over and sit with me while we wait for him," Mom says.

I check for Dad's reaction to her suggestion. He nods his head at me, approving the idea. "Of course, I can do that."

"And it'll give you a chance to see Nate again. I'm sure he'll be there."

"Enough with the matchmaking, Qianyang," Dad huffs, then stands from the table. "Come on, Rosie. Let's go play a game of pool while your mom finishes up dinner."

Dad slips an arm around my shoulder and guides me upstairs to the game room. I can tell the weight of the fire and losing his business is a drain on him emotionally and physically.

He leans on the edge of the pool table and grabs my hands.

"You want to talk about it?" I ask.

"Actually, no. I need a distraction and not the 'let's push my only child back together with that slacker Nate Bell' kind."

I laugh. "Dad, Nate's not a bad guy."

"No, he's not for someone else's daughter. Just not mine," Dad says, then narrows his eyes as he looks at me. "Please tell me you're not thinking about giving that guy another shot."

"We are just friends, and that's the way we both want it to be."

"So what is going on with your love life? I swear, I watch you working on that vineyard, and you remind me of myself. I lived, ate, and breathed that brewery to the exclusion of everything else."

"Until you met Mom."

"Until David hired your mom to be the Head of Excelsior Prep. If it wasn't for that, I'd probably be a lonely old fool. I still remember the day he brought her around to taste the best beer in Texas."

"Love at first sight, right?"

"Only on my end. I had to work hard to get her to give me a second look. It was three months later before I convinced her to go on a date, and I could show her the error of her ways."

I smile, imagining what they must have been like before I was born.

Dad says, "Sometimes you need help from fate to show you what you need in your life."

"You think so?" I think of Santos. He's in Kimbell. For the first time in years, I know where he is. With a few phone calls, I could probably find out where he's staying and why he's here, but I haven't made those calls, and I'm not sure why.

"What's going on, Rosie? You got a new man in your life?"

"Not exactly."

Dad perks up. "Tell me."

"Remember the guy I met in Napa a couple of years ago."

"Yeah, you really liked him. He was the one related to the President of Mexico and had political aspirations of his own."

"That's the one," I say, not surprised that Dad remembers Santos. I had gushed about him for months after I came home, knowing that there was no chance for me to have a relationship with him. "He's in Kimbell."

Dad frowns now. "Why?"

"I don't know."

"Think maybe he came here looking for you?"

A flutter ripples through my chest. The thought hadn't crossed my mind. At all. But could Dad be right? And if Santos is here to see me, why didn't he come inside the cupcake shop to talk to me?

"No," I shake my head. "He didn't know my real name. He thought my last name was Rose."

"He didn't have to know that to find you. Your name is pretty unique, even if he didn't know you are a Robinson. With your winery getting so much attention, maybe he's passing through town on his way to Fredericksburg. You know, to see you."

"Were you always this hopeless of a romantic?"

"I want my girl to be happy professionally and personally. You need to find him and see if the spark is still there between the two of you. Your life can't be the winery all the time. You need to make time for finding love, too."

"What if he's not interested in me anymore, and I make a fool of myself?"

"What's worse? Knowing or wondering for the rest of your life?"

"Wise man, you are," I say, leaning into his embrace.

CHAPTER 8

ARLOW-ROSE

"How long has it been? Two hours now?" I stand up from the couch for the hundredth time in the past hour and walk toward the cabinet, stretching the length of the back wall. In the far corner, a variety of snacks, coffees, and teas rest in a basket next to cans of soda and a coffee machine. Reaching for one of the coffee pods in the basket, I pick it up and contemplate if I should really drink a third cup. My nerves are shot as it is.

"Put that away. Get a bottle of water," Mom says, ending my internal debate. She pauses typing on her cell phone to glance up at the clock behind me. "It's been a little over two hours."

"I don't know how you can work at a time like this."

"Because Excelsior Prep pays me to ensure that every child gets a superior education, Harlow-Rose. That doesn't stop just because we're going through a family crisis. Have you checked in with the vineyard?"

"They know to text me if they need me," I say, dropping the pod. Reaching for a bottle of water, I twist the cap off and take a sip. The lukewarm liquid almost causes me to gag. This was not at all how I expected the morning to go. Nate had been here when we arrived and made it seem like the interviews would be quick. A formality while they continued to try to track down Joe Little, the unofficial prime suspect. Why were we still here hours later?

"Your interview only took thirty minutes. Why would they need to talk to Dad for so long?"

Mom lowers her phone and looks at me, her expression passive. Her smooth, alabaster skin is without a wrinkle or concern—due to her regular botox treatments. I've seen that look on Mom's face too many times to count. Armageddon could be brewing, and Qianyang Robinson would never let anyone see her sweat. It was a quality I usually admired, but right now, it seemed cold.

Here I am on the verge of breaking down, cycling through worst-case scenarios of what could be going on behind the door of the interview room. But that's my own unfounded speculation and conjecture. There's no indication that anything is wrong. How many times had Mom told me to focus on the facts? Don't be rash. Think things through. Pause before acting. Be smart, not emotional.

"If you would calm down and think rationally, you'd recognize that Scott would have tons more relevant information to share about the brewery than me. He built the business and works there every day. I'm not involved in the company at all," Mom says.

"You're not worried that the interview has gone on for hours?"

"If there's anything that your dad knows that can help them figure out who destroyed his business, then I'm fine with him talking to them all day, if necessary."

I slump against the cabinet, realizing Mom is right. Crossing the room, I sit next to her and lean my head on her shoulder. "Sorry for being a brat."

"Try not to make a habit of it."

I chuckle. "I'll see what I can do."

"Let's talk about something else. How's the lake house coming along?"

"Slow," I say. It's been a few days since I got an update from Zaire, and I make a mental note to go by her office and check-in at some point this week. "Tile was completed in the bathrooms, kitchen, and laundry room, so that's good progress."

"Any chance you can move in early? I hate that you're living in that cramped space above your winery. My girl deserves better than that."

"It's not so bad, and no, more like I'll be moving in a few weeks later than scheduled—"

A knock raps on the door, then a man pokes his head inside. He's one of the investigators we met when we arrived, Officer Gary Logan. He's a forgettable-looking man with kind eyes. "Sorry to interrupt. We're wrapping up with Mr. Robinson now, and we'd like to interview you next."

He looks directly at me.

"Why would you need to talk to my daughter?" Mom asks, her cheeks blazing a deep pink as she bolts up from the couch and stands between the officer and me.

"She is part of the family that owns the brewery—"

"I don't work for the brewery. I haven't since I was in high school," I explain, but that doesn't seem to matter to Officer Logan.

"Harlow-Rose has her own very successful winery in Fredericksburg that's not affiliated in any way with Elm Street Brewery," Mom adds. "You'd be wasting your time and my daughter's by questioning her."

"While all of that may be true, Ms. Robinson would inherit the brewery if anything were to happen to you or Mr. Robinson. Because of that fact, we consider her part of the ownership structure and would like to interview her." Gary gives us a forced smile. "It's just a formality."

But something in the way he says it makes it clear it's not a formality. They think I could know something about the fire, and I'm not sure why. Resisting the interview would probably do more harm than good. I rise from the couch and stand by Mom's side.

"It's okay," I say, resting an arm around her. "This shouldn't take long."

Mom stares daggers at the officer as I follow him out of the waiting room. We walk down a long hallway painted a dull white. There are no pictures on the walls. Only a series of closed doors with small plaques next to each, denoting a room number. Officer Logan stops at the last door on the right and steps aside. "You can go on in. Officer Estrada is waiting for you."

I take a deep breath, surprised by the jolt of nervousness that courses through my body. Stepping over the threshold, I feel like I've run into a brick wall and sputter to a clumsy stop. The man sitting at the conference table across from me sends jolts blazing through my veins.

Santos?

I exhale a shaky breath and try to force my legs to move, but they don't obey. I drink in the sight of him as he types quickly on a laptop resting in front of him on the table.

My pulse quickens, and I can't tear my eyes away from him.

How could this be? None of this makes any sense.

He finally looks up at me.

A bolt of energy sizzles between us, causing my legs to turn to mush. I reach for the chair that's a little too far in front of me and stumble before gripping my hands on the back of it.

Those dreamy, honey brown eyes bare into my soul.

Only a few feet separate us, but without the glass like there'd been at Elevation Cupcake Shop last night.

My hands ache from squeezing the cushioned back of the chair.

How could he still be so handsome? Or even more devastatingly so?

I size him up. He's wearing a crisp button-down white shirt with the sleeves pushed up above his elbows, showing his strong muscular arms. The smell of his cologne wafts toward me, hurtling me back to memories of Napa. Memories of only inches separating us as we lay underneath the golden sun and talked for hours.

"Ms. Robinson, please have a seat," Santos says.

Neither his expression nor his voice registers any recognition of me.

Disappointment doesn't begin to explain what I'm feeling.

Has he forgotten me? Forgotten the incredible week we'd spent together in Napa Valley? Or had it only been special to me? Maybe Santos had weeks like that with tons of other girls, and I was one of too many to be memorable.

His gaze drops from my face to the chair I'm holding, then back up at me. Suddenly awkward, I pull the chair back and sit. I rest my hands on my lap and hope he can't see how flushed I am to be near him again. I swallow hard and wait for what comes next. Hoping that I'll get some kind of explanation for how it's possible that he's here investigating the arson at my family's brewery.

Nonplussed, Santos maneuvers the laptop toward his right, keeping it in reach. "Can you log the interview reports from the day? I can handle this one on my own."

"Yes, sir," Officer Logan says. The door shuts with a loud bang behind me.

I flinch.

And just like that, we are alone.

After two years of not seeing each other.

My mind races with all the questions I need answers to all at once. Confusion threatens to paralyze me, but I can't let another second pass without figuring what is going on.

I say, "Do … you … not remember—"

"Ms. Robinson, before we get started, there are a few preliminary items that I want to make clear," Santos says. His tone is professional and curt. "This is information that we freely share with any witness or person that could be connected to an ongoing investigation. First, I'm Officer Santos Estrada of the Lasso County Fire Marshal's Office."

He pauses.

His words linger in the air between us.

Definitely not the nephew of the President of Mexico. I struggle to reconcile everything I thought about Santos with the brutal truth of who he is being thrust at me now.

Santos continues, "I'm the lead arson investigator assigned to this case and will be overseeing the entire investigation. My primary goal is to determine if the fire at Elm Street Brewery was deliberately set and if so, ensure that the individual or individuals responsible are charged appropriately for the crime."

I remain quiet, not knowing what to say or even if I should say anything.

"While Texas is a one-party consent state and I have no obligation to inform you that this interview will be recorded, I do like to be upfront and make you aware that audio recording is occurring of our entire interview," Santos says, then points to a black digital recorder connected to the laptop with a long black cord.

"Do you understand?" His voice is softer, tender as he waits for my response.

"Yes." I push the word out of my mouth even though I don't understand. I can't possibly understand what's happening. I feel like I've been transported to some crazy alternate universe, and I want out of this. Now.

"Lastly, I wanted to interview you about the fire because Scott Robinson identified his wife and you as heirs to the Elm Street Brewery Company. You could have information that may be critical to our investigation, whether you realize it or not. Do you have any questions at this point?"

"No."

"Okay, let's begin. Would you please state your name and city of residence for the record?"

"Harlow-Rose Robinson. I guess I'm temporarily living in Fredericksburg at my winery until construction on my house here is finished. That's about three hours ..." I stop. If Santos is from Lasso County and not Mexico, he knows exactly where Fredericksburg is.

"Thank you," Santos says, his brows knitting in a sexy furrow as if picking up on my thoughts. "Can you tell me where you were on the night of the fire and how you learned about it?"

I take a deep breath, then recount everything that happened that night as well as what I did yesterday before arriving in Kimbell to support my parents through this tragedy.

With precision, Santos weaves through a series of additional questions about the state of my relationship with my adopted parents, my knowledge of the brewery operations and finances, and my recollection of my father's interactions with his employees, including Joe Little.

I squirm under his scrutiny, the intensity of his gaze and the disconcerting back and forth from friendly to professional that he takes in questioning me.

He's different from the man who swept me off my feet two years ago in a lot of ways, but in others, he's the same man I remember. Over the past hour, I see more than a few hints of him. The cute way his eyebrow raises when he's amused by something I say. The relaxed vibe he exudes. His quiet confidence.

With every passing minute, I find myself drawn to him despite the subject of our conversation.

Yet, he can't be the Santos I thought I knew.

I don't know who this man is.

"Thank you for your patience and your candor. I need to ensure that I'm aware of any other heirs to the brewery other than yourself." Santos shifts in his seat. For the first time over the past hour, he seems unsteady. He rests his elbows on the table and leans closer to me. "Are you married?"

I whisper, "No."

A hint of a smile plays at the corners of his lips. "Children?"

I shake my head.

"I'm sorry, for the recording, I'll need an audible response."

"Oh, of course. No, I'm not in a relationship with anyone and have no children." I say, then instantly regret my response.

Why did I give him more information?

He isn't asking if I'm dating someone. He needs to know if there are any other family members he might need to question, like a spouse or grandchild, for the investigation only.

I shudder.

What he must think about the extra information I volunteered?

Information that he doesn't care about.

If he cared, he wouldn't have let two years pass by without reaching out to me, especially since we were only hours away from each other. Dad was right. It would've been impossible for *him* not to find *me* if he had tried to look. But he didn't.

"Thank you, Ms. Robinson. That's all I need … for now." Santos reaches over and presses a button on the digital recorder connected to the laptop.

He leans back in the chair and takes a long, deep breath. The sexy smile I lost my mind over two years ago appears on his face.

"It's been a long time, Harlow. Too long."

His eyes soften and lock onto mine, making it impossible for me to look away. A rush of conflicting emotions rains down within me.

"I can't do this." I stand up, almost knocking the chair over.

I push away from the table and pivot, racing toward the door as fast as my legs will take me.

A strong hand rests against my arm, gently stopping my progress.

Santos is so close I can feel his breath against my neck.

He turns me to face him.

Too close.

Close enough for me to stroke my hand along the stubble of his jaw. To trace the edges of his sensual lips with my fingertip. To kiss him like I've dreamed of doing for two years.

"Don't go. Not yet."

"Why shouldn't I?"

"Because I owe you an apology."

Pent up rage I didn't know I had erupts within me. "For what? Being a liar? Pretending to be someone you weren't? To feel something that you didn't? Don't bother. I don't need or want your apologies."

Santos's hands slip from my arms and fall to his side.

The void of his retreat fills me with sadness.

A shadow of hurt and regret clouds his features.

"Look, figure out who burned my family's brewery to the ground and go back to wherever you've been hiding this whole time." I open the door of the investigation room and storm down the hallway.

CHAPTER 9

S *ANTOS*

~

"DID YOU EXPLAIN TO HIM HOW THIS WORKS?" ASKS THE sassy Latina waitress with long dark lashes and bright red lips. She slams two twelve-ounce plastic beer mugs down on the table, one in front of me and the other in front of Ronan.

I stifle a crude whistle as I take in the toned legs in cut-off shorts, flat stomach, and nice rack of the waitress, then raise an eyebrow toward Ronan. My first time at Baker Bros Bar-B-Q, and now I understand why Ronan suggested the place to bring both of us out of our funks.

"Please." Ronan gives the waitress a sly grin. "You do the honors."

"Alright, fellas," the waitress says, then claps her hands above her head, giving us another sensational view of her body. "At Baker, the first round of beers is always on the house. But you have to follow our two rules. If you don't, you'll see the cost of two rounds on your bill at the end of the night. Got it?"

I chuckle under my breath. This should be interesting.

The waitress raises one finger in the air. "First, you must come up with a toast for the drinks and scream it out loud so the rest of the restaurant can hear."

I lean back in my chair.

Things are starting to make sense. When I arrived at the restaurant for dinner, I'd heard a lot of yelling and had chalked it up to the place being rowdy. Not that it wasn't, but I could see that it was encouraged by this tradition.

"And two." She raises a second finger in the air. "You have to chug the beer without stopping. You fellas up for the challenge?"

"I think we got this." Ronan gives her a wink.

"Great, then I'll be back to take your order in a few minutes."

I reach for the cold mug and wrap my hand around it. "Do they really charge you if you don't follow the two rules? Seems hard to keep track of."

"Trust me, I've been burned before with the guys on my shift, and we never made that mistake again." Ronan swipes at the condensation pooling below his beer mug. "They have spies or something. So, what are we going to drink to?"

I hunch over. "How about 'misery loves company?'"

Ronan wags a finger at me. "Perfecto. On the count of three. One. Two. Three."

Roaring the toast at the top of my lungs, my words mingle with Ronan's. I press the mug against my lips and chug until it's empty. Slamming it down onto the table, I gaze at my old friend. "Tastes like they still have Elm Beer in stock."

"That's all they serve. Not sure what they'll do when the inventory runs out. No way they'll get the brewery back up and running any time soon."

"Especially since they can't get started until I finish up the investigation and the insurance guys do their thing." I grab the menu and scan the sparse contents. Baker Bros is a carnivores' paradise with every type of barbecue meat you could think of served along with three sides: jalapeño baked beans, potato salad, and white bread. If you want different sides, a note at the bottom of the menu directs you to walk three blocks to Gwen's Country Café. If you want dessert, another note directs you to walk two blocks to Elevation Cupcake Shop.

"Give me that." Ronan snatches the menu from my hand and puts it back behind the roll of paper towels. "Your first time at Baker Bros, you gotta get the brisket tips. It made the place famous."

"Brisket tips it is." My stomach signals its agreement with a loud growl. "Now tell me why you're in a funk tonight. What's going on?"

"Nikki got some kind of record deal in the UK." Ronan drags a hand down his face. "One of the ladies at the daycare is a huge fan of the song. The twins heard it, and some kind of way recognized her voice. Now they're missing their mom all over again."

"Man, I'm sorry about that," I say. Ronan had married a rolling stone musician who'd tried to settle down with him but ultimately felt the call of her hopes and dreams as a singer stronger than any bond she had to stick around to be with her husband and kids. "Did you try reaching out to her? Maybe she'll come back."

"That ship sailed a long time ago. A courier delivered divorce papers to the firehouse a year ago this week. She changed all her numbers and stopped checking in with her parents. She didn't want any of us to stop her from pursuing her dreams. She ain't coming back. Not to the boys or me."

"A year ago? Why didn't you tell me?"

"You were in the middle of the trial. You had enough on your plate. I wasn't about to dump all my problems on you when you had enough of your own, brother."

"Still, I would've been there for you," I say, feeling bad for being caught up in my own issues to have missed this big change in Ronan's life. I push the empty beer mug to the edge of the table. The waitress appears out of nowhere to scoop it up and replace it with another full glass. Ronan gives her our order, and she sashays away from the table.

When I look back at Ronan, I'm glad to see more anger and annoyance on my friend's face than hurt or sadness. Nikki had always been trouble, and despite everyone warning Ronan to stay away from the songstress, he'd fallen hard for her. The fact that the relationship had shattered, leaving Ronan alone to raise their twin sons, was a surprise to no one.

"Enough about my crap. Is it hard for you to be back here in Kimbell? Is that why you're miserable tonight?"

I contemplate his question for a moment. No doubt being back in Kimbell was weighing on me emotionally. Excluding staying at the bed and breakfast with Alma, I'd avoided all the people and places in town that would trigger an onslaught of memories of Papi.

For the most part, everyone in the town had been kind, if not aloof, to my presence over the past few days. They all know why I'm here and that it's a temporary intrusion on their regular lives. But I know that could all change the longer I'm in town. If the investigation stretches over weeks, or God forbid, months, things will be a lot harder. As much as I'd rather not experience any of that, it isn't the reason my life has imploded.

"If only it was that simple," I say, still debating on whether I should bother Ronan with this or not.

"Complex means one thing. A woman." Roman guesses correctly. "And I think I know which mousy VP of Creekside bank has pushed you over the edge. Luke told me what happened. Can't believe she came at you like that."

I laugh out loud. "Trust me, I've already forgotten about Victoria and her ridiculous suggestion. I need money, but not that bad."

"So who is it then?"

"Actually, it's someone from here."

Ronan's eyes narrow as he scrutinizes me. "Why am I not surprised that it only takes you three days to snag one of Kimbell's finest. Who did you make fall instantly in love with you now?"

I roll my eyes. If only Harlow had fallen for me, maybe she wouldn't have shut me down so quick this afternoon.

I give Ronan the finger, then say, "So, I got to know someone and never thought I'd see her again."

"One-night stand?"

"Not exactly."

"Now I'm really intrigued."

"I ran into her here. I didn't know she was from Kimbell when we met," I admit, slumping down in the chair. I grab the mug and take a long swig of beer.

"Stop being dramatic and spit it out, brother. Who is she?"

My focus locks on the foam in my beer as I mumble, "Harlow."

"Harlow-Rose Robinson?" Ronan's voice hits a higher note. "The beer princess?"

"Y'all call her 'beer princess'? That's rude."

"Nowadays, she's called the 'Queen of Wines.' Brother, I hate to break it to you, but Harlow-Rose is way out of your league," Ronan says, pity in his gaze. "I can see how you could fall for her, though. She has this thing about her. Girl-next-door charm, pretty face, and sweet personality to match."

"Tell me about it. We are complete opposites." I exhale and finish off the second mug of beer. "She's sophisticated, intelligent, worldly, and ..."

"Rich."

"Yeah, very rich," I agree, but deep inside, I know Harlow is different. She's not a rich, spoiled brat using her money and power to secure advantages that others don't have. She doesn't look down on others with less or treat them like they're something on the bottom of her shoe. The days I spent with Harlow showed me that she was an exception to the rule of all the deplorable behavior I'd witnessed from rich people my entire life.

Ronan continues, "She's not the type of girl that has ever considered dating working-class schlubs like us. Not that she's pretentious or anything like that, because she's not. She's real sweet. We just can't reach her orbit to be recognized."

I don't disagree with the assessment at all, which makes me feel worse.

"Did you know she dated Nate all through high school?"

"The billionaire slacker wanna-be firefighter?" Something inside of me twists into a tight knot. That punk doesn't seem like Harlow's type. I can't wrap my head around the two of them being together. But maybe I can't wrap my head around anyone being with Harlow.

Except me.

"He ain't so bad. Trains hard with us and holds his own fighting fires. Still can't figure out why, though."

"They stopped dating after high school?"

"Yeah, she went to college at Stanford, and he stayed in Texas and went to SMU. They are still good friends, so the break-up was amicable."

"She said she wasn't dating anyone now," I remember her slip as I asked her about any other heirs to the Elm Street Brewery Company.

"Can't say I remember her being linked to anyone since she got back to Texas a couple of years ago. In California, she dated a couple of guys who are all Silicon Valley billionaires now. I think one proposed to her, but she turned him down."

"I guess she's focused on her winery and not her love life." I sober at the thought.

"Maybe. She's living in Fredericksburg most of the time. She could be dating someone up there."

"And keeping it a secret?" I scoff.

"She obviously kept whatever happened between the two of you a secret. When did y'all have a chance to hook up?"

"I told you it wasn't like that. No hooking up or anything, just a … connection." I struggle with how to explain what transpired between Harlow and me. Connection sounds so common when what we experienced was deeper than I'd ever felt in my life.

"Fine. When did y'all connect?" Ronan pauses as the waitress sets plates piled high with brisket tips in front of each of us. A scrawny busboy holds the sides in his hands, then lines them in the middle of the table.

I give them a nod of thanks as they walk away to check on other guests.

Ronan stuffs brisket into his mouth, waiting for me to respond.

I eat a few pieces of the succulent meat. "This is ridiculously good."

"Told you. Now back to you and Harlow-Rose."

"Remember Napa Girl?"

"Harlow-Rose is Napa Girl? I thought Napa Girl owned a winery in, well, Napa."

"I guess I just presumed the winery was there."

"Just like you let her *presume* you were the nephew of the President of Mexico."

"Kinda like that."

"You saw her today? When you brought Scott Robinson in for questioning?"

I nod. "He mentioned that the brewery would go to his daughter, Rosie, if anything happened to him. Not to his wife."

"So, of course, you had to interview Rosie."

"Exactly, and I had no clue that Rosie was actually Harlow."

"No one would guess that a white guy and his Asian wife would have a black daughter," Ronan acknowledges.

"Tell me about it. I almost died when she walked in. I'd already pressed record on the audio and couldn't afford to have anything between us on tape. So, I kept it professional. Asked all the necessary questions and a bunch more that weren't needed."

"How long did you question her?"

I shrug. "About two hours."

"Damn! You got it bad, and that ain't good."

"After I'd run out of questions, I stopped the recording. We probably had a few minutes before Gary came back in, so I tried to talk to her. You know, apologize for not being honest about who I was when we were in Napa."

"What happened?"

"She wasn't having any of it."

"Can you blame her? She had a great time with a guy a couple of years ago, then finds out he lied about who he was when he's interviewing her about her family's brewery going up in flames. It's a lot to take in, especially for someone as sheltered as Harlow-Rose."

"Just wish I had a chance to talk to her again. Explain what I was going through so she understands why I did what I did."

"What will an apology do? Trust me, it's not going to make you feel any better." Ronan wraps several pieces of brisket into a slice of white bread. "And if you think for one minute saying I'm sorry will get her to run back into your arms, you're crazy. There aren't enough zeros in your net worth to win over a woman like Harlow-Rose Robinson."

I hear Ronan, but I can't reconcile his thoughts on Harlow with the woman I spent five days with in Napa. I know she believed I came from a wealthy family related to the President of Mexico, but none of that seemed to truly matter to her. She was so different from what I expected someone of her wealth and stature to be. She was down-to-earth, open, and welcoming. She was the kind of woman I could see myself falling for. Hard.

"I have to do something. I'm going to run into her again as the investigation progresses. Her family owns the brewery."

Ronan sits up straight, pointing a finger at my face. His expression serious. "Don't let the blip of time that y'all were together ... years ago ... compromise your investigation or your career. You can't be intimately involved with someone so close to the crime you're investigating. Plus, she already told you she wasn't interested in your apology. If it's one thing I've learned if a woman tells you she's done, believe her. Walk away, brother, before you do something you'll regret."

I eat more brisket instead of responding to Ronan.

Deep down, I know he's right. But I'm not sure I can stay away from Harlow. Memories intrude on my thoughts.

"Don't go. Not yet."

"Why shouldn't I?"

"Because I owe you an apology."

"For what? Being a liar? Pretending to be someone you weren't? To feel something that you didn't? Don't bother. I don't need or want your apologies."

How could Harlow believe that it was all a lie? That my feelings and everything we shared were fake. I may have lied about my family name, but everything else had been real, authentic, and pure. Spending the week with her in Napa had been the only time since Papi died that I didn't feel lost and alone. Harlow had given me a reprieve from grief and showed me exactly why life was still worth living.

The minute she stepped into the interrogation room, those feelings had come back with a vengeance, stronger than ever.

Ronan curses under his breath. "I'm not getting through to you. I can see it on your face."

"I'm not sure I can be in the same town with Harlow and not try to clear the air between us."

Ronan shakes his head. "If you can't be in the same town and not try, then I guess there's no way you can be in the same restaurant and not do the same."

"What?"

Ronan points a piece of brisket toward the door to the restaurant, directly behind me.

"Harlow-Rose Robinson has arrived."

CHAPTER 10

ARLOW-ROSE

~

"Hey, Harlow."

My head snaps up from my cell phone. My attention on Zaire's text splinters into a million pieces as I'm instantly lost in the sensual, honey eyes of Santos.

Fumbling my phone, it clatters against the table and comes to rest in my lap. My insides twist into tight knots as I take in the full sight of him.

Could it be that he's gotten infinitely more gorgeous since this morning when he'd been all business grilling me about the fire at Elm Street Brewery? He's ditched the crisp white shirt and dark trousers for more casual wear. A black San Antonio Spurs t-shirt barely contains his broad, muscular chest and rock-hard biceps. His black jogging pants hang low on his hips, hugging his toned legs.

Santos slides into the booth across from me in one fluid motion.

I don't have a second to protest. Heat flushes against my face, and I resist the urge to pick up the menu and fan myself. Excitement slithers along my skin. I force myself to remember that I am still mad at him no matter how sexy he is.

Angry.

Furious.

He lied about who he was.

All the memories I've been clinging to about the connection and chemistry we'd shared had been a figment of my imagination. He toyed with my emotions and got me to open up to him about personal things. Things I'd never shared with anyone before. I thought he'd opened up to me, too. But now I'm questioning everything he ever told me about himself.

Had they all been lies?

A game he played as he enjoyed making me fall all over myself to be with him in Napa.

Picking up the phone, I scan Zaire's text again.

Running late. Problem at the lake house. Don't panic. Will be there in fifteen minutes.

I don't let myself think about what could have gone wrong this time at the house I'm having built on Lake Lasso. As I type a response, I send a silent prayer that she would truly be here soon to rescue me from doing something I'll regret.

Hope everything is okay. Hurry, it's getting crowded.

I slip the phone into my purse and gaze beyond Santos, hoping for some interruption or distraction—a waiter or busboy coming by to give me a chance to gather my thoughts and corral my wayward emotions.

No such luck.

I plaster on my face what I hope to be a bored look and wait for Santos to explain why he's ambushed me.

He licks his lips, sending another army of butterflies skittering through my body. The booth in the back of the upstairs section of the restaurant is suddenly too secluded, too dark … too intimate. I wanted to be away from the rowdy crowds on the main floor, but now I know that was a big mistake.

Four empty booths separate mine from the next occupied table.

I'm basically alone with the man who'd dominated my thoughts for almost two years.

"I don't mean to bother you," Santos leans back against the booth with a casual relaxation as if he owns the place. He's entirely at ease as his eyes drift from my face down to my chest and back up to my eyes. "Sorry, you're … breathtaking."

"Do you have more questions for me, officer?" I ask, ignoring the flip flop fluttering in my stomach.

He pauses. I can almost see his brain processing my question as an adorable frown appears between his eyebrows. He stiffens and sits up straight in the booth. "I really shouldn't be talking to you like this. Not here. Not with you being an integral part of an open investigation."

"So why are you here? What do you want from me?"

Santos runs a hand slowly down his face, but not in time to hide the sensual smile that plays at the corner of his lips.

"Carpe Diem" rings through the air from four guys at a table below. I follow Santos's gaze as he stares at the group chugging their beers. A long moment passes, then he turns his attention back to me.

I feel the familiar tug and wonder what it would feel like to touch him again. Laying underneath outstretched limbs of enormous oak trees, I'd caress his face as we stared out at the calm, pristine waters of the lake. His head resting against my chest, we would talk for hours on end until the sunlight faded into night. I'd held onto those memories for almost two years until they were obliterated this morning with his lies.

"Forgiveness," Santos says after the yelling and hollering dies down.

"Oh, is that all?" I roll my eyes and cross my arms over my chest. Inching back toward the corner of the booth, I try to put more distance between me and Santos's overwhelming handsomeness. But it's too late. A dazzling smile spreads across his face.

I bite my lower lip to stop myself from smiling back.

What is wrong with me?

Yes, I find him mesmerizing.

Yes, if there was a picture in the dictionary of "Harlow-Rose's Type of Man," Santos's photo would be the only one on the page.

Yes, a part of me wants to let go of all my confusion and give in.

But I can't. He made a fool of me in Napa.

Why would I open the door for him to do it all over again?

Or worse?

Not even try.

"There's no point in revisiting the past. Like you said, you shouldn't be talking to me about anything other than the arson investigation of the brewery. My dinner companion will be here soon, so—"

"You're here on a date?" I detect the slight edge in his tone and can't help but feel triumphant. I relax as the power balance shifts in my favor. I don't have to be rattled by Santos. Nothing about this reunion is how I ever imagined it would be, but I'll get over that.

Eventually.

I don't answer but stare back at him.

Recognizing that he isn't going to get an answer to that question, he says, "I really came up here to apologize to you. I don't have any control over whether you forgive me or not."

"That's not necessary." I pluck at a loose thread on the vinyl of the booth and avoid looking at him. A quietness settles between us. It's comfortable and almost pleasant as if we are falling back into old patterns. Or accepting that this is how things will always be between us. Welcoming and easy.

I glance up.

"I lied to you about who I was, and I'm sorry for that." He reaches over and rests his hand on top of mine. "After everything we shared with each other, I should have trusted you with the truth before I left."

"So why didn't you?"

"Honestly?"

"Yes, Santos. Now is the time to be completely honest with me."

"Everything over those five days had been perfection. At least for me. I didn't want to introduce anything at the end that would change that. Especially since I knew or, I thought I knew, that we'd never see each other again."

"So, what's the harm in a little lie? What if I had tried to find you?"

"Did you?"

"I thought about it."

"But you realized that it would be too hard."

"Only because I thought you were the nephew of the President of Mexico! There was no way the Santos I thought I knew would walk away from his obligations in Mexico City, and there was no way I was going to abandon my winery and my family. We were from two different worlds."

He squeezes my hand, then laces his fingers with mine. I should pull away, but I can't. His touch feels too good.

"My background is different, but the conclusion is the same," he says.

"What does that mean?"

"We really are from two different worlds." Hurt cascades across his face. "I don't fit in yours, and you don't fit in mine."

Santos looks down at our hands intertwined. His thick dark lashes cast a shadow across his sculpted jaw. The urge to caress his face rises strongly within me. I want to tell him that he's wrong. He never gave us a chance to see if we could fit in each other's worlds. How could we have been so in sync in Napa but not be able to recapture what we shared here in Texas? Especially if we'd known that we were from not just the same state, but the same county, too.

Would our relationship be different if he'd trusted me with the truth?

Would we be in a relationship?

Or could he be right?

Maybe the reality of Harlow-Rose, owner of a small winery in the Texas Hill Country, and Santos, arson investigator, wouldn't have held the same mystique. We could've fizzled and faltered, ending things after realizing that the magic only existed in Napa Valley.

"I still wish you had told me," I say. Maybe then I wouldn't have spent the last two years wanting a man that didn't exist. I pull my hand away from his. "I can't imagine how you kept all the stories about who you were straight. You deserve an Oscar for that performance."

"There was no performance in Napa. I never lied to you about anything that mattered," Santos challenges. "I'm Mexican, but not related to the President. Everything else I shared with you was a hundred percent … me."

I throw my hands in the air. "Okay. Fine. You apologized. I forgive you. It was two years ago. We've both moved on with our lives. None of this matters now."

"It matters to me," Santos says, his voice rising as he taps his fingers against his heart. "Before you left the fire station, you said that I pretended to feel something that I didn't really feel when we were in Napa. There's no way in hell I could fake all the ways you made me feel. How you changed me. Made me see that life was worth living even as I felt lost in darkness. It was your positivity, your hope, your optimism that pulled me through. I'll never forget that. I never forgot you."

"I never forgot you either." The words tumble from my mouth before I can stop them.

"Do you know how many times I thought about looking you up online? To try to find you?"

I shake my head and look away as tears prick my eyes.

"But I knew it was pointless. I have nothing to offer an intelligent, accomplished woman like you, Harlow. So, I let myself be okay with sharing those five days with you since that's all we'll ever have." He runs a hand through his dark curly hair, then sighs heavily. "I'm here to find whoever set the brewery on fire and make sure they're convicted, not to reconnect with you."

I recoil, stung by the blunt finality of his declaration.

My jaw clenches as I struggle to stop the floodgates of pain from rushing through me.

Santos eases out of the booth and looks down at me. "Still, I want you to know that I've never felt anything like what we had in Napa with anyone else. You're a special woman, Harlow, and an impossible act to follow."

This time, it's me watching as Santos turns and heads back down to the restaurant's lower level.

CHAPTER 11

SANTOS

~

I FLIP OVER AND KICK THE COMFORTER AND SHEETS OFF my legs. The air is stifling and humid, despite the whirring of the ceiling fan set on high. A sliver of moonlight cascades through the curtains of the window. All is quiet inside Crockett Manor, except the thoughts racing through my mind.

I glance at the clock.

Just past two in the morning, and sleep still alludes me.

After my visit to Harlow's table at the restaurant, the rest of the night had quickly gone downhill. I'd said all the right words, the things I'd rehearsed in my head after seeing her in Kimbell for the first time. Some stupid part of me had thought apologizing would be the closure I needed to put her and our time together behind me. But being alone with her again, without the investigation looming over us, had the opposite effect.

In seconds, my mind had logged and memorized everything about her.

Toned, shapely legs peeked out from underneath the table. Toenails painted a pale pink, wagging back in forth within the strappy sandals she wore. The white halter top that hugged all the curves of her chest. Her smooth, dark caramel skin glistening under the soft wall sconces.

But that gorgeous face had been my undoing.

Her full lips covered with gloss had a hint of shimmer, and a light coating of mascara on her long lashes was the only make-up she wore. Arguably, she didn't even need it. Her beauty was timeless and natural, drawing me like a moth to a flame.

This was the Harlow of my dreams since the night I'd flown back from Napa and re-entered the disaster that was my life. The Harlow that pushed me to get out of bed when I felt like becoming a recluse and disappearing from the world. Thoughts of her always inspired me to push on for another day, for another chance to live up to being the man that Papi had wanted me to be.

As soon as I got back to the table, I didn't need to tell Ronan the conversation hadn't gone like I thought. Like any good friend, he fed off my misery with a healthy dose of his own. We upgraded from Elm Beer to Tito's vodka and stumbled out of the restaurant when it closed at midnight.

I looked for Harlow, but she was long gone.

Two hours later, I'm fed up with tossing and turning, trying to get thoughts of her out of my head. I should've listened to Ronan and left well enough alone. It will be hard enough interacting with her throughout the investigation of the brewery fire. Why did I have to make things worse by talking about what happened between us two years ago?

Flipping over onto my stomach, I bang my fist into the pillow until it's almost flat in the middle. I know what I wanted to happen after I apologized to her. I wanted her to look at me with disgust and disdain. To show me that I never should have pretended to be someone she could be interested in. To blow out the flame of hope that's been burning within me for two years, once and for all.

Problem is Harlow didn't do that.

I stared right into her dark mahogany eyes and saw the same desire burning there that I'd seen when we were in Napa. It's like the truth had changed nothing for her. Sure she was pissed and shocked, but she wasn't repulsed by me or my actions. I could almost see the tug-of-war of emotions she battled, especially when I held her soft hand in mine. The chemistry was still there, linking us to each other whether we wanted to be or not.

Does she care that I'm Santos, the arson investigator, and not Santos, the President of Mexico's nephew? She's a millionaire, for God's sake, and I'm drowning in six-figures worth of debt with no way out. Why would she give me a second glance?

Or another chance?

I grab the pillow and push it against my face.

I want another chance with Harlow.

A chance that I know I can't have.

The odds are stacked high against us.

She was raised rich and privileged, then grew up to be even richer. She only dates men as successful and wealthy as she is, if not more so. Doesn't matter how attracted to me she might be. There are things that she'd expect from a relationship that I would never be able to give her. I can't get my life back together after the foreclosure on my house. I'm trying to avoid filing for bankruptcy.

With everything dragging me down, did I really need to get assigned to investigate the fire at her family's brewery? What kind of cruel twist of fate is that?

Now, I have to deal with the frustration of being around the woman I can't have for weeks and maybe even months.

I bolt up from the bed.

There's only one way to clear my head.

Minutes later, I slip into a pair of jogging shorts and a sleeveless exercise shirt. Lacing up my running shoes, I tie them tight, then grab my key and cell phone. Stuffing them in my back pocket, I ease out of the bedroom and make my way outside Crockett Manor.

The night air is sticky and dewy with humidity, coating my skin in a slick sheen. Pushing my earbuds into my ears, I scroll to one of my running playlists and settle on heavy metal filled with top hits from Metallica, Black Sabbath, Iron Maiden, and Slayer.

The intense guitar riffs make it nearly impossible to think, which is precisely what I want. Glancing to the left and right, I jog in place for a few seconds, then decide to head down Main Street toward the town center and Bell Park. I push the pace faster than usual, keeping up with the tempo of the music blaring in my ears.

Soon, I'm passing Elevation Cupcake Shop and Baker Bros Bar-B-Q, now darkened and deserted. I turn onto Market Street, race past the Police Station, several antique shops, and restaurants, and head straight toward the park. Old fashioned street lamps illuminate the pathway, and I'm drawn to the quaint gazebo in the distance. It's painted white and decorated with a string of lights around the perimeter of the octagon. It was one of Papi's favorite places in Kimbell. He'd cajole Alma into making a picnic lunch and meet us there whenever I came to town for the weekend to see him.

I normally avoid places that remind me of Papi in Kimbell, but something about the gazebo is drawing me toward it now. Maybe because the park is empty at this time of night.

Or maybe because someone has the same idea that I do.

I slow my pace and confirm that someone is indeed sitting under the soft lights inside the gazebo. Whoever it is has their head bowed, oblivious to the surroundings. Kimbell isn't known for having a homeless population, so it's not likely that the person is a vagrant. I can't imagine who could be there alone or why at this time of night. The officer in me can't resist checking it out in case the person is in distress or needs some medical assistance.

Turning my music off, I circle around toward the steps that lead into the gazebo, careful not to startle whoever is inside. Before I reach the steps, I see exactly who it is. The one person I was running from turns out to be the one I was running to.

"Harlow?" I call out to her.

She doesn't look up. She can't hear me over the sound of her own whimpered cries.

A myriad of worse-case scenarios line up in my mind, starting with whoever she'd been meeting on her date earlier tonight. Had it been that punk, Nate Bell? A low simmer of rage begins to boil within me. Had Nate hurt Harlow? Done something to make her cry?

Propelled by an insatiable need to protect her, I take the steps two at a time and drop to my knees in front of where she sits. "Harlow, what did he do to you? Did he hurt you? Was it Nate?"

Harlow flinches as she looks at me. Her eyes wild with surprise. Quickly, she runs a hand under her running nose and swipes at the tears falling from her eyes.

"Nate? No. What are you talking about?" Her eyes search mine for an understanding that I can't give her.

"You're crying," I say, swiping my fingers across the wetness still on her cheek. "Did something bad happen on your date?"

She closes her eyes slowly and exhales.

I hold my breath waiting for her to look at me again.

When she does, I'm grateful to see a hint of amusement beyond the pain.

"I wasn't on a date," Harlow says, then pats the wooden bench next to her. "I was supposed to meet Zaire for dinner. She's one of my oldest and closest friends."

Taking her cue, I rise and sit next to her. Adrenaline is still flooding my veins. I'm on high alert for danger despite the new information.

"Why are you crying? What happened?"

She glances at me. "What are you doing here in the middle of the night?"

"I thought answering a question with a question was banned."

A soft chuckle escapes her lips. "Look at me breaking my own rules."

"That was your pet peeve, not mine," I remind her. "But I'll answer you first. I couldn't sleep." I don't add that my insomnia was a direct result of incessant thoughts of her running through my mind. "Your turn." I hope she doesn't cop out and tell me she'd rather not answer, which is what she prefers people to say if they felt the need to dodge a question.

"When Zaire had to cancel our dinner plans, I decided to take a walk. Some kind of way I ended up at the brewery." She shakes her head as a fresh bout of tears springs to her eyes. "I should've gone home, but by that time, it was too late. I couldn't believe what I was seeing. It was so much worse than what my parents had told me. So, I went around toward the back, near the forest, and scaled the fence. I was there for hours walking through the rubble and ashes."

The right thing for me to do is tell her that the area was fenced off for a reason. It's still the location of an active arson investigation, and we're still gathering evidence to analyze. Her being on-site could've contaminated evidence critical to my case. But I can't bring myself to be the strict arson investigator right now. I don't have the heart to scold her. Not when she looks like her entire world has been destroyed.

"It's all gone." She whispers. Her body shakes as the tears she was trying to hold back are unleashed.

Tears prick my own eyes at her pain. A pain I'd do anything to make go away. I slip my arm around her. Relief floods through me when she doesn't flinch or move. I lean in closer and do what I've wanted to from the moment I first saw her standing inside Elevation Cupcake Shop. I pull her into my arms and hold her tight. Her face presses against my chest as she clings to me. A lifeline when she needs it most.

I'm reminded of how perfectly her stunning curves feel against my body. But somehow, the feeling is infinitely more intoxicating than I remember.

I never want to let her go.

I lose track of time as I hold her, content to be here for her as long as she needs me. Her tears have stopped, but she hasn't pulled away from me. I sneak a glance at my watch. She's been nestled next to me for almost half an hour.

"Guess I should let you go," Harlow says, catching me.

"Never," I say, then press my lips against her hair. I shouldn't indulge in this ... whatever it is ... with Harlow, but I can't help myself. "I know how hard this is for you."

She sits up and stares at me. Those lovely dark brown eyes acknowledge that I'm right.

"You remember when I told you about the family business I wanted to take over from my dad," she says.

I massage slow circles against her neck as I nod. "You wanted to prove to him that he could trust you to take over the business when he was ready to retire. It was your single focus."

"Until you helped me see a different perspective. Letting that dream go is what freed me to make my winery the success it is. Still, I have so many memories of the brewery. I never imagined a day when I wouldn't be able to walk into the beer garden, head down the hallway to my father's office, or check on the production coming out of the brewery. Those are things that I've been doing since I was a little girl, and I hadn't stopped. Now I'll never do them again."

"The fire took away the buildings, but it can never take away your memories. Those are in your heart forever. Your family will rebuild, and you'll be able to make new memories to add to the old."

"Like taking my first drink of beer when I was five at my birthday party. That raised a bunch of eyebrows and sent my mother into a tizzy."

"I'm guessing your dad didn't mind."

"Not one bit. After I'd swiped his can, he took it back but poured a little bit in my teacup to drink for the rest of the party. I remember feeling so sophisticated. It was years before I realized beer isn't the type of drink you sip from a cup."

I laugh out loud, imagining what five-year-old Harlow was like prancing around, sipping beer from the teacup. "I'll bet you were adorable."

"As a matter of fact, I was. I have the pictures to prove it."

"No hangover the next day?"

"Actually, no. I've always been able to handle more liquor than anyone would guess."

"Maybe one day I'll get to see those pictures."

Harlow rubs a hand along her neck as she looks away from me. "Maybe."

I decide not to press my luck. It's almost four in the morning and time for Harlow to get home. Standing, I reach a hand out toward her.

"Come on, let me walk you to your car."

Harlow looks up at me with wide eyes. It takes me a moment to register that she's not looking at me at all. She's looking at my arm. My bicep, to be exact. The one that is completely exposed since I'm wearing a sleeveless t-shirt. Completely bare for her to see the tattoo that stretches across the entire width of my arm. My mouth goes dry.

"When did you get that?"

She stands in front of me as her hand slides along my arm. Her warm touch sends a jolt through me. I watch as her fingers trace the outline of her winery logo. The same logo I'd drawn on a crumpled napkin.

"Long time ago."

"Why?"

"So I'd never forget the time we spent together."

I step closer to her and caress the side of her face, cupping her chin in my palm. The intense intimacy I see in her eyes matches everything churning within me. My thoughts are consumed with kissing her even though I know it's a bad idea.

The worst idea I could ever have.

I can't let anything happen between Harlow and me.

As much as I want her, I need my job. It's the only reason I'm hanging on by a thread, living pay check to pay check to pay off the mountain of debt I have. I've built a good reputation and should be up for a promotion at the end of the year, especially if I nail whoever started the fire at the brewery. I can't risk it.

Harlow's lips part in anticipation.

That's the red stop sign I need to know I have to step away.

Increasing the distance between us, I say, "Where did you park?"

"I rode my bike down here." She points to an expensive sparkling red electric bike resting against the outside of the gazebo. It looks top of the line and no doubt costs as much as a small car. Anyone trying to attack her would have a hard time catching up once she took off.

Harlow gives me a small smile. "Really, I'll be fine getting home."

Disappointed that she won't need an escort, I step aside and watch as she descends the steps and gets onto the bike. She switches the motor on then turns back to me.

I walk down the steps and lean on the side of the gazebo.

"Thank you, Santos."

"For what?"

"Being the man I remember from Napa."

CHAPTER 12

H*ARLOW-ROSE*

Leaning back against the leather seats, I press the button to close the convertible roof of the Maseratti and watch as the glorious blue sky overhead begins to shrink from view.

Inhaling deeply, I can't stop wondering what Santos is doing. He's been on my mind ever since I saw him at the gazebo a week ago. As I cried my eyes out, he was a welcomed sight. A friendly face, a dry shoulder, a caring and compassionate heart ready to help me pick up the pieces of the shattered memories of my family's business.

A couple of hours had been all it took to wipe away any doubts that he was the man I'd fallen for years ago. In hindsight, I don't understand why I got so caught up on his family. None of that mattered. It wasn't what had brought us together back then or … now.

But we weren't together.

We couldn't be.

At least not yet.

Santos's role as the lead investigator of the fire meant any personal relationship between us could compromise his career. I would never do that to him. Still, I can't stop myself from yearning to be with him again. Every day since the night at the gazebo, I've had to talk myself out of coming up with some excuse to request an update on the investigation. Spending most of the week in Fredericksburg preparing for our tours and tastings had distracted me. There was double the number of guests as the first weekend, and we'd had to turn some away.

Once the mad rush was over, Santos had crept back into my mind. So much so that I decided to drive back to Kimbell and check on my parents during the week. They were shocked to see me but didn't question my need to be close to them during this time. And I truly was worried about them. If they needed to be interviewed again, I wanted to be there with them and not just to see Santos.

Who am I kidding?

I'm here because I want to see Santos again. It's been a whole week, and I'm about to drive myself crazy. Part of me hopes that he can figure out who set the fire over the next few days. Once the investigation is closed, there would be nothing standing in the way of us exploring whatever it is that still exists between us after all this time.

And there is no denying that something is there.

For God's sake, the man has my winery logo tattooed on his arm.

If that doesn't say we are connected, I don't know what will.

"Stop thinking about Santos," I mutter, then fling the door open.

Stepping out into the sunshine, I stop to survey the massive development that has sprouted along the shores of Lake Lasso.

Zaire Kincaid's vision for the area had come true. A series of commercial buildings stretch along the harbor, designed to blend into the natural surroundings with maximum use of windows and light. Kincaid Real Estate offices are to the far left, next to a coffee shop, a boutique clothing store, a kayak, and boat rental hut, and a dock that extends out into the lake. To the right is Kimbell's only five-star restaurant—Thorn, which boasts fresh seafood flown in daily, and a museum scheduled to open in a couple of months. Across the lake, a series of vacation homes and waterside villas hug the shoreline, with more under construction.

Lake Lasso is the perfect size for boating, fishing, and relaxing, but not so large that locals will be overwhelmed by out-of-towners coming to vacation in the area. Despite the massive growth, the site embodies the familiar laid-back charm and refreshing character that Kimbell is known for. No matter how far I've traveled and the many places I've lived, this little town would always be home to me. Being here fills me with a familiar calm and peace.

"Harlow-Rose?" A male voice calls from behind me. "Is that you?"

I spin around and see the smiling face of Lance Bassett. "Hey, Lance!" I cross the sidewalk to give him a hug.

Lance returns my embrace, then steps back and looks at me long and hard. "I'm sorry to hear about what happened at the brewery. Are the police any closer to figuring out how the fire started?"

I shake my head. "They think it was arson."

"You're kidding me." His mouth falls open.

"I wish I was," I push my hands into the pockets of my jeans. Talking about the arson inevitably makes me think of Santos, which is exactly what I'm trying not to do.

"Any suspects so far?"

"Joe Little. Dad fired him a few weeks before the fire."

"Joe? Really?" Lance drags a hand down his face. "Well, it's not so far-fetched. The guy could be … unpleasant and definitely had a quick temper."

"Dad thinks that's ludicrous, though."

"Have the cops talked to him?"

"No one knows where he is. He's disappeared, but I'm sure they want to bring him in for questioning," I say. Unease snakes through my body at the thought of anyone wanting to hurt my family in such a devastating way. "Enough about that. What brings you to town? It's not a holiday and not anyone's birthday, from what I remember."

"Well," Lance raises his hands. "I'm moving back home."

"Really?" I don't bother to hide my surprise. "I thought you were doing well in Chicago working at that prestigious firm where the Obama's started their careers."

"I was actually doing quite well there, but life has a funny way of showing you what really matters. I have everything that should make me happy, but I'm not. The law firm is awesome. Chicago is a great city, but the daily grind and the hustle to claw my way up and make a name for myself feels pointless," Lance admits. "I work hard every day all day just to come home and be miserable and alone with my legal briefs every night. When I think about my life five, ten years down the road, I realize that it's not the future I want. So I decided to walk away while I still had a chance to make my life into something I really wanted."

"And does that life include … Jasmine?" I ask, thinking of my old rival. For as long as I can remember, everything had been a competition between her and me.

"I hope so." Lance smiles, but it doesn't reach his eyes. "I'm meeting her at Thorn to gauge if I have a shot at getting her back."

"If you ask me, she'd be crazy not to. She was less abrasive and annoying when the two of you were together. You're more than she deserves," I say, unable to hide my disdain for the brash, loud E.R. surgeon. Jasmine would never be one of my favorite people. Lance, of all people, knows that.

"Thanks," Lance says, though he doesn't seem convinced. "I gotta go. She'll be here any minute."

"And she'll be in a much better mood if she doesn't drive up and see you talking to me," I say, laughing. "Good seeing you."

Lance laughs. "You too."

I head in the opposite direction and enter the glass doors of Kincaid. The cool air conditioning envelops me as I step inside the open space.

"Hey, Harlow-Rose," I hear my name in the sing-songy voice of Zaire's long-time receptionist.

I turn to see her walking toward me. "Hi, Simona. I'm doing a drive-by to see if I can squeeze some time on Zaire's calendar. Did she tell you she ditched me for dinner last week?"

"She did, and she feels horrible about it. She'll be glad to see you now, though. She's been on that same call for over an hour. Go on in and give her a reason to wrap it up."

"You sure? I don't want to get in between a woman and her money."

"Girl, please. Zaire makes money in her sleep. Go on back."

I give Simona a quick hug then follow the carpeted walkway toward the large corner office overlooking the lake. Stopping in the doorway, I stare at Zaire sitting at her desk, typing feverishly on her keyboard. A headset is on her head as she expertly gives orders in the sweetest, most patient tone to whoever is on the other line. Her hair is cut in a low fade, a style that only a woman as beautiful as Zaire could pull off. Dressed casually in a scoop neck sweatshirt emblazoned with her company logo, I make a note to do a sweatshirt swap with her. Couldn't hurt to cross advertise for each other's businesses.

I knock lightly on the door.

Zaire looks up then stretches her hands in the air, beckoning me to come inside. She says, "I gotta go. Do not leave until everything on that list is done. We can't afford to fall further off schedule. Bye now."

Jumping up from her chair, she dashes over to me and wraps me in a fierce hug. "Hey, honey! I'm so sorry for ditching you at dinner the other night."

"It was a week ago," I remind her, then wiggle her back and forth.

"Come on, sit," Zaire says, then presses a button that automatically closes her office door. I do as I'm told, curling my legs into the oversized plush chair. She presses another button, then says, "Simona, get Troy to cover my next call and sit in on it yourself. I'll need detailed notes of what I missed."

"You got it, boss," Simona's voice comes back through the line.

Zaire flips the computer screen off then turns to me. "I'm a horrible bestie. I can't believe I let so much time pass without checking on you."

"You did check on me. We text every day."

"It's not the same. How are you, honey? Really? I mean, you look fabulous and not at all like a woman whose family business burned down to the ground."

I shrug, then look at the floor. I'm tired of being emotional about the fire. Santos being here has amped up more feelings.

"Oh, honey. The fire is just a setback. Elm Street Brewery will come back stronger than ever."

"I know. I grew up with that brewery. It's always been there, and now it's a pile of debris. It's hard to see it like that. But you're right. Once the investigation is over, Dad will start to rebuild and get back everything we've lost," I say, and I do believe that. Even though the road will be hard, based on the damage. Changing the subject, I ask, "So tell me what happened at the lake house?"

"A stupid deer crashed through the windows that I had installed. And don't look at me with those big eyes. I don't know if the deer survived or not. He did a hit and run on your house. I had to order a replacement and get the blood cleaned up. Everything is back like it should be now," Zaire says. "But that's not why I missed dinner."

"Another crisis?"

"You know, I'm still working on identifying ownership of the land around the lake," Zaire says. "The county records are a hot mess, mostly in paper and spread in warehouses all over the place. Right before our dinner, I was all set to buy property from one family only to find out that they didn't own the land after all. Luke Diamond shows up with his copy of the deed and drawings of the area. Diamo owned the land I was about to buy. It's prime lake shore property, and it was snatched out of my hands at the last minute. But what's worse, I spent the next several hours trying to get Luke to sell me a portion of the land, and he turned me down flat."

"Luke is sentimental. If his grandfather amassed all that land, there's no way he's going to sell it. It's the reason he moved back to Kimbell in the first place."

"We all loved Diamo, but I promise you, I could've gotten him to sell me the land a lot faster than clawing it out of the grasp of his grandson," Zaire says, clearly exasperated. "He's hoarding a significant chunk of prime real estate, forgoing a huge payday to be sappy and nostalgic. Anyway, speaking of Nate, have you seen your sexy ex lately?"

My mouth drops open. "Were we?

"Talking about Luke is like talking about Nate. They're BFFs. Now answer my question. Don't think I haven't noticed how cagey you've been in some of your texts."

I wrap a strand of my curls around my finger, twisting it tight, then watch as it springs loose when I let go. "I ran into him at Elevation last week."

"And?"

"And what?"

"Any sparks?"

There were sparks alright, but none between Nate Bell and me. That was the night I'd seen Santos for the first time in two years.

"Not with Nate."

"But with someone else? Anyone I know?"

"Kind of." I bury my face in my hands. "Napa Guy is back in the picture."

Zaire squeals loudly. "Did you find him in Mexico City? No, did he find you here? Has he been looking for you all this time? It was the wine, wasn't it? He saw your wine had won all those awards and reached out."

"Will you give me a chance to explain?" I ask as my heartbeat quickens. Zaire is so used to controlling every situation around her, she often forgets to just shut up and listen.

"Be quick about it. I need details now."

"Well, first, he's not who I thought he was." I give Zaire the rundown of everything I learned about the *real* Santos. That would've been a good place to stop, but I need a second opinion about my confusing emotions. I tell Zaire about running into Santos at the gazebo and how that one meeting had dissipated all my anger. "So, am I crazy?"

"Depends," Zaire leans against her desk. "How does he make you feel?"

"He's so easy to talk to. Confide in. I feel so comfortable with him. There's this connection that I've never felt with anyone else."

"Then that's your answer."

"Just like that."

"Well, yeah," Zaire says, leaning back in her leather chair. "Let's state facts. We are business owners. We are millionaires. We are not looking for men to take care of us in the traditional sense. We take care of ourselves professionally and financially. But what we do need is a man who knows how to emotionally support us and uplift us. Connect with us on a spiritual level. Be a great lover and an even better friend. You don't need Santos to be rich or part of Mexican political royalty. You need him to be the guy who can't sleep at night because deep down, he can sense you're hurting, and he's compelled to find you and comfort you. And that's exactly what he did."

"Wow, that's a stretch. I think he had insomnia, and it was a coincidence."

"I don't believe in coincidences. What's your next move?"

"I have to wait until the investigation is over. Getting involved with the lead arson investigator of the fire at my family's brewery isn't good for him or me."

"Good point. Well, for your sake, I hope it wraps up soon."

"Me too." There's a soft knock at the door. I turn to see Simona in the doorway. "That's my cue to leave. You owe me dinner."

"Simona, book dinner for Harlow and me at Thorn next week," Zaire says, then turns to me. "I got you, honey. I won't cancel next time."

I blow an air kiss at her, then weave through the building to the outside. Stepping out into the bright sunshine, I stop in my tracks.

Santos is across the sidewalk near the boat rental hut, and he's … in deep trouble.

CHAPTER 13

S *ANTOS*

~

I LET MY GUARD DOWN, AND THAT WAS A BIG MISTAKE. Wound up from pouring over the evidence in the Brewery fire case and anxious about not locating Joe Little, who is shaping up to look guiltier by the day, I left the fire station early and went for a long run. Weaving through the streets of downtown Kimbell, I detoured through a wooded area that led to Lake Lasso. Now I wish I'd headed back to Crockett Manor and taken a nap instead.

"Answer me! What are you doing here?"

I inhale a long breath and stare down at Dr. Jasmine Jones. Trembling with rage, her dark brown curls flutter in the wind as she has a death grip on a large, iced coffee. Deep down, I knew this confrontation was possible but had hoped to avoid it. Over a week of not crossing her path had come to a screeching halt as I stood near the kayak rental hut on the shores of the lake.

I raise my hands in the air. "Look, I don't want to get into anything with you. Why don't you go on about your way, and I'll do the same."

"You think it's that easy?" Jasmine demands. "I can't believe you would show your face back in Kimbell after what you did! Nobody wants you here."

"I'm here for work. As soon as I'm done, you won't see me ever again," I say, keeping my voice steady and calm. I don't want to exacerbate the situation. I glance over at the guy dressed in khakis and a polo standing near her, looking confused. A boyfriend, maybe. Perhaps I can get the guy's help in diffusing this situation.

Stepping toward the guy, I say, "Hey man, I'm not trying to cause any trouble. Why don't the two of you—"

"Are you really talking around me to Lance? You would disrespect me like that and not speak to me directly. Why am I not surprised?" Jasmine huffs, taking a couple of steps toward me. "You destroyed my family, and you want Lance to swoop in and cart me off, so you don't have to answer for the horrible things you did."

The horrible things *I* did?

I swallow hard. I can feel the tension and rage blazing hot up the back of my neck.

Has she lost her mind?

What I did was get justice for *my* family. The judge and the jury agreed with me. I'm not going to stand by and let Jasmine attack me for doing what is right.

I pause and force myself to take a deep breath. Nothing good could come from battling with her. The fight was over, and I won.

We both know it. She's hurting, and that's not my fault. But that doesn't mean I can't be the bigger person and walk away from her now before things get out of hand.

"Jas, come on. Let's go," Lance pleads with her. "Don't do this."

"You don't understand, Lance," Jasmine says. "You weren't here to see how he ripped our family apart because he couldn't deal with the fact that his—"

"Don't say it," I grit through clenched jaws. "I swear to God, don't you—"

Her retaliation is swift.

The large iced Frappuccino slams into my face, drenching me as the coffee covers my skin, soaks into my t-shirt and running shorts, then drizzles down my legs. I swipe the sticky liquid from my face. When I can see again, my eyes lock on something in the distance.

Not something.

Someone.

Harlow-Rose.

She's here.

Right when I need her most.

I won't go to her.

I can't allow myself the indulgence, but seeing the care and concern in her eyes is enough to deflate my anger and make me think more rationally.

Another cup of coffee sloshes against my neck and splashes down my shirt.

"Please, Jas, don't do this," Lance pleads, gripping Jasmine's arm to hold her back from hurtling some other object at me.

She jerks away from Lance's grasp without much effort and stalks over, stopping mere inches from me.

I don't budge. Staring into her dark eyes, I see my own feelings mirrored in them. I understand her rage and indignation because I feel it too. We will forever be on opposite sides of the issue, unable and unwilling to see the other's point of view.

"You need to leave Kimbell, do you hear me?" Jasmine screams. "You aren't welcome here. Go away!"

"I'm not going anywhere," I say, flinging ice cubes from inside my shirt to the sidewalk below.

"You bastard!" Jasmine raises her hand to slug me, but she's whisked off her feet before she can connect the blow.

"No, put me down!" She screams, fighting to free herself. I watch as Darren Manning, a volunteer firefighter, throws Jasmine over his shoulder and carries her across the parking lot to his F-250.

Crisis averted.

A hand rests against my arm. The warm caress sends excitement racing through my veins. I glance down at the delicate fingers, then gaze up the arm to the face of the woman touching me.

"Harlow, I—"

"Come on, let me get you out of here," Harlow says, casting a disdainful glance over toward Jasmine.

Darren secures Jasmine in the passenger seat of his truck, despite her protests, and stomps over to the driver's side.

Harlow looks back at me then slips her hand in mine. My resistance fades, and I follow her down the sidewalk. She presses a button on her key fob. The lights of a sleek, shiny burgundy Maserati flash.

I pull back, causing Harlow to falter, but she doesn't let go of my hand.

"I'm drenched in coffee." I fumble over my words. "I can't get into … that."

"Sure, you can." Harlow dismisses my hesitation with a gentle squeeze. "It's only a five-minute drive to my house. I can always get the car detailed later, if necessary."

"Are you sure?"

"It's just a car." Harlow shrugs. "Come on."

I walk to the other side of the luxury coupe and open the door. I've never been in a car that costs twice my annual salary before. This should be interesting. Stepping to the side, I wring the excess coffee from my shirt and shorts as best I can then ease down onto the soft Italian leather.

Harlow starts the engine and steers out of the parking lot. Silence fills the car, but it's the comfortable kind. I lean my head back and close my eyes, trying to shake the frustration from the encounter with Jasmine Jones.

Before I can get too comfortable, Harlow says, "We're here."

I glance ahead at the stunning house set on the opposite side of Lake Lasso from the commercial park. It blends beautifully in the space, constructed with limestone and boasting tons of windows. Towering pine trees surround the secluded property. I follow her out of the car and onto a wide outdoor porch.

"Construction is finished, but my friend Zaire still has to get the interior decorating done before I can move in," Harlow says, chuckling. "So, there's no furniture. But I do have running water, and the appliances have been installed. You can take a shower while I wash the coffee out of your clothes."

"Why are you doing this?"

"I don't know what happened between you and Jasmine, but I do know that she's … difficult. She shouldn't have come after you like that. It wasn't the time or the place."

"Her anger is justified."

"Is it?"

"You don't think so?"

"Something about the look in your eyes as she tried to goad you into an argument tells me no." Harlow unlocks the door and steps inside, holding it open for me.

I cross the threshold into the luxurious interior. Most of the outer walls are floor-to-ceiling windows giving a one-hundred-eighty-degree view of the lake no matter what part of the house you're in. The architecture is stunning. The layout is interesting and varied, a maze of corners, angles, and arches that convey an open and airy feel, almost as if you're still outside.

Harlow rests a hand against my face, bringing me out of my awed stupor.

"Are you okay?" She asks, caressing the side of my cheek.

I lean into her touch, feeling for the first time in so long that I am. The stress of seeing Jasmine, the looming debt, and the loneliness that clung to me are nowhere around when I'm with Harlow. I'm soothed by her presence and more at ease and comfortable than at any other time. How did she do that for me? And did it matter?

"I am now. Thanks for getting me away from there."

"Anytime."

"Really?" I raise an eyebrow. A hint of a smile emerges on my face.

Harlow loses the fight of hiding her own smile and gives in, wowing me with the brilliance of her grin.

"Yes." She removes her hand from my face, slips a finger into her mouth, then frowns. "Pumpkin spice, yuck. I knew Jasmine had terrible taste, but this proves it."

I erupt into laughter, then lick my lips slowly. I can't help but notice how much that simple move seems to captivate her. Her eyes lock onto my lips. I stare at Harlow, memorizing every contour of her face. My heart swells, and all I want is to pull her into my arms and kiss her like there's no tomorrow.

But there is the pesky thing of the ongoing arson investigation at her family's brewery holding me back. I don't just need the job financially. I actually love the work. I can't jeopardize my career and livelihood. Not even for Harlow.

I say, "You're right. Definitely pumpkin spice. The flavor of fall that we both hate."

"Come on, let's get you cleaned up," she says, beckoning for me to follow her.

I pass through the wide-open space that houses the family room and enter what I suspect is her master bedroom. She opens a door and leads me through a closet that's about the size of my apartment, then into a massive en suite bathroom. A large jacuzzi tub dominates the center, flanked by his and hers sinks and cabinets. Tucked toward the back wall is the shower with overhead Vichy jets extending from the ceiling and the side walls.

"I was testing out potential color schemes, so I happened to have a few sets of towels here," Harlow explains, pulling out three oversized plush towels in pale green, bright blue, and peach. She extends them toward me to select.

I'm drawn to the pale green and lift it from her hands.

"Good choice. Toss your clothes out, and I can have them washed and dried by the time you finish showering," Harlow says.

Without thinking, I lift my t-shirt over my head and hand it to Harlow. She sucks in a sharp breath as her eyes travel over my chest. I resist the urge to flex my muscles and put on a show for her to enjoy.

"Santos …"

"Not like you haven't seen any of this before," I tease. The memories slam into my mind, making me dizzy with desire for her.

"Don't do that."

"Do what?"

"Try to distract me with your amazing body, and it is stunning, when I can see you're hurting. Do you want to talk about it?"

I blow air out of my mouth and slump down on the edge of the jacuzzi. Harlow sits next to me. Close enough for me to feel the warmth of her against my skin. To feel her support and unconditional acceptance. Now is the time for me to talk about this. Really talk about it, and Harlow is the only person I want to do this with.

"Remember when we were in Napa, and I told you that my father had … passed away," I say.

Harlow nods then laces her fingers between mine. That gentle touch soothes me, making the conversation feel effortless.

"Papi moved to Kimbell after we found out St. Elizabeth's was the best place for him to get treatment. For years, he was at least not getting worse, but we knew he was terminal. There was no cure, but he still kept fighting to hang on as long as possible. Lived ten years. Much longer than any of the doctors predicted," I pause, squeezing the bridge of my nose.

Harlow's arm slips around my neck as she presses her head against my shoulder.

"The last few months, as he battled the disease, he was in constant pain. No amount of pain killers could dull it enough for him to be comfortable, and he began to lose hope. I took out a second mortgage on my house and maxed out my credit cards to pay for all kinds of treatment. We tried western medicine, eastern healing. Anything to help his last days be easier. His doctor and I talked almost daily about how to help him, and the topic of assisted dying came up. There was no way I was going for that. I made it clear to the doctor that was not an option for us and to not bring it up to Papi. We'd have to find another way to ease his pain until he passed away on his own."

"Did the doctor …"

"Yeah, he did. He went behind my back and left a lethal secobarbital prescription by Papi's bedside. I talked to Papi that night, and he said the doctor had brought some medicine that would help take away his pain," I paused, emotion clogging my throat. "Usually, I picked up all of Papi's prescriptions, and trust me, they weren't cheap. So, it was weird that the doctor had given him a prescription without me being involved. Felt like something was wrong. So, I called the doctor."

"It was Dr. Uriah Jones, wasn't it? Jasmine's father."

"Yeah. He started going on and on about how it was time for me to let go and let my father be at peace. I panicked and drove as fast as I could to Kimbell, but it was already too late. Papi was gone."

"I'm so sorry. I can't imagine how hard that was for you. I'd heard that Dr. Jones was sentenced to prison, but I didn't know your father was the victim."

"Some people don't think my father was a victim. They think that Dr. Jones was giving him a peaceful and dignified way to die."

"What do you think?"

I tip my head back and search her ceiling in vain for an answer to that question. The question that has haunted me ever since I called the cops on Dr. Jones.

"I honestly don't know anymore," I say, revealing the truth that weighs on me. "Papi never talked about it with me, but maybe it was because he couldn't. How do you tell your only son that you're tired of fighting a disease and want everlasting rest? He knew I wouldn't want him to do it. I thought if he'd left a letter or something to let me know he wanted what Dr. Jones had offered, I could find a way to be okay with it."

"But there was no letter."

"No. I don't have any definitive proof that it was what Papi wanted or not. Maybe there's something in the house he used to live in. I've been putting off going over there to go through his things."

"You think you might find something?"

"I don't know. Maybe."

"It must be hard wanting to find the truth, but also not really wanting to after all this time. I can understand why you'd avoid that place, but in the end, I think it's much better to know one way or the other. You really should go and see what's in the house," Harlow presses me.

"I'm planning to … later," I say, which isn't entirely a lie. I've told Alma the same. I just haven't made any definitive moves to make it happen since I've been here. "All I know is that Dr. Jones paid for the secobarbital with his own money and left it on Papi's bedside, and that is a crime in Texas. I wanted to make sure he experienced the consequences of his actions."

"And that's why Jasmine hates you. Her dad committed a crime, lost his medical license, and went to jail, and she blames you."

"She said it's what Papi wanted, and her dad was being compassionate. Maybe she's right. Maybe she's wrong. It doesn't matter anymore."

"Because getting justice didn't make your pain or hurt go away."

"And it didn't bring back my father," I say. "I lost over a year of my life focused on making Dr. Jones pay for killing my dad. Through it all, the only light in my life was the memory of the week I spent with you in Napa. That's why I got the tattoo. It reminded me that there was still some good in the world, even if I couldn't see it."

"I see good in you, Santos."

A mirthless laugh escapes my lips. "Trust me, you don't need someone like me in your life. It would never—"

"Never say never," Harlow interrupts and stands. "That shower over there is like heaven on earth. Turn on all the shower heads and press the button for the aromatherapy steam. In an hour, you'll feel like a brand new man."

I watch as she walks out of the bathroom.

I marvel that somehow, I already do.

CHAPTER 14

H*ARLOW-ROSE*

"This is really good beer," Santos says, holding the bottle of Elm Beer up toward the moonlight.

I stare at him, sitting casually in my custom-made teak wood Adirondack chair, and can't deny how right it feels for us to be here like this. Together. Like he fits perfectly into my life even though I know he'd argue that I'm wrong.

I toss another piece of wood onto the fire pit and watch the dazzling orange and yellow flames dance up toward the sky. Grabbing the last bottle, I hand it to him and take his empty one.

"Dad says the barley is his lucky ingredient," I say, then rest the empty bottle between the debris collecting on my back patio deck. It joins the other remnants of trash—discarded empty pizza box and two plastic to-go containers that once upon a time held Kimbell's best cinnamon rolls. "He's bought it from the same family since he opened the brewery and swears by it. But it's his special brewing process that makes the beer so good. He's just too modest to say it."

Santos unscrews the cap off the beer and tosses it into the fray of trash, then takes a long swig. I watch as his neck bobs from drinking the liquid and imagine what it would feel like to pepper his neck with kisses. To have the smooth hairs of his beard brush against my lips. I have to stop doing this. We've been out here, underneath the moonlight, talking for hours with no sign of stopping. The longer I'm with him, the more wayward and wanton my fantasies are becoming.

Santos interrupts my latest fantasy. "He let you in on his trade secrets?"

"I'm probably the only one who knows them all. As much as he pushed me away from running the brewery, he never held back on everything he did to make it a success. I've worked in about every area of the company. I'd hang out there almost every day, watching and learning."

He hands the bottle toward me. I take it eagerly, pressing my lips on the cool glass where his had been, and drink the beer.

"Think that's why your winery is taking off now?" Santos asks, a sneaky grin playing at his lips. "I looked up some articles about you online last week. You're a winery marvel. Overnight success."

I flush, thrilled that Santos had been thinking about me as much as I had thought of him in the week since seeing each other at the gazebo.

"A seven-year overnight success," I say, crossing my arms over my chest. "But I do think being around Dad's business helped."

"Business is business, right?"

"Yeah, that's the easy part. The accounting, the marketing pieces. It's operations that are so different," I say, groaning. I run my fingers through my tight curls as Santos stares at every move I make. Lifting a hairband from my pocket, I force my hair into a puff at the top of my head and secure it in place. I take another sip of beer.

"So, what's the hard part?" He stands and lifts the bottle of beer from my hand. Our fingers brush, leaving a trail of heat on my skin.

"For me, making wine is so much harder than beer. There are things about the process that people would never think of. Guess how many hours I work a week?"

"Fifty?" He raises an eyebrow, making his handsome face sexier.

"Try seventy. I work seven days a week. I can't take a day off. I work with my team making sure the land is cultivated, the vineyards are thriving, testing the chemical content of the grapes, planning out our offerings four and five years into the future. It's exhausting," I rub a hand against my neck.

"And you love every minute of it," Santos says, tossing the empty bottle to the ground. He reaches for my hand and pulls me toward him. As he eases down onto the chair, he pulls me down with him.

I'm sitting sideways on his lap with his arm resting around my waist. Every part of me wants to jump for joy, but then I'd miss out on being this close to him again after all this time. I force myself to relax and enjoy being with him.

I ask, "Is it that obvious?"

He squeezes my hair puff, then nods. "It's impossible for you to hide when you're truly passionate about something. I picked up on that when we first met in Napa, and I see it stronger now. That's a good thing."

"And what are *you* passionate about?" I ask, wanting to know more than the general topics we'd covered already.

"Nothing really." He says, then stares at the stars dotting the night sky. His hand strokes slowly across my back in a hypnotic motion.

"I don't believe that. There's got to be something that makes you want to wake up in the morning and get at it." I rest my hand against his arm, where the tattoo of my winery logo is etched on his skin. My voice softens. "I get that it's not work for everyone, but there's usually something."

Santos is quiet for a long moment. Only the sound of the fire, hissing, and crackling, permeates the air. I'm content to let him ponder my question as long as he needs to because knowing his answer is important. Like it could be the bridge to something special between us, and I'm eager to cross.

"You really are going to wait until I answer, aren't you?" His honey eyes rest on my face. A hint of trepidation behind his gaze. I want him to know that he can trust me with anything. His deepest and darkest thoughts. Nothing will make me think less of him. I contemplate telling him that, but I know what will happen next. The lecture about how we can't get involved because of the investigation. He'd probably demand I take him back to Crockett Manor, and this wonderful night will be over much sooner than I want. Instead of saying what I really feel, I take a safer route.

"I have all night. I already texted my team and told them I'd be coming in late tomorrow."

"Fine," Santos says, shaking his head. His gorgeous honey eyes turn a shade darker as he looks at me. "Family. I grew up with a big one. I was the oldest, and I had a younger brother and younger twin sisters. We were so close and did everything together."

My heart lurches as I suspect there's more tragedy that Santos has gone through than I ever knew. He never mentioned having siblings in all the time we've spent together.

"Growing up, my house was the one all my friends wanted to come to after school and on the weekends. My mom would make the best Tex-Mex you ever tasted in your life. Enchiladas, empanadas, fajitas. You name it, she'd mastered it. The boys would play soccer in the street while the girls sat in the yard playing dolls."

"Sounds so fun." And nothing like my upbringing. Fun was always tied to something educational. There wasn't play for the sake of playing.

"Don't get me wrong. We were poor as dirt. My parents and four kids living in a two-bedroom shack in the worst part of San Antonio. But none of that mattered because we had each other." Darkness passes across Santos's face. "But all that ended when a teenage driver slammed into my mom's car after she'd picked up my brother and sisters from a friend's house late one night. They were all killed."

I open my mouth, but no words come out.

"After that, it was just Papi and me. It took a long time for me to get over the loss, probably because we never got justice. The teenager was from one of the wealthiest families in San Antonio. We heard rumors that he was drunk, but his family protected him long enough so that it couldn't be proven. In the end, it was ruled an accident, and no charges were filed," Santos says, then strokes a hand along my cheek. "I didn't tell you that to depress you or to open up any old wound for myself. I was ten when it happened. Papi and I had years to work through all of our anger and pain and move past it. It's just he was the last family I had. I'm alone now, and I guess I'm kind of struggling to figure out what's next. What is my reason for waking up in the morning? It used to be to make him proud. He wanted me to be the first in our family to graduate from college. I did that. He loved that I chose to be a firefighter and to help people. He was more proud when I became an arson investigator and could put away the bad guys. Without him here, pushing me along, it's like I can't think about anything but clawing my way out of the debt that I'm in. After that, who knows."

"Can I hug you?" I ask, knowing that I have no words that could make any of this better for him.

Santos laughs a hearty laugh that lets me know he truly is okay. "You're sorry you asked?"

"No, actually, I'm not." Slipping my hands around his shoulders, I lean in and embrace him. The heady scent of my soap mingled with his raw masculinity is intoxicating.

"You give great hugs. Did I ever tell you that?"

I giggle. "Good to know." I release him, then shift on his lap. The slight pressure from his hand tells me he doesn't want me to get up, so I stay in place. "I do think you'll find your way, though. Everything that your family gave to you is still inside here." I press my hands on his heart and feel it pounding underneath my touch. "Knowing the question is half the battle of finding the answer."

"Always with the positive spin."

"I am who I am. But seriously, I, for one, know that family doesn't always come to you in the traditional sense. You have to be open to recognizing the new family around you. People like Ronan and Luke and definitely Alma. She sounds like quite the character."

"She is. I was really glad Papi found her later in life. It was good to see him in love again," Santos says. "He used to tell me all the time to get out there and date. Date as much as you can. It's the only way you can find the right woman for you. I'd ask him, how will I know she's the one if I'm dating every chica on the planet? Seemed like a recipe for being labeled a player and ending up a bachelor for life."

Curious, I ask, "So what was his answer?"

"I can't give away Estrada Family secrets." He teases, tapping me on the nose.

"Do you think the answer he gave you was right?"

Santos's stare turns intense, and I feel my body temperature ratchet up several degrees.

"Absolutely." His definitive response sizzles between us. The look in his eyes convey exactly what I hope, but what we could never say. At least not yet.

Santos clears his throat. "Now enough about me. Tell me about you and growing up adopted."

"Yes, I have an unusual family. Black girl adopted by an Asian mom and a White dad doesn't happen very often."

"Was that hard for you?"

"Yes and no. I mean, I never had to go through any shock of finding out I was adopted. It was pretty obvious, even if my parents didn't do a good job of explaining it to me when I was really young." Feeling bolder, I lean onto his chest, resting my head against his shoulder. His grip tightens around me. "The hard part came when I was a teenager and found out more details about my birth parents."

"Did you ever meet them?"

"No, I still have no clue who they are."

"They wanted the adoption to be closed. No information shared with you."

"It wasn't that kind of adoption."

Santos looks intrigued but doesn't say anything.

"Here's what I know. Two kids check into a motel on the outskirts of Kimbell. The person working there said they barely looked like teenagers, maybe thirteen or fourteen years old. The boy was scrawny, and the girl was fat, or so they thought. They had enough cash for the room, and times were tough, so the worker never reported that they were there."

"Runaways. It's a shame the motel clerk didn't call the cops."

"The next morning, they found the bed bloody and me in the middle of it. No sign of the kids. I was taken to the hospital and checked out. My mom volunteered there and saw me. She said something in her told her that I was her daughter. I never had to spend a day in foster care. I went home a Robinson, and they finalized the adoption after a year of trying to search for my birth parents with no luck."

"Did you ever think about them coming back to find you?"

"I was thirteen when they told me the details, and it kinda wrecked me for years. I was so scared they would come back and force me to leave the only family I knew and loved. I didn't want another mom and dad. The ones I have are perfect for me."

"Legally, there wouldn't have been anything they could do since they abandoned you. The Robinsons would have continued to be your parents."

"That's what everyone told me, but you know how it is when you're young. It took a while for me to believe it, and now, I don't fear meeting them."

"But you also don't see a reason to seek them out?"

"Nope," I say, then glance up at the brightening sky. "Sun is about to come up."

"Whoa, we really talked all night ..."

"Want me to drive you back to town?"

"You're not tired?"

I shake my head, noticing that he looks as wired and awake as I am. There's no way I could think about sleeping and miss spending this time with Santos. "I'll force myself to take a nap, then head back to Fredericksburg this afternoon."

"You're leaving?"

"Construction on the restaurant is picking up, and I'm expanding the tours and tastings to Fridays starting this week."

"Sounds like you'll be a very busy woman."

"If you need a break on the weekend, you should come down to the winery." I hold my breath, wondering if the invitation crosses some kind of professional line for him.

But there's no hesitation in his response. "I'll do that."

CHAPTER 15

ARLOW-ROSE

"STOP IT WITH THE GOOFY GRIN," I SAY, STARING AT myself in the mirror. My curls are particularly unruly this morning, mashed against my head in an unflattering style that I wouldn't dare be caught dead with outside. This is Santos's fault. If I hadn't been on the phone with him until the early morning hours for the third consecutive night, I would've done my regular nightly routine of tying up my hair and wrapping it within a silk bonnet.

Instead, I have less than two hours to make myself presentable before customers start arriving for the tours and tastings. My goofy grin spreads wider. I pinch myself and wonder how did this happen so fast. One minute I'm rescuing Santos from Jasmine's wrath, and the next, we're talking until the sun comes up at my lake house.

When we were in Napa, I'd thought we had so much in common. This week has shown me Napa was just the tip of the iceberg. As I pulled up in front of Crockett Manor to drop Santos off around dawn, he grabbed my cell phone and typed his number into the contacts. Tossing it back in my lap, he exited the car and said, "Call me," before shutting the door.

Too wired to sleep, I'd driven straight to Fredericksburg and worked a full ten-hour day before crashing in my studio apartment nestled upstairs above the main tasting room floor. Sleep had clawed at me, but I couldn't forget Santos's words. Before I could talk myself out of it, I dialed his number. Another marathon conversation later, and I finally drifted off to sleep sometime past three in the morning. The following two nights had been the same. We talked after we finished our busy days until late into the night. Each conversation undulating from serious to silly, frivolous to significant, as we get to know each other better. And knowing more is plunging me into the deep end of feelings I've never felt for any man.

Shaking away the thoughts of the sexy arson investigator, I glance at the clock. Again. It's almost nine, and my team will be expecting me downstairs soon. I can already hear them bustling below, getting everything ready for the opening at eleven.

I wonder what time Santos is coming today. He'd reiterated again last night that he's coming but didn't give me a sense of when. To say I'm nervous is an understatement. He'd heard all my early plans for the winery two years ago and probably understands my vision better than anyone. Knowing what he thinks of how it all turned out is more important to me than I want to admit.

"Stop thinking about Santos, Harlow-Rose!" I yell at myself, then resign to completely put him out of my head. There's work to be done.

I quickly brush my teeth then wrangle my spritzer from underneath the full bathroom cabinet. Spraying my hair with water and then curling cream, I watch the tight curls spring back to life, gorgeous and shiny. Twenty minutes and a quick shower later, I'm donning a red winery logo t-shirt and leggings as I jog down the steps to the tasting room floor.

A large circular bar dominates the center of the space with three stations of glass racks. Walking into the interior, I survey the inventory of wine being put out by one of the bartenders, pleased that my team had followed my meticulous instructions exactly. It's times like this that I am very much so Qingyang Robinson's daughter. Micromanaging is her specialty. And now it's mine.

Across from the center bar are several enclaves, one filled with logo merchandise, another with specialty foods that complement the wines, and two with casual seating. Wide, large windows are evenly arranged around the perimeter, allowing the beauty of the hill country to flood inside.

I press my hands on my hips, watching the flurry of activity as I greet each worker and swell with pride. It's bittersweet to experience my greatest success as Dad goes through the worst moments with his own company. Elm Street Brewery is as much his life as Harlow-Rose winery is mine. A sourness fills my stomach, knowing how hard it is for Dad to wait. His frustration was evident when I talked to him a couple of days ago. The longer the arson investigation goes on, the longer it will take for him to get the insurance money to rebuild the brewery. Waiting isn't a Robinson Family virtue. We are doers.

Just another reason for me to hope that Santos finds whoever set the fire and closes the investigation as soon as possible.

A loud knock raps against the heavy wooden door.

I jump, my head jerking toward the sound. Obviously, whoever is outside doesn't realize that the winery won't open for another hour and a half. I wave away one of the staff and head to the door to explain to the eager customer myself.

I pull the door open and poke my head out.

"Good morning," Santos says, a playfulness in his eyes.

"Hey. I didn't think you'd be here this early," I say, my voice hitting a higher octave.

"My guys have been working hard, so I thought it would be nice to give them a Friday off. Let them have a three-day weekend." Santos leans against the door frame. "Plus, I had something I really wanted to do today."

"Well, I guess that settles it. Come on in." He brushes against me as he walks inside, leaving a wake of his sensual scent to tantalize me. My heart thuds in my throat as I take him around and introduce him as my "friend" Santos to my team. They're too busy with prep work to give the sparks shooting between him and me a second glance, which is a relief.

"Can I take a look around?" Santos asks.

I nod, then watch as he weaves through the various areas, pausing to peruse some, lifting containers, running his hands over merchandise with a slight nod. As he comes back to where I'm standing behind the bar, I realize that I'm holding my breath, wanting to know what he thinks.

"I never forgot your plans for this place. How excited you were back in Napa when you talked about your vision," Santos says, then leans over the bar.

"How'd I do?"

"Impressive," he says, then gazes around the room again in awe. "It's like I see the essence of everything you told me you wanted, but you amped it up a notch. Raised the bar for yourself and met it. Good to see you carved out a small part of the brewery to have here, too."

"It's part of my story and the tour. I want people to know that I grew up learning the business of alcohol, beer, and spirits long before I went to school and got a Master of Viticulture and Enology," I explain. "And if they like beer, they can get a bottle of one of Texas' best." At least for a few more weeks. My inventory of Elm Beer won't last much longer, and nothing is being produced to replace it for me or any other businesses and stores that sell it. I bite my tongue, not wanting to bring up the investigation. There's no way Santos would tell me any details on why it's taking so long. I don't want to ruin the mood.

"Let me help out today," Santos asks.

"You want to work with me?"

"I'm a quick learner, and you're a very smart businesswoman. I know you're not about to turn down free labor."

Definitely not when it comes in a package that looks like Santos Estrada.

I step from behind the bar and walk to a rack of winery t-shirts in red. Flipping through the sizes, I find an extra large and pull it off the hanger. Might be tight for his broad shoulders and muscular chest, but it would give us a treat as he works.

"If you're going to do the part, you have to look the part," I say, tossing the t-shirt at him.

Santos catches it in one fluid motion.

I have to stop myself from drooling as he slips his shirt off and replaces it with the winery t-shirt. He tosses his shirt at me. I fold it and place it on one of the shelves behind the bar.

"Perfect," I say. "Now follow me. We're going to give you a crash course on how we do things at Harlow-Rose Winery."

I turn and wave at Gina Owen, my second in command and the woman who helps me run a tight ship on the retail side of the business.

"Hey, so Santos has decided he wants to roll up his sleeves and help us with the work today," I say.

Santos gives Gina a sexy wink, then melts me with his devastating smile.

Gina says, "Well, we sure won't turn down any help. How about I switch up the schedule and have you work with him inside on the tastings, and I'll do the tours this time."

"Great idea," I say, then lean back against the bar.

"What do I need to do?" Santos asks.

Gina launches into a whirlwind of instructions, peppering him with the dos and don'ts for the tastings. He falls in sync next to her, maneuvering around the bar with ease, picking up quickly on all the instructions. After Gina is satisfied that he understands the process and order to serve wines, she leads him to the main floor area. I listen in as she explains how we keep the traffic flow within the tasting room from becoming overcrowded and how to greet guests and follow up with them regularly.

"I think I got it," Santos says, then gives me a reassuring look.

"And Harlow-Rose will let you know if you mess up," Gina says. "She's very good at that."

"Gina!" I say, but don't disagree. It's part of the reason that our tasting and tours have run so well over the past two weeks. Following protocols without any deviation is critical to establishing the Harlow-Rose Winery brand.

"I'm not worried," Santos says, his eyes locking onto mine. "I'm very good at taking directions." He licks his lips slowly as his eyes rake across my body. My temperature shoots through the roof, and my face flushes from his subtle flirting.

"Well, get in place because we're opening in five minutes. A line has already started outside." Gina leaves us alone to check that the other workers are in their assigned areas then opens the large wooden doors of the winery.

The hours fly by until the heavy stream of guests has become a manageable trickle. One sweet older couple has been drinking their way through each of my wine varieties, buying bottles along the way. They were up to the fifth variety and hadn't gotten to the Cabernet yet, which by design is the last wine of the entire tasting and served with a delectable piece of 80% dark chocolate.

"Sweetheart, look," the gray-haired woman with bright brown eyes gives Santos a warm smile. "He has a tattoo of the logo on his arm. That's so romantic. I hope your ..." She glances at his hand to see it devoid of a wedding band, then continues, "girlfriend appreciates it."

I flush, my eyes growing wide as heat envelops my neck and cheeks for the hundredth time today. I place a glass in front of the woman's husband and pour it full of pinot noir with a shaky hand. "We're not a couple."

"You're not? Could have fooled about everybody in here," the husband chimes in. "The two of you are giving off some strong relationship vibes."

I can feel Santos's gaze but refuse to turn and look at him. I grab a complimentary plate of cheese and crackers and sit it between the married couple's two wine glasses. "Pecorino and manchego go perfectly with this wine," I say, ignoring the husband's comment even though I'm in complete agreement with both of them. There's no way to explain to anyone why Santos and I are in limbo. Only Gina knows that he's the arson investigator for the brewery fire. The other workers think he's an old friend of mine.

I freeze as Santos speaks.

"No, we're not a couple. But we should be."

My mouth goes dry, and I press my hands against the bar. Did he just say that out loud?

As if to answer my internal question, Santos slides his arm around my waist, cradling my body next to his. I register the strength of his solid, defined, muscular body in an instant. I'm breathless and overwhelmed by how good this feels. How right it is.

The woman starts clapping. "I have a feeling that you're going to get the girl really soon, young man."

I sneak a glance up into Santos's honey eyes, and I'm struck by the passion I see emanating from him.

"Y'all need anything else?" Santos asks the couple but never takes his eyes from me.

The woman shakes her head.

"We're good for now, thank you," the husband says.

"Good. I think it's time for me to get the girl."

If his arms weren't supporting me, I'm sure I would've fainted to the floor.

I take stock and notice that only a handful of people are still meandering through the tasting room. It's almost closing time.

As Gina passes by, I say, "Can you close up without us?"

She gives me a salacious, knowing grin. "Of course. Get out of here."

Santos holds my hand and leads me out of the winery.

The blustery humid wind blazes across my face as we head out to the vineyard. It's mid-September, but the temperatures are still scorching. Weaving through the rows of grapevines, we veer left at the fork and meander toward a massive oak tree in silence. A carved wooden bench seat circles around the trunk.

"Have a seat," Santos says, releasing my hand.

Grateful for the shade and to give my wobbly legs a break, I collapse down onto the bench and press my back into the sturdy oak. Santos sits next to me, his hands fidgeting as he stares across acres of my land.

"I found my reason to wake up in the morning," he says after a long silence.

"Santos, that's wonderful," I say, joy infecting my words. "I knew you would if you took the time to listen to yourself. Are you going to tell me what it is?"

He turns slightly, his honey-eyes a shade darker and twinkling with devotion. "I'm looking at her."

"Oh." I wish I'd had a better response, but my mind is reeling.

"This week, I was reminded of how you inspire me to be a better man and how much I love being the person I am when I'm around you. Even the crap I'm still dealing with from the foreclosure and the debt doesn't seem insurmountable anymore. That's because you make me believe that things will get better for me. That I can overcome anything. No one has ever made me feel like that, but you, Harlow."

I shift to face him as the words rush from my mouth. "You make me feel the same way, Santos. It's crazy that it took my family's brewery being destroyed for our paths to cross again. Sometimes it feels weird to be grateful for the fire, but I'm not going to lie. I do. It brought you back to me. I know Dad will rebuild Elm Street Brewery better than it was before. But this … between us. I never thought I'd get this chance. Now that you're here, I don't want to lose you again."

Santos leans forward, resting his hands on my waist, and

presses his forehead against mine. His voice is pained as he whispers, "This won't be easy."

"Anything worth it never is." My heart swells as he pulls me closer, his arms wrapping around the small of my back. I rest my hands along his massive arms, stroking his skin slowly.

"I shouldn't get involved with you until after the investigation is over, but I don't want to wait."

"I would never do anything to compromise the investigation. I want you to figure out who burned our brewery." I'm desperate to convince him not to put on the brakes and force distance between us.

"I know you wouldn't, but it doesn't change the fact that it creates the perception of a conflict of interest for me," Santos pulls back and stares into my eyes. His face sober. I can read in his expression the potentially dire consequences of us exploring a relationship with each other too soon. "Besides you, my job is the best thing I have in my life. I'm up for a promotion at the end of the year and, with it, a nice raise. But it's not just about the money. I believe in the work I do. There were three workers in that building when it went up in flames. It's a miracle that Luke and Nate were able to get them out alive. They risked their own lives to do it. Whoever set those dominoes in motion needs to be brought to justice. I will do that."

My shoulders sag, and I look away. If I look at him, I won't do what needs to be done. "Santos, we both know you'd never let our relationship interfere with your work. But I'm not sure how far this can really go until the investigation is over." I wrap my arms around my stomach, ignoring the dull ache building. "I can wait."

"Can't believe I'm going to suggest this …"

I look back at him. "What?"

"We can see each other in secret."

"You mean, sneak around?" A spark of hope flutters inside me.

"Look, I'm not crossing any lines by telling you that the brewery fire is one of the most complex we've dealt with. I can't promise you that the investigation will be wrapped up in the next few days or weeks. Do you really think we can stay away from each other that long? Or longer?"

My pulse quickens. "Absolutely not."

"So … you're okay with keeping us a secret for a while?" Santos asks, his eyes pleading with me to give the answer he wants. The only answer that I'd ever give to him because it's what I want, too.

"Yes."

Before the words have escaped my lips, Santos's mouth is on mine.

The kiss is explosive, pouring out every ounce of the longing that has built up between us over the past two weeks, mingling with our memories from Napa. His hands cup my face as his lips enthrall me. His kisses are at once gentle and blistering, fueled by the unbridled passion that has been waiting to be unleashed between us.

I welcome the sweet taste of his mouth, urging the kiss to deepen as I squeeze my arms around his neck. Santos's reaction is instantaneous as he kisses me like it's the only thing he ever wants to do in the world. As I lose myself in him, I know beyond a shadow of a doubt that there's no way I want to be away from him ever again.

CHAPTER 16

~

MY CELL PHONE BEEPS. I HOPE THAT IT'S A TEXT FROM Harlow. She doesn't text a lot, so the other officers don't start to suspect anything. But I went the extra distance and have her saved in my phone under Alma's name in case anyone gets nosy. That does make for some careful actions on my end not to mix up my messages for Harlow and send them to the real Alma by mistake.

The pop-up on the small screen deflates me as I see a preview of a new email to my work address. I flip open my laptop and log in. It's from the testing facility alerting me of further delays in processing the test results.

More delays that I don't want and can't afford.

We sent in hundreds of samples for extensive testing almost a month ago and are still waiting for results. Finding out if there are any incendiary chemicals or residues in the soot and debris gathered from Joe Little's office is critical to the investigation.

My relationship with Harlow is in limbo until I can get these answers. It's been two weeks since we decided to see each other secretly. Despite the stress of sneaking around, I have no regrets. The alternative never would've worked. Too much had happened between us for me to stay away from her completely while this investigation dragged on.

Part of me thinks starting our relationship this way is better. The secrecy and trying to find time together away from the prying eyes of my team and the entire town of Kimbell, including her family and friends, is more than exciting. It's connecting us on a deeper level, drawing us closer and closer. In the past couple of weeks, we've synced our friend finder apps to allow us to find each other without having to text details. There isn't much to do late at night after work, but we've seen five movies and shared a few dinners at a restaurant in Fredericksburg. The times I cherish most are when we spend the evening walking through the rows of grapevines at her vineyard in comfortable silence, content to be in each other's presence. And when we can't sneak away to see each other, we fill in the gaps with late-night phone conversations.

Conversations that rivet me as I get to know more about the beautiful woman who has completely stolen my heart. All the differences that I thought would turn her off from wanting to be with me don't matter. She looks beyond the superficial and treats me with respect, like equals, regardless of the fact she can waste more money in a day than I earn in a year. She doesn't care that I'm broke. She cares about me. Harlow is exactly the woman I want and need in my life. As soon as this investigation is over, I'm going to make sure that the entire world knows it.

But that means I have to stop daydreaming about her and focus back on the case. Kicking my feet onto the desk, I lean back and stare at the laptop resting on my thighs.

I scroll through the witness interview reports, each with yellow highlights denoting critical information that form a timeline of who was at the brewery before the fire. My notes from the most recent interview of Ace Lallo, a maintenance worker for the town of Kimbell, solidify what I already know.

I need to find Joe Little and question him about the fire.

With Ace's information, that makes six witnesses that put Joe Little in the vicinity or entering the brewery in the early afternoon on the day of the fire. This is after Scott Robinson, and his employees had left for Lake Lasso to have their quarterly team meeting and happy hour. Interestingly, Scott left the brewery about an hour after the others and arrived at the retreat late. The timing overlaps witness reports about Joe, which means that they could've been in the offices at the same time. Maybe even seen each other or talked. Scott didn't mention it, but that doesn't mean it didn't happen.

Too many people saw Joe Little there and noticed because the whole town knew he'd been fired a few weeks earlier. Some presumed he was picking up personal belongings, while others made a mental note to tell Scott Robinson the next time they saw him.

Usually, I prefer to have more objective evidence that a suspect was near the fire. Unfortunately, the security cameras mounted around the corporate offices and brewery were dummies, designed to deter but not actually record any activity. The brewery didn't have a security guard. The perks of being located in a small town where everyone knows everyone and crime is nearly nonexistent.

I glance at the papers strewn across the desk, then place my laptop on the mess. There is no doubt that a dust explosion occurred in the primary production building of the brewery. Interviews from the employees revealed a deterioration of protocols over the past couple of years. Cleaning of the facility had waned, and there was a damaged silo leaking grain that hadn't been fixed in months.

Several workers mentioned regular maintenance on equipment that had been postponed and signs that others were malfunctioning. Increasing amounts of dust in the air had started to irritate the workers, causing allergies and coughing spells. But nothing was done by Scott Robinson to fix things up. Production continued, as usual, creating a perfect storm of ingredients to set off the chain reaction of explosions from the grain dust accumulating inside the plant.

But had the fire started in the production facility? Or was it fire from the corporate office that spread and ignited the dust instead? The intense burn patterns we found in Joe Little's former office were a potential indication that the fire started there. It wouldn't take much for flames to make their way to the interconnected air ducts and cause the dust in the back buildings to ignite. Because of the intense explosions in the production area, it was almost impossible to determine if the fire started there or in the corporate offices. At least not without the test results.

Pushing away from the desk, I roll the chair to a stop against the wall and stand up. My muscles are stiff from sitting in the same spot for the past few hours, and my stomach is crying out for some sustenance.

Gathering the papers, I stack them into neat piles, place them in the appropriate file folders, and then lock the drawer. I head down to the second floor, where the firefighter breakroom and living quarters are housed.

As I descend the stairs, I can hear tense conversation from inside. Stopping at the information board, I scan the schedule, and I'm relieved to see that it's Shift A on duty tonight. Ronan's shift. It never hurts to see a friendly face. Plus, I can find out the latest gossip on where Joe Little might be hiding out.

I round the corner and stop short as the door to the break room swings open with a loud bang.

Darren Manning stalks out the door, shoulder checking me and sending both of us stumbling backward.

"Watch where you're going," I growl, not deterred by the brazen stare Darren gives me. A look that would make the average man wither. I'm not the average man, and Darren knows this. I'm not intimidated or impressed by the former Super Bowl MVP and two-time defensive player of the year.

Darren steps closer, looking down at me. "There's no reason for you to still be in town."

I scoff. There is one perfect reason for sticking around Kimbell, and her name is Harlow. But I'm not sharing that with Darren or anyone else.

"Evidence collection is done. The whole town has been interviewed. You can take all of that and finish the investigation from the Fire Marshal's Office," Darren continues, anger and frustration clouding his face. "If I find out that you're sticking around to make Jasmine's life a living hell, you'll regret it."

Dr. Jasmine Jones isn't on my radar. I haven't given her a second thought since she threw iced coffee on me a few weeks ago. Modifying any part of my investigation to accommodate Jasmine's hatred of me will never happen, but that doesn't mean I can't understand how she feels on some level. I'm not entirely unsympathetic to the pain she is going through losing her father. But being without the man you looked up to as a role model for two years is a lot better than losing him for the rest of your life. Jasmine should think about that. Explaining any of this to Darren is pointless.

I decide to take the high road. "Trust me, I don't want to see Jasmine as much as she doesn't want to see me. I'm here for one reason only, and it has nothing to do with her."

Darren doesn't look convinced, but he finally turns and walks away down the darkened hallway.

Turning around, I enter the break room. Tension is laced in the air as the guys sit around the table in uncomfortable silence. Four boxes of pizza lay on the counter, calling to me.

"Mind if I grab a couple of slices?" I ask to no one in particular.

Luke looks up as if shaken from a trance. "Help yourself. There's plenty left."

"I'm surprised to see you still here so late, brother," Ronan glances up from scribbling on a notepad. "I thought the team had left hours ago."

"They did," I say, lifting each of the lids on the pizza boxes. Meat lovers, pepperoni lovers, and two supremes. Closing the lids on the first two boxes, I take four slices of supreme pizza and arrange them on a plate. Punching three minutes on the microwave, I start nuking the food and turn back toward Ronan. "I think better after everyone is gone."

"Joe Little still a primary suspect?" Wiley Alexander asks, leaning back in his chair. I don't know him well, but he has a reputation of being a goofball and an irresistible ladies' man.

"No suspects yet until we get test results back, but he is a person of interest."

"A person of interest who hasn't been seen in Kimbell since the day of the fire," Luke says, implying what everyone suspects. Joe's disappearance is believed to be akin to a criminal fleeing the scene of his crime. If I could go by public sentiment, Joe Little would already be locked up behind bars for arson. Something about Joe setting the fire still disturbs me. Doesn't quite fit the pieces of the puzzle. I'm not saying that all criminals are masterminds, but if Joe did torch the brewery, he did an amazing job of leaving breadcrumbs right back to himself for it. Would he have done that, though?

"If you're sticking around for Joe Little to return to Kimbell, you're wasting your time." Nate Bell speaks without bothering to look up at me. "He's not coming back. Finishing your investigation from the Fire Marshal's Office would be more considerate to the people who live here."

I push down the annoyance bubbling within me.

Was everybody in this town on Jasmine's side? The rules in the state are clear. A jury of Dr. Uriah Jones's peers had found enough evidence to convict him of breaking the law.

But some kind of way, they all viewed me as the bad guy.

"Where and when we conduct our investigation is based on our judgment and not the whims and moods of the town where the fire has occurred," I say, as the microwave beeping pierces the air. I take the sizzling slices of pizza out. "There's no reason for me to avoid or limit the time I spend in Kimbell."

I cross the room and sit down directly across from the billionaire slacker. Nate glares at me, a challenge in his eyes that feels more personal than I'm expecting. Is Nate's subtle hint for me to get out of town related to Jasmine? Or could it be that some kind of way he's picked up on the budding relationship between Harlow and me? I don't think she would've told him anything, but I doubt she could hide the truth if he asked her directly. Harlow has no poker face. If Nate knows or suspects that Harlow and I are sneaking around, what exactly would he do with that information?

The thought makes me uneasy.

The Bell Family keeps a low profile across the state. Most Texans are completely oblivious to how much money and power they wield. I have no doubt that Nate could have my superiors yanking me out of Kimbell and performing the rest of the investigation back at our HQ with one phone call.

"I think you could've been more compassionate. It's too soon after the conviction for you to be strutting around town," Nate adds with finality, then rises from his chair. He walks over to the sink and places his dirty dish inside. "I'm going to work out with Darren."

Ronan, Luke, and Wiley watch as Nate leaves the room. The tension in the air dissipates the moment he's gone.

But it does nothing to lift my darkening mood.

Harlow's spoiled, billionaire ex could be a problem for me.

In more ways than one.

CHAPTER 17

HARLOW-ROSE

~

I RUB MY HANDS ABSENTLY UP AND DOWN MY ARMS where goosebumps pepper my skin despite the humidity of the late afternoon. My plan isn't foolproof by any means. I debate back and forth whether I should do this. Somewhere deep inside me, I know it's the right thing to do.

Standing in front of the dilapidated shack of a house, I peer out at the narrow dirt road surrounded by towering, overgrown pine and oak trees. I'd been confident and committed to this plan for the entire drive from Fredericksburg to Kimbell.

Now, as I watch the late model truck speeding toward me, kicking up dust and debris, I'm second and third and fourth guessing my decision. As the truck idles to a stop next to my Range Rover, Santos emerges, slamming the door behind him. Towering pine trees rustle in the wind, casting long shadows across the dirt driveway. But no shadow is dark enough to mask the anger I see etched on his face.

"We can't be here," Santos whispers through gritted teeth. His gorgeous honey eyes dart back and forth across the abandoned property as if someone will jump out from the forest. "Do you know what would happen if someone catches us here?"

"I needed to see you."

"Why here? How in the hell would we explain how you know about Papi's house? This is too risky."

"Please, hear me out. No one comes up here anymore."

"Alma told me that this is prime real estate. The Crockett Family is trying to sell this land, which means potential buyers could pop in anytime to check it out." Irritation is laced in Santos's tone as he crosses strong, tanned arms and bulging biceps over his chest. I stifle a smile as the bottom edge of his tattoo peeks from underneath his t-shirt sleeve. I want to point out that the tattoo is a bigger risk of being caught, but I don't. There's no need to piss him off more than he is.

"Zaire told me that nothing can happen on this land until the Crockett's can produce the deed of ownership, which they haven't done yet. So, interest in the property has gone silent."

"You told Zaire about me?" The frown creasing his forehead deepens.

"No," I say, feeling the entire situation slipping out of control. Panic grips my chest as I reach for him. "Not exactly. She knows our past, but that's it. Real estate is what she does, so things like this come up in our conversations all the time. I swear, she has no clue that you and I are …"

His features soften. "That we are …"

It's impossible to ignore the flutters in my stomach. Passion pulses between us as his words linger in the air. I lick my lips slowly, knowing how I want to finish that sentence but not sure if I should.

I take the safe route. "Sneaking around."

What we are really doing is much more special than that. It's not cheap or superficial. We're not hooking up. Not yet anyway. There are no unrealistic expectations and no pretenses between us. We accept each other as we are, which I find immensely liberating.

"Fine. Why did you want to meet … in person … in the middle of the day?" Santos asks, still annoyed.

I'm not surprised by his reaction. We've worked hard to keep our entire relationship under wraps. Meeting in Kimbell is something that generally would be strictly off-limits until after the arson investigation is complete. But these aren't normal situations.

"Last night, you got pretty upset on the phone," I say, slipping my hands in his. "I was worried about you." I step closer, then ease on my tiptoes to place a gentle kiss on his lips.

He relaxes instantly from my touch. Our mouths linger, allowing the kiss to take on a life of its own until we break from each other, heaving breaths.

"Sorry to lay all that on you and for being rude. I know you want to support me, and I appreciate that, Harlow. I really do."

Last night was the first time I realized that Santos was still going through the stages of grief over his father, even though it had been over two years since Papi's death. The grief was complicated by his uncertainty of whether going after Dr. Jones had been the right thing to do.

Because of that guilt and confusion, I knew in my heart that he was robbing himself of reliving the best memories he had with his dad. When I woke up this morning, I was convinced that encouraging Santos to go through his father's personal items once and for all could be the thing that would give him some kind of closure and help him move on.

Did I question whether it was really my place to push him like this? Absolutely. He'd been avoiding this singular task since Papi's death. Forcing him to face his fears could cause a rift in this new relationship we're trying to build with each other. But even with all those risks, I had to try.

I care too much about him to watch him suffer and not help in any way I can. After all the time we've spent with each other, I know that if there is anyone who could convince Santos to face these demons, it's me. That's the only reason I'm taking such a big risk that could backfire on me.

Santos's arms surround my waist and pull me into a tight hug. His words are warm against my ear. "Because of you, I got through all those emotions last night. I'm good today. I promise."

I squeeze him tight, then pull back slightly. "I think there's something you can do that would make you good not just today, but every day going forward."

"Really?" He raises an eyebrow. "What's that?"

I look past him at the rundown house. "You should go inside and see what Papi left behind."

Santos tenses in my arms. He shakes his head. "I can't. Not today. I need to get back to work."

"I'm sure the team can handle it if you play hooky for a good cause this afternoon," I say, refusing to let him bolt. "This isn't just about finding something to explain why Papi died. It's also about reminding you of all the good times you shared with him.

Finding keepsakes that you'll cherish forever. You need to do this."

"I don't want to."

"But you need to," I insist. "And you won't have to do it alone."

"You'll stay with me?"

Forever, if you'll have me, is what I want to say. But of course, I don't. Placing a quick kiss on his soft lips, I say, "That's the plan."

I watch his expression lighten, a sign that he may be warming up to the idea.

"I brought a bunch of trash bags and boxes from the winery, and I have an organized system that will make this go smoothly."

"Why am I not surprised?"

"Mom taught me the virtues of always being prepared and having a solid plan," I flash him my best smile. "Anything not worth keeping will go in trash bags. Then there will be two labels for the boxes. One for keepsakes, things precious to you that you want to hold onto now or later in the future. The other will be for items in good shape to be donated."

Santos turns to look back at the house and exhales slowly.

"And I brought food from our favorite restaurant in Fredericksburg."

"Maisie's Table?" He turns back to me. A sexy tilt to his face as his honey eyes focus back on me.

I nod enthusiastically. "And a bottle of wine, of course." The tide was turning in my favor. "You go open up the house, and I'll grab a few boxes to get us started."

Santos hesitates.

"Or we can both grab some boxes and go into the house together."

"Let's do that," he says, then follows me to the back of my SUV.

We walk along the broken concrete sidewalk up to the front door with boxes and bags in hand. Santos fishes a key from his key ring and opens it. A loud creak fills the air as it opens slowly.

He looks back at me, and I send him all the courage and support I can. It must be enough because Santos turns around and enters the house.

The place is much smaller on the inside than it looks from the outside and reeks of the staleness of being shuttered for years. It's cluttered, but in a way that feels like a well-lived in home. I imagine everything is as it was when Papi was last here.

Santos stands in the middle of the living room, his shoulders slumped. I wrap my arms around him and lean into his back.

"You okay?"

"Only because you're with me."

"Where do you want to start?"

"This is the biggest room in the house and has the most things, so it's as good a place as any."

I label the boxes and place them in the corners, then settle onto the sofa as Santos begins to go through the remnants of Papi's things.

Hours later, we sit surrounded by a mountain of mementos, pictures, papers, and knick-knacks. A half-empty bottle of merlot from my vineyard rests against the living room wall, next to a dish of nearly devoured chicken fried steak sandwiches, mashed potatoes, and fried green beans.

I listen as Santos tells me another story from his childhood, holding up an action figure that had lost a leg and seen better days. His face is flushed from the joy of the memories, and I can't help but laugh.

"What? It's not funny. Papi whooped my butt for breaking the leg off this toy. I was sore for days."

"But it taught you to value the gifts that you were given."

"Especially since gifts were few and far between when I was a kid. We were really poor. I remember wearing clothes and shoes until I wore holes in them. When I had my growth spurt, I got teased for my pants being too short. But Papi couldn't afford to buy me new ones. I didn't have a mom around to let the hem out or anything." Santos says, but there isn't a hint of sadness in his tone. Those experiences made him the man he is today, and there's no shame or sadness attached to them anymore.

I stretch my legs and realize that the opposite wall is only a yard from my feet. The house is so tiny. Once again, I realize how blessed I am for being adopted by my parents. They showered me with the best gifts and the finer things in life, but that isn't what I love most about being their daughter. They gave me unconditional love, like Santos's dad had given to him. It's the greatest gift a child could be given, outweighing even the best or worst of circumstances.

Santos climbs to his feet and tosses several items into the charity box, then puts the broken action figure into the box with "KEEPSAKES" on it. There isn't much in that box, but everything in there came with a precious memory. Memories that Santos shared with me.

"So, I ran into Nate at the fire station yesterday, and it was kind of awkward."

I lean forward, not entirely surprised that Santos and Nate crossed paths. But in all our conversations over the past weeks, we never wasted time talking about previous relationships. We both shared what we learned from those prior experiences, but not in gory detail, and definitely not sharing any names, which I prefer.

I ask, "Why was it awkward?"

"Because he's your ex."

"How do you know that? You're investigating me and not just the arson?"

Santos laughs. "I kinda told Ronan about you, way before we decided to … sneak around. He mentioned that you and Nate had been a couple for a long time."

"That's true, but it was a very long time ago. We were high school sweethearts, I suppose."

"Nothing happened between y'all after high school?"

"No, even though his mom and my mom are always trying to play matchmaker to get us back together."

Santos stares at me, but I can't read his expression. "Is he still interested in you?"

"No," I laugh, but Santos's expression stays serious. "I mean, not that I know of." Why did I say that? The grim expression turns darker. "Look, I've known Nate my whole life. He and I are just friends now. If he wanted to pursue a relationship with me again, he wouldn't hesitate to let me know, and he hasn't done that."

"You sure about that?"

"Trust me, I've known that guy long enough to accurately predict what he would and wouldn't do."

"And you've known me for only what six, seven weeks over the past two years. Doesn't really compare, does it?"

"No, it doesn't," I say, reaching for his hand, cradling it in my own. "Nate and I have never shared a connection like the one I have with you. Nothing compares to this." I press my other hand against his chest. "Please tell me you're not jealous of Nate Bell."

"What if I am?"

"You shouldn't be," I say, unable to hide the smile from my face.

Santos bites his bottom lip, eliciting a boyish charm that competes with the overwhelming sensuality that radiates from him. I'm drawn to him like I've never been with any other man, and the feeling is escalated by his raw and unfiltered attraction to me. His gaze drifts down to my hand pressed against his chest. His heart quickens under my touch.

"If only it was that easy, Harlow. I'm not sure how much longer I can stay away from you."

Santos lifts my hand and places a soft kiss against my palm.

I shudder from the passion in his touch. I slip my arms around his neck and lean into his hard body. Our lips are inches from each other. His hands encircle my waist, holding me tightly. He leans forward and presses his forehead against mine. My body ignites in anticipation of what could come next, and I know I'm so ready.

"Almost done," Santos announces, pulling away from me.

And just like that, the mood is shattered, and we're back to the task at hand. I ignore my disappointment and give him a sweet smile.

He puts more distance between us, heading to the bedroom. His voice floats from the hallway. "I'm going to grab the rest of the stuff out of the closet. Shouldn't take too long to go through it."

I fall back onto the couch with a loud thud. My fantasies will have to sustain me for a while longer. Picking up a stack of papers and folders tossed in a pile between the boxes, I sort through them. Papi was a huge boxing fan and kept all kinds of articles and magazines on the top boxers over the years. Oscar De La Hoya was clearly the man's favorite, but nothing he'd saved over the years would be worth any money, which was why Santos added it to the trash pile.

I flip through a couple of Ring Magazines and watch as an

envelope tumbles from between the pages. My heart catches in my throat.

I thought if he'd left a letter or something to let me know he wanted what Dr. Jones had offered, I could find a way to be okay with it.

I flip the envelope over and see Santos's name scrawled on the outside in shaky penmanship. Could this be what Santos had wanted from his father all along? Had his dad written him a letter before he died?

"What's that?" Santos asks.

I scramble to my feet, holding the envelope as if it's fragile. "It's for you." I stretch the envelope toward Santos.

He stares at it but refuses to move a muscle to take it from my hands.

"Do you recognize the handwriting?"

He nods. "It's Papi's."

CHAPTER 18

SANTOS

~

THE ENVELOPE BURNS AGAINST MY PALMS. HOLDING IT
tightly, I press it against my chest and exhale. The silence in the
house is deafening, and I almost regret asking Harlow to leave.
Almost.

Her hand presses against my face, and she leans in to give me
the sweetest kiss.

"Call me if you need ... anything." Harlow hesitates. She
doesn't want to leave me alone. I can see the fear in her eyes. The
worry that I won't be able to handle whatever is in the envelope
that my father left.

She's right to be worried.

It's the reason why I'm sending her away.

If the contents blow my world apart, I don't want her to be collateral damage. She deserves a better version of me. Not the man I am now. The one trying to claw from under a mountain of credit card debt, living from paycheck to paycheck, while the death of my father still weighs heavily on my heart. Her warmth and light aren't bright enough to pierce the dark, coldness infecting me. A part of me wishes she hadn't found this envelope. This ticking time bomb of perhaps Papi's last message. Why couldn't she have left well enough alone?

I nod, but I have no intention of calling her.

She has the emotional, spiritual, and financial resources to handle anything I could throw at her, but why should she do that? Her family is in chaos from the fire at the brewery. They need her, and I'm a distraction that she shouldn't be dealing with.

"I'm headed back to Fredericksburg. We have our first private booking tomorrow night. A big party that we need to prep for," Harlow adds. She's lingering, probably hoping that I'll ask her to stay, but I want her to go. I need her to be too busy to think about me or what I'm going through.

"Drive safe." I push the words from my mouth, then turn my back on her. I can't deal with the envelope and Harlow at the same time. I can only take so much emotion pulsing through me, and she makes me feel too much.

"Santos."

"Yeah?" I don't turn around.

"Wait until you're ready before you open the envelope. Really ready. Don't force yourself to see what's inside until then."

I glance over my shoulder and lock eyes with her. A silent thank you passes from me to her without any words uttered. A hint of an encouraging smile curves her lips, and then she's gone.

A brisk wind rushes across my skin, and I glance up at the dark gray clouds moving overhead. The air smells of rain. I force the memories from last night out of my mind and plunge the shovel into the flower bed. I want to finish before the thunderstorms start.

After ditching work yesterday afternoon, I was a no-show again today. Texting Byron this morning, I let him know I was dealing with a personal matter. He didn't take the news well since we're under increasing pressure to find the brewery arsonist. But right now, I don't care about any of that. My only focus is tending to Papi's yard.

A tangle of weeds and crabgrass cover the dirt, but the vincas Papi planted years ago still manage to thrive. A steady rhythm falls over me, and before I know it, there's nothing left to do. Carrying the overstuffed trash bags around the side of the house, I turn to survey my work.

Papi would be proud.

The grass is cut low. Weeds gone. Flowers blowing in the wind. The entire house and yard are spotless like Papi used to keep it. Hours of hardworking leave me more at peace. Less haunted by the contents of the envelope, although I'm still not ready to open it. I'm not sure when I'll be, and that's okay for now.

Heading to the front door, I hear my cell phone ringing from inside. I push the door open and glance at the stacks of boxes lined neatly around the living room next to the furniture. While I'd prefer to rent a truck to move all the boxes at one time, that is a luxury I can't afford. But there's no rush. I can grab the boxes that I'll be donating to charity first and come back and get the ones I'm keeping later.

Crossing the living room, I stop at the small dining table and glance down at my phone. Four missed calls in the last fifteen minutes, all from Harlow. I pick up the phone as a text comes through.

Can you call me please? I'm okay, but having an emergency …

I yank the phone into my hand and call her back.

"Hey," Harlow says.

"What's wrong? Where are you?" I ask. My heart pounds in my chest. I kick myself for not taking my phone outside while I was working. I hear heavy rain in the background.

"My car broke down."

"Where are you?" I ask again, scrambling to find my keys. Thunder rumbles, and I lose her response in the noise. "Where?"

"On 122 headed west. The road is flooded. I didn't realize how deep it was, and I drove through the water. The engine started to shake and sputter, and I didn't know what to do. I steered the car onto the side of the road, but now I'm scared to start it up again."

"Don't. You'll fry your engine if water gets into it. Are you somewhere safe, off the road?"

"Yes, I'm in front of an old gas station."

"Is roadside assistance on the way?"

"Yeah … but from Houston. The nearest dealership is there, which is fine, but I need to get to Fredericksburg. That private event I told you about is tonight. I promised the client that I'd be there. I can't miss this. The tow truck driver will take me to Houston with the car, not Fredericksburg. That's why I called you."

"What's the last town you passed?" I listen as she gives me directions. It's not too far from here. "Even if I leave now, you'll still be an hour or so late to the event."

"That's better than not showing up at all."

I glance down at my dusty, dirt-stained t-shirt and jeans. I really should grab a shower first, but that would make her later.

Panic and worry lace her words, and I'm compelled to do whatever it takes to stop her feeling that way. Even if it means reeking when I pick her up. I'll have to keep the windows down.

"I'm on my way."

Forty-five minutes later, I pull into the parking lot of an abandoned gas station. Weeds as tall as trees have grown up through cracks in the sidewalk in front of the boarded-up building. The burgundy Maserati is at an awkward angle near the road. Harlow waves at me through her window as I park my truck. For a moment, I'm struck with the realization that she's never been *inside* my run-down, old pick-up.

Embarrassment races up my neck, making me hot and irritated. I look over at the seats, yellow cushions visible through the tears in the faded black fabric. Dust coats the dashboard, and the windows are clouded with grime and dirt.

Shaking my head, I open the door, pull the trucker cap down on my head, and jump out.

At least the rain has calmed down to a soft drizzle.

Harlow opens the door, and I swear my mouth drops open to the ground. She's wearing a shimmering gold sateen cocktail dress with a one-shoulder neckline. The dress stops mid-thigh, showcasing her toned legs. My eyes travel down the length of her to the tips of her gold-painted toes perched in strappy stilettos. She beams at me as she raises her umbrella and prances across the gravel.

"I'm so glad you were able to come." She's about to throw her arms around me when I hold up my hands to stop her.

"You can't hug me," I say, regretting the decision to not take a quick shower. "I'm filthy."

"I don't care," Harlow giggles then throws her arms around

me. She buries her head in my neck and squeezes me tight. "Thank you for rescuing me."

I slip my arms around her waist and hold her. She fits perfectly.

"You're officially late, and it's going to be another hour before I can get you to the winery."

"I texted Gina and let her know," Harlow says.

I reluctantly let her go then lead her around to the truck's passenger side. Opening the door, I glance down at her soft curves in the dress. "You look stunning."

"In this old thing?" She twirls around and shakes her hips a bit.

Keeping myself in check around Harlow has been a struggle over the past few weeks. I can't help but want to peel that dress off her as she puts on a show for me. I close my eyes for a moment, forcing the thoughts away. I fight the overwhelming urge to drive Harlow back in the other direction to her lake house, where we can be alone. Where I could do all the things I've been wanting to do to her body from the moment I saw her standing inside Elevation Cupcake Shop. I'm amazed that I've been able to restrain myself for this long, especially with her tempting me without realizing it.

But I hold back because I know how special Harlow is.

She's different from all the other women I've had in my life.

And she means more to me than all of them combined.

I laugh away my lust over her glorious body, then lift her in my arms and place her on the seat. "Sorry about ..." I wave a hand at the inside of the truck.

Harlow shrugs as if she rides around in hoopty trucks every day. Could she really be unfazed by how crappy it looks? I don't pause to think about it and hurry over to get in. It takes a few cranks to get it back running, mostly because I'm distracted by the sight of Harlow's smooth legs crossed one over the other.

Finally, the engine roars to life, and I gun it onto the road, leaving the Maserati behind. My hand grips the steering wheel, eyes locked on the road as dusk eases into darkness. The lights illuminate the road ahead, cloaking the interior cab in blackness. But that doesn't stop me from feeling Harlow's eyes on me.

"What are you looking at?"

"You, silly. What were you doing today that got you all ... dirty?"

I raise an eyebrow. The way she says the word dirty is filled with salaciousness and no trace of disdain. A thought starts to invade my mind of Harlow helping me get clean, but I force it away. The last thing I need is to deal with my body's reaction over an arduous and long hour drive.

"I stayed over at Papi's last night. When I got up this morning, I gave the place a good cleaning inside and out. Cut the yard, cleaned the flower beds, and put out the trash for pick up next week. It's back to looking how it did when he was living there. You know, before he got sick."

"I bet that felt good."

I nod, swallowing past the lump in my throat. Doing all the things I remember my father doing helped me feel close to him again. Thoughts of the envelope and whatever was inside flew out of my mind.

"I didn't open the envelope."

"Okay."

"You think I should've opened it by now?"

"I think you should open it when you're ready, Santos. Only you can know when that is. Until then, don't worry about the envelope. It's been there for two years or longer. It can wait a few more days or weeks or months for you to see what's inside."

When she puts it like that, I relax. "Enough about the envelope. Tell me about this private event."

"Gina booked it. Some company out of California having a reunion of sorts. The owner wanted me to sign bottles of wine and take pictures with the guests. Can you believe that?"

"You're a celebrity now. I can't believe you're still willing to hang out with a nobody like me."

"Trust me, you're far from a nobody. At least not to me."

I want to see the expression on her face, but the shadows inside the truck and the dark night prevent me. I relax even more, longing to ask her what I was to her, but I stop myself. I refuse to open up a topic that I can't see through. Instead, I settle into the familiar and comfortable routine of being with her.

After a long moment of silence, Harlow asks, "Can I ask you something?"

I shift in my seat, anxious about her approach. Normally, she asks without regard to whether I want to deal with her question or not. It piques my curiosity, although I know I might regret it later. "Is this going to be deep? I'm not sure I want to get deep right now."

"Come on," Harlow says, her voice light. "We have another twenty minutes before we get to the winery, and I've been wanting to ask you this ever since we decided to sneak around."

"So, you've been holding out on me?"

"A little."

"What's your question?"

"What do you want to happen with us after the investigation is over?" Harlow sounds confident, but I detect the slight tremor in her voice, and it causes my heart to squeeze in my chest.

I want to give her the answer she's looking for, the answer we both want to hear, but I'm not sure that I can. So I hedge.

"I hope we'll keep in touch this time," I say, infecting my words with humor that falls flat in the cab of the truck.

"That shouldn't be a problem. We know the complete truth about each other now. You're Santos, hot Texas Guy and arson investigator from San Antonio and living in Conroe."

"And you're Harlow hyphen Rose, gorgeous Texas Girl, winery owner from Kimbell and living in Fredericksburg."

"I do not live in Fredericksburg!" A swipe of her hand hits my forearm, sending a jolt of electricity coursing through my body. "I live in Kimbell and travel to my winery for work only."

"From what I can tell, you're there a whole lot more than you're in Kimbell."

"Only because the lake house is taking much longer to get finished and moving back in with my parents in the meantime is not something I'm willing to do. No matter how many times they offer my old room."

"I can imagine that would put a crimp on your love life."

"Would it?"

I walked into that one. If her love life consisted of us, I could say that she could live in a monastery, and it wouldn't have been able to stop us from being together. The attraction that keeps us tethered to each other.

"Harlow, I don't know if—"

I pause, not sure how to put this into words.

She's quiet.

I can only make out the contours of her face, the edges, and the round curves. Even in the shadows of darkness, she takes my breath away.

But I know she's not going to help me out. She'll wait patiently with those pretty legs crossed until I figure out how to tell her what I really feel.

"I want to be with you. I want to know that we have a future. But right now, I can't say that will happen. Too much is … uncertain."

"I don't agree."

I chuckle under my breath. Of course, she doesn't. Harlow had never had a time in her life when she didn't get what she wanted. It may have taken longer than she would've liked, but she got it just the same. I don't have to see the intensity in her chocolate brown eyes to know what she wants.

"I'm in debt over my head, Harlow. I took out loans, maxed out credit cards, and tried anything to make Papi better. When that didn't work, I doubled down to make his last months and weeks easier. I don't own anything of my own. I barely have enough money to scrape by after paying all the bills. I'm working hard to get my life back together and be the kind of man that can be good for you. But then you found that envelope, and I feel like I got jerked back in time. All those nagging doubts and the anger is bubbling up all over again, straining for a release. I'm not going to let that come out on you."

The air in the truck is tense. I hate that I dumped all my garbage onto her. Whoever said talking about it would make you feel better lied. I feel like crap.

Harlow lets out a long sigh.

I hold my breath waiting to hear her response.

"None of that changes how I feel about you or what I want for us. You don't have to deal with any of that alone. I could help you—"

"No!" My voice is harsh, and I'm relieved to pull up to the entrance of the winery. Luxury cars are packed in the parking lot.

Money drips off the clothes and demeanor of the guests milling around in front of the entrance.

"That stuff doesn't matter, Santos."

"Yeah, it does." I slam on the brakes in front of the fancy limestone mansion that is the Harlow-Rose Winery tasting room and store. Out front, a banner has been erected and blows in the wind as strobe lights float across the shiny surface.

Congratulations Harlow-Rose!

Shock registers on her face, and I realize what's happening, too.

A surprise party to celebrate all of her accomplishments. The guests must be friends and family. I see her parents beaming behind a stream of people pouring out from inside. I leave the truck running, then get out and jog around to the passenger side. Three hard yanks, and I'm able to get the door open. I reach a hand toward her, then feel shoved to the side.

A cocky baritone floats from behind me. "Whoa, Harlow, you sure know how to make an entrance."

It's Nate Bell. He slips his hands on Harlow's waist and helps her out of the truck, then turns to me and gives a quick nod. "Thanks for coming to the rescue."

I can tell he doesn't recognize me.

Or he doesn't bother to look at me.

He looks through me as if I'm not human, tossing the words casually before whisking Harlow toward the waiting partygoers.

"I can't believe this," she says.

"You're so hard to surprise, but we pulled this thing off," another guest says as Harlow walks into a group hug. The look on Nate's face sours my stomach. He's the kind of guy Harlow deserves, not me.

"Appreciate you helping our girl out," a frat-looking guy with slick blonde hair and an Australian accent slaps a hand on my shoulder and forces something into my hand. "We're lucky one of her workers was close enough to get her here before the night was completely ruined." He gives me a toothy grin. "A little something for your trouble."

He turns away and follows the crowd that has ushered Harlow inside and out of view.

I glance down into my palm.

Five crisp folded one hundred dollar bills.

Crumbling them in my fist, I drop them to the ground and drive off.

CHAPTER 19

ARLOW-ROSE

I STARE AT THE PHONE, WILLING IT TO RING OR DING OR something. Give me some kind of response from Santos, but it lays there silent.

Should I try to call again? Or could that make matters worse for him?

I'm so torn. I don't know what to do.

I glance around the tasting room. Remnants of last night's celebration are all over the place. Streamers, balloons, and glitter litter the floor. Empty plates and discarded wine glasses rest on various surfaces. In the hour since I awoke from passing out after the party, I've already scheduled a cleaning crew to be here in two hours, called Santos twice, and sent him three text messages.

Arriving at the winery and seeing all my friends from Stanford and my co-workers from Mondavi mingling with my family and friends from Kimbell had been a thrilling surprise. Everyone here to celebrate my success has been humbling and exciting.

Too bad I couldn't fully enjoy the evening.

All night long, as I drank way too much wine and partied, my thoughts were never far from Santos. Worry clawed at me that someone recognized him when he dropped me off at the front doors. No one mentioned him or asked me about it, but that doesn't mean they didn't notice. It wouldn't protect him from becoming today's fodder for gossip in Kimbell. And it definitely wouldn't guarantee that a phone call wasn't made to the Lasso County Fire Marshal's Office saying that he was seen with me last night.

This was everything that Santos had warned me about. Over the weeks, as we deftly avoided being caught, I've become complacent. It never crossed my mind that I shouldn't have called him when my car broke down. Mom or Dad could have easily come and got me, but no. I wanted to see Santos. I wanted another chance to be alone with him. To see how he was doing. To share time and space with him. Flooding out my car on accident was as good of an excuse as any.

But none of this is good for Santos.

Not if it means he's at work right now being reprimanded by his superiors for conflict of interest while investigating the brewery fire. I hope he's swamped at work. Not dealing with the aftermath of caring so much about me that he took a risk he shouldn't have.

If he is in trouble, I can talk to his boss. Tell him he happened to be driving by when my car flooded, and he was being a Good Samaritan. Anything to help him get out of the mess I may have caused him.

But I can't do anything until I hear from Santos.

Until he finally calls me or texts me to tell me what's going on.

I recheck the phone.

Is it a good thing that none of my friends from Kimbell have reached out to ask me about Santos? Maybe they didn't recognize him? When he arrived to pick me up, he was a dirty mess, though still sexy. He wore a baseball cap covering most of his unruly dark curls. A stark contrast from the clean-cut attire he wore when he was working the case.

If anyone would've recognized him, it would be Nate.

He practically pushed Santos out of the way to help me out of the truck. But Nate never said a word about seeing Santos. He definitely didn't question me about why Santos had been the one to rescue me and drive me back to the winery.

So, I ran into Nate at the fire station yesterday, and it was kind of awkward.

Is he still interested in you?

You sure about that?

I slam my hand on the counter.

Nate is perceptive enough and has known me long enough to figure out that I've been sneaking around with Santos. Even though I can't imagine when he could've seen us. We've been careful not to slip up around Kimbell, but I know we were probably too lax here in Fredericksburg. Maybe Nate saw us here around town.

And ... if Nate is interested in rekindling our romance from long ago, he wouldn't hesitate to get rid of his competition by any means necessary. Turning Santos in for an inappropriate connection to one of the key parties in the brewery investigation would be right up Nate's alley. My ex-boyfriend would never utter a word to me about it, either. Why would he? He'd know I'd be upset, which would reduce his chances of us getting back together.

But is that what's going on here?

I feel like a crazy woman, cycling through a myriad of possibilities without any definitive evidence about what is truly going on.

"Come on, Santos, call me back," I plead at the cell phone.

The soft creak of the door opening floats through the air.

Could it be Santos?

Stumbling from behind the bar, I briskly walk to the foyer of the tasting room as the door opens wider. I freeze. My heart thuds in my chest. My mouth slacks as the last person I ever expected to come to see me steps inside.

"Jasmine?" My voice croaks. "What are you doing here?" Dread seeps through me. She hates Santos. If she's found out about our relationship, she won't hesitate to tell his boss to get revenge for her father going to prison. This is a nightmare.

She chuckles. "You can't even pretend not to be shocked to see me."

"Well, it is unusual."

"Because you and I aren't friends and probably never will be."

I shrug in agreement. This visit isn't a coincidence. I feel it in my bones that it has something to do with Santos. As much as I don't want to deal with Jasmine, I need to find out why she's here. I'm hoping it's not as bad as what I'm thinking.

"So, what brings you to Fredericksburg."

"I don't know. Needed a change of scenery, I guess, and wanted to see what all the fuss over your vineyard was about."

I stare at her but can't read her blank, nonchalant expression. I don't believe for one minute that this is a random visit. She knows exactly why she's here, but she's not ready to drop whatever bomb she has planned for me. Not yet. I can be patient, though.

Jasmine glances around, her eyebrows raised. "Did I miss the party?"

"Yeah, it was quite the surprise. A bunch of my friends came down from California to celebrate all the awards my wines have won this past year," I say. Maybe alcohol will loosen her up. "Would you like to try my cab? It's won the most awards."

Jasmine closes the door behind her and heads to the bar. "That would be nice."

As she eases onto a stool, I grab the keys to the wine cellar. Minutes later, I'm back with a couple of bottles and place one in front of her.

She picks up the bottle and runs her finger along the label. "Nice logo. Did you design it?"

"No." I look away.

"Ah, but someone very close to you did."

"You could say that." I pop the cork and grab two wine glasses. Pouring the deep burgundy liquid into each, I push one toward Jasmine and lift the other to my lips. "So, I hear Lance is back in town."

"Yes, he is," Jasmine says, then squeezes the bridge of her nose.

"He's always been so in love with you. It must be nice to have him back."

"Nice isn't exactly the word I'd use for it." She gulps the wine then beckons for another pour.

"What would you use?"

"Confusing, infuriating, and distressing," Jasmine takes another gulp of wine.

"That's three words."

"You know how in the movies when the girl is torn between two guys, it's all romantic and fun to figure out which great guy she'll choose. You look at her and think, why can't that be my life. How could she ever go wrong with too amazing men fawning all over her?"

My eyes grow wide. I didn't know that Jasmine was dating or interested in anyone. I'm guessing Lance didn't know either before he got back to town. No wonder his arrival is creating havoc in her life. So much havoc that she's here confiding in a frenemy instead of one of her friends.

"Not so fun when you're the girl, I suppose."

"And when you're not in the slightest bit torn on how to choose between them." Jasmine twirls the wine in her glass, her eyes locked on the sloshing movements.

"I'm sure you'll figure out the best way to explain your feelings to both guys."

I want to know who the second part of the love triangle is. Honestly, I'd be pressing my luck to think she'd confide in me that much, so I hold my tongue.

Jasmine shrugs then narrows her eyes. The conversation so far has been easy but not entirely comfortable. I take a sip from my own wine glass and wait, wondering what she might say next.

"I don't know how much you know about my dad's conviction earlier this year," Jasmine starts.

"Honestly, I was too busy with the winery. We've never been close, so I didn't feel the need to keep up." I say, leaving out that I wasn't really interested in her life. "I'm sorry that he's in prison, though. It must be hard for you."

"My dad was never a top doctor in any field—"

"But you are, winning top awards in emergency medicine for the past few years."

"Glad I'm not the only cyberstalker in the room," Jasmine laughs, an infectious and airy sound that makes me smile.

We were always too busy competing to ever see that maybe we could've been friends.

"Anyway, my dad was the best at caring for his patients, hands down. He taught me what it meant to be a compassionate doctor. Becoming the best in a specialty requires intelligence and technical skills honed over thousands of hours of experience. Connecting with patients as humans and not as a number is completely different. He taught me that, and I feel lost without seeing him every day at St. Elizabeth's."

"I can understand that. I always envied your relationship with your dad. Don't get me wrong, I love my dad to death, but he was all about encouraging me to get out in the world and make my own path without any help like he had to do growing up. At sixteen, he ran away from home and found himself in Shiner, Texas. Fell in love with beer and wanted that to be his ticket to success."

"Looks like he nailed it."

"Yeah, but it was never in his plans for me to follow in his footsteps. He didn't want me to do anything in the beverage industry, unlike your dad."

"I think Uriah would've had a heart attack if I used that 'big brain' for anything other than medicine," Jasmine says, mimicking her father's accent and speech cadence.

"You sound just like him."

"Mr. Robinson never wanted to leave the brewery to you?"

"Nope. He told me he wanted to give me the best in life so I could go out there and create something better than his small-town brewery. I was destined for bigger and better things."

"Like internationally renowned and award-winning wines?" Jasmine raised an eyebrow.

"Perhaps."

"Looks like both of our fathers did a pretty good job."

"I think so," I say, beginning to see my dad from a different light. "What do you think of the Cab?"

"I'm in love. I'll need to buy a bottle to take back with me."

"It's on the house," I say, then lean my elbows onto the bar. "Why are you really here, Jasmine?"

She sucks in a sharp breath. "Just because we're not close doesn't mean I want you to be blindsided."

Panic slides down my body. I press against the counter to keep myself steady. "Blindsided about what?"

"The investigation of the fire at the brewery."

My heart kicks up a notch as I watch her struggle with the right words to say. Fear infects me, and my body trembles.

Jasmine says, "The arson investigator on the case is the same man who's responsible for putting my dad in prison for two years."

"Okay," I say, trying to hide the fact that this is not news to me. Santos and I had talked about his role in Dr. Jones' arrest and conviction many times over the past few weeks. He was torn and unsure that he'd done the right thing pursuing the charges even with assisted death being illegal in Texas. It was the reason he hadn't opened the envelope I'd found. He wasn't sure how he would handle knowing if his Dad really did seek out Dr. Jones' help to end his own life. He wasn't sure if knowing would bring him closure or more devastating heartbreak.

"I don't know Santos, and I don't want to know him. But I can tell you a bit about my experiences with him as the charges against my father were investigated and with the trial," Jasmine says, then proceeds to give me a play-by-play of the year-long battle between her family and Santos that ultimately ended in her father being convicted. Nothing in her story had been much different from what Santos had told me.

"He's relentless when it comes to justice, only seeing things in black and white instead of the shades of gray that the rest of us live in."

"That's a good thing, I think, for the investigation. We want him to figure out who set the fire."

"Do you?"

"Of course," I rise up and cross my arms over my chest.

"I was complaining to Darren the other day about why Santos was still in town. Why he hadn't gone back to County headquarters or anywhere else to continue the investigation now that all the evidence has been collected from the site. Do you know what he told me?"

"Please, spit it out."

"Darren said that most business fires determined to be arson are set by the owners to get insurance money. Santos is sticking around Kimbell so he can watch you and your family. Gather evidence that your dad set the fire on purpose."

"No, that can't be right."

"It's the only reason for him to still be here. At least, that's what Darren thinks, and I tend to agree. Santos has the highest success rate in arson cases for the county for a reason. I don't know what's going on at the brewery, but gray areas happen all the time. You need to watch your back around him and protect your family. I'd hate for you to watch your dad go to prison like I had to watch mine."

"Jasmine, I appreciate you coming here to tell me all of this. But there's no way my dad set the brewery on fire. His business isn't in any financial trouble. Even if it was, he knows I have enough money to help bail him out of any problem."

"But would he ask you to? Or would he try to deal with it himself?" Jasmine raises an eyebrow then drinks the last of the wine from her glass. "I need to get going. Can I get the extra bottle of wine?"

I reach below the counter and hand her the bottle.

"Thanks, Harlow-Rose," Jasmine says, tucking the bottle under her arm. "I really hope me coming here turns out to be a waste of time for you. But if not, don't say I never tried to help you."

I slump back against the bar as the door closes with a loud thud.

Could Santos be secretly investigating my family as the prime suspects in the arson? Wouldn't he tell me if he was? Or is maintaining his job and career more important than helping me protect my family?

The answer to those questions is crystal clear.

He's told me over and over that he isn't in a position to pursue a relationship with me. He's pushing me away because of his financial debt and the pain over his father's death. But what if the arson investigation of my family's business is another reason? Would he pursue a relationship with me at the same time that he's trying to gather evidence against my family?

My thoughts wander to Joe Little. The man who was the CFO of the brewery until a couple of weeks before the fire. Why had Dad fired Joe? Was it conflict over the strategic vision like Dad had said? Or could the brewery have been in financial trouble, and Joe knew it?

The better question is, did Dad have a reason to set the fire at the brewery?

CHAPTER 20

S *ANTOS*

~

Rolling over in the bed, I reach for the clock and turn it toward me. It's the afternoon, and my head feels like a jackhammer is trying to break free from my brain. I glance down to the floor at the bottle of Tito's and groan.

My father's favorite vodka. He used to joke that it was named after him, and thus, the bond between man and spirits was that much stronger. Indeed, as I lost myself in the smooth vodka, I felt closer to Papi than I had in a long time. It could've been the last twenty-four hours doing things that Papi had loved to do in his life—hard work, landscaping, and enjoying Austin's finest handmade liquor.

Or could it have been not being seen and dismissed as some

menial worker who had no value? Papi had experienced that all his life and never once complained, but he wanted better for me. It had angered me to watch it over the years. I'd plead with him to stand up for himself, but he'd shrug it off and say in the end, what they thought of him doesn't matter.

I turn over in bed and stare up at the ceiling fan. Both of them, blurred and shaky in my drunk vision. I could care less what they thought of me, but I cared too much about what *she* thought of me.

Harlow hadn't shown an ounce of hesitation before she dismissed me as one of her workers like her friends presumed. Not even a backward glance of sorry. She'd been whisked away into the winery, and I stood on the curb feeling like a fool.

I set myself up for this.

Falling for a girl from a completely different background.

Her's is a world of the rich and privileged. Where they don't understand what it's like to struggle to put food on the table, pay for your medical bills, or live in fear that you'd lose your job.

A world that is hard to get into, and once in, no one wants to get out. They look down their noses on the rest of us like we're beneath them. Last night, I saw her in the world where she belonged and got a gut punch. She isn't different than the rest. She doesn't have more heart or compassion.

I'm not special to her.

She is just like them.

My mouth twists, and my eyes burn with emotion I don't want to feel.

Even if I got my life together, paid off the debt, and rose in the ranks within the County Fire Marshal's Office, it wouldn't change one thing between us. Last night showed me that. It's time for me to suck it up and move on. Let go of any idea that Harlow and I can have a future.

There's a knock at the bedroom door.

I know who's on the other side, but I'm in no mood to see Alma.

Not like this.

She doesn't care, though. The door pushes open, and she flips the switch, bathing the room in harsh bright light. There's a tray in her hands holding a glass of water, two pills, orange juice, and plain toast.

"What's wrong, mijo?" Alma places the tray on the bedside table and forces the pills into my hand. "This is the third day you've skipped out on work. Your team is starting to worry about you. So am I. Tell me. What's going on?

I pop the pills in my mouth and accept the glass of water.

"I saw someone's true colors last night and didn't like what I saw."

"Ah, this must be the young lady you've been staying up late to talk to on the phone at night for the past few weeks."

"How do you know about that?"

"Thin walls. I like to check on you. Make sure you're okay. What changed?" Alma asks, then leans over to pick up the empty bottle of Tito's from the floor.

"We're too different. It's not working out."

She shakes her head. "I swear the older you get, the more you remind me of Tito."

"You say that like it's not a good thing."

"Usually it is, but you have some of his bad tendencies, too."

"Like what?"

"Getting your answers from a bottle of vodka instead of confronting the situation ahead of you. Your father used to make me so mad doing that. We'd have a misunderstanding, and then the next thing I know, he's holed up in his house refusing to talk to me because he's figured out the solution to our problems all on his own." Alma's face flushes with a hint of anger and pinch of joy at sharing a memory about Papi. "And his solution was always to run away and break things off between us."

"I remember that. But he always came back to you."

"Only after I forced him. He hated confrontation and so do you. But it's a natural part of any healthy relationship. You won't always agree, but you have to find a way to keep communication open, especially during those times."

"She and I technically are not in a relationship."

Alma gives me a look that says she's not buying what I'm selling. I look away, staring at the dirt and grime caked under my fingernails from yesterday's landscaping.

"Have you talked to your lady friend about how you feel?"

"There's no point in talking about it."

"Why not?"

"Because coming here was a mistake," I blurt out. "Everything in this stupid town is toxic to me. Well, except you, Alma."

She raises an eyebrow and bats her lashes at me.

"You know how you've been on me about cleaning out Papi's house? Well, I did it the other day because she convinced me it was time."

"Smart lady. I think I like her already."

I cringe.

Alma knows Harlow, or better said, she knows "of Harlow." They don't exactly travel in the same circles, which is part of the problem I'm having with Harlow.

"When I was there with her, everything felt easier. She helped me sort through all his stuff. We lined up boxes against the walls and labeled them. Then we went through each room, grabbing stuff and deciding what I wanted to keep and what could be thrown out. The memories came hard and fast, but it wasn't sad like I thought it would be. It felt good to talk about him and the things we used to do together."

Alma beams at me as she grabs my hands and gives them a gentle squeeze.

"But all of that changed when she found this tucked into the folds of one of those boxing magazines he loved to read." I reach into the back pocket of my dirty jeans, which I didn't bother to change out of last night.

"I recognize that handwriting." Alma traces a finger along the lines that formed my name large on the front of the dirt-stained paper. "Tito left that for you."

"And I haven't opened it because I'm not sure I'm prepared for what could be inside." I squirm and sit up straighter in the bed. Sweat collects in my palms, and my heart pounds in my throat as I force myself to look her in the eyes. "What if I was wrong? What if my pain and grief blinded me from the truth? A man is in prison right now because of me, and maybe … maybe he shouldn't be."

Alma gazes at me then runs a hand along the side of my face. "This isn't about Dr. Jones."

My stomach sours, knowing that Alma is on a one-way trip to giving me a dose of tough love.

"When Tito was getting sicker by the day, and none of the fancy medical treatments were working, you did everything you could think of to keep him with you longer. You're scared that maybe it had become too much for your father. That he made a *choice* to leave you. Maybe that letter will help you understand why."

"Is that what you think happened?"

"No. My heart won't let me believe that Tito wanted to leave us. I was right by your side throughout the entire trial because I feel the same way you do," Alma says, then swipes at a tear rolling down her cheek. "But I can't ignore the possibility that it could be true. That Tito could've explained everything in that letter he left for you."

"Maybe it's better not to know." I let the envelope fall on the bed between us. Part of me wants to ask Alma to open it and read it instead. But I know she won't.

"Only you can decide that." Alma picks up the plate of toast and places it in front of me. I lift the square and take a bite.

"So, who is this mystery woman?"

I force the bread down my throat and say, "Harlow-Rose Robinson."

The gasp that escapes Alma's lips brings a sad smile to my face. Even Alma recognizes that a guy like me ending up with a girl like Harlow is a long shot under the best of circumstances. Last night showed me that we're far from the best and closer to harsh reality.

Harlow and I work when it's just us.

Alone.

But a relationship like we both want doesn't exist in a bubble.

We'd have to make it work with the pressures and prejudices around us and within us. I doubt that either of us is strong enough to endure that, which is why I need to walk away from her.

"Now you see why this is so hard?" I ask, seeking validation of what I'm feeling.

Alma nods her head. "I still think you should talk to her. From the moment you started having those late-night phone calls, you've seemed much more like yourself again. Like the Santos before Tito's illness got really bad. I like seeing you happy, and she does that for you."

"Until she doesn't."

Alma slaps a hand on my wrist and stands, obviously fed up with me being hard-headed. "Finish eating that food. It will make you feel better."

As the door closes behind her, I lean over and grab my phone from the table, wondering if maybe Harlow had tried to call and explain how crappy she'd treated me.

Flipping it over, I let out a sigh.

The battery is dead.

CHAPTER 21

ARLOW-ROSE

Stabbing my spoon into the bowl of Tin Roof ice cream, I scoop a large glob of the decadent dessert and stuff it into my mouth. The kitchen dining nook with windows overlooking Mom's rose garden in the backyard has always been one of my favorite spots in the house. A place where I could come to work through issues I couldn't talk about to anyone. I shouldn't be back in Kimbell with all the work that needs to be done at the winery, but after Jasmine's visit, coming home felt like the right thing to do.

I want to be close to Mom and Dad.

Especially if Jasmine is right about Santos. The more I think about everything that's happened between us, the more the little bombshell Jasmine dropped makes things clearer.

I want to be with you. I want to know that we have a future. But right now, I can't say that will happen. Too much is … uncertain.

Every moment I've spent with Santos has been completely certain. We don't have to say the words to know how much we mean to each other. That's why his feeble attempt to blame pulling away from me on his financial situation is ludicrous. Knowing the truth about our different backgrounds didn't change anything for me, and I thought it didn't change things for him either. My upbringing of private schools, learning multiple languages, ballet lessons, family vacations to Europe compared to his in public school, struggling to learn English as a kindergartner, playing soccer in the streets with friends, and taking trips to the lake to fish with his dad had become more fodder for jokes between us. Not something to keep us apart.

The man I've spent hours on the phone with each day over the past few weeks is confident and secure. He's not intimidated in any way by my net worth.

Too much is … uncertain.

The only uncertainty hanging over us is the arson investigation.

Jasmine's words haunt me.

Santos is sticking around Kimbell so he can watch you and your family. Gather evidence that your dad set the fire on purpose.

Is Santos secretly investigating Dad?

Is that the uncertain thing that could keep us apart?

If he thinks Dad could be arrested for arson, that absolutely will put an end to any chance of a relationship between us.

How could I ever forgive him for that?

"Harlow-Rose?"

I jump in my seat and turn around. Mom's shrewd eyes study my face intently. When I was little, I thought she actually had the power to read my mind. That's how good she is at figuring out what's troubling me. If I'm not careful, she'll get me to tell her everything I suspect about the arson investigation and my secret relationship with Santos before I can finish off this bowl of Blue Bell ice cream.

"You're stress eating." The words were an indictment. "Why are you here? Shouldn't you be at the winery prepping for the tours tomorrow?"

"Good to see you, too, Mom."

Her glare changes from shrewd to suspicious as she crosses the kitchen and enters the dining nook. I turn back around and watch the pale pink roses flutter in the wind.

"What's wrong?"

"Nothing," I say a little too quickly. "I wanted to check in on you and Dad."

"You were on edge at the party last night. I could tell something was wrong then, and I see it all over your face now," Mom says, then sits down at the dining table next to me.

She runs a hand along my face then tucks strands of my curly hair behind my ear. The simple gesture comforts me, and I relax.

"Fine. You don't want to talk to me. Go talk to your father. His bowl of ice cream is as big as this one." Mom says, snatching the half-eaten bowl from in front of me.

"What's wrong with Dad?"

She gives me a look, and I know Dad probably gave her the same response as I did.

"Where is he?" I ask.

"In his office." Mom busies herself at the sink, dumping out my uneaten ice cream. I hear her mutter under her breath, "I don't understand how eating until you're bloated helps take stress away."

Pushing away from the table, I leave the kitchen, taking the hallway up toward the front of the house. Passing through the smaller of our three living rooms, I enter the library and make my way to the double French doors that lead to Dad's office.

I debate whether I should tell Dad that he could be the prime suspect in the arson investigation. Knowing that my father is already stressed about something causes me to hesitate. Mom would've told me if Dad was worried about the delays in wrapping up the arson investigation. That means it must be something else. Something that Dad doesn't want to share with her. Yet.

But would he share it with me?

Maybe.

I slow my pace as I approach the slightly opened door.

I hear Dad on the phone. His voice oozes with desperation as he pleads with whoever is on the other line.

"The money is in your account like I told you it would be," Dad says. His fingers drum against the desk, echoing in the cavernous space. I press my back against the wall, where he can't see me.

"Damn it, Joe. Twenty-five thousand is all I can do for now. The whole point is for people to not get suspicious, including my wife!"

There's silence. Dad's breaths are heavy with anger as several minutes pass.

"Give me two weeks, and I'll make another transfer. You just stay off the radar. The last thing I need is for you to be brought in for questioning. It's the only reason why I agreed to this ... arrangement!"

I jump as the sound of the cell phone clattering against the desk floats through the air. My blood runs cold as I process the conversation. Dad is paying off Joe Little to avoid the arson investigation. Tears prick my eyes. This can only mean one thing.

Dad is responsible for the fire at the brewery.

He burned his own business to the ground. But why? What does Joe Little know that could lead the investigators to Dad?

I take a deep breath then step out from the wall.

The intercom buzzes in Dad's office.

Mom's voice comes through. "Scott, the dishwasher is flooding the kitchen. Please come quick."

"On my way, babe."

Scampering back further into the library, I pretend to walk toward the office doors as Dad rushes out.

"Hey, Rosie," Dad pauses. "I didn't realize you were back in town."

"Just came to check on you and Mom."

"You're the best, sweetie." Dad gives me a warm hug. "You wanted to talk to me?"

I nod my head.

"Go on inside while I take care of the dishwasher for your mom. It'll only take a few minutes."

I nod again, then stare as Dad disappears down the hall.

Heart thudding in my chest, I rush into his office and see his cell phone sitting near the edge of the massive mahogany desk. I pick it up and type in his password. My hands shake as I access his call log and see a number he called about five minutes ago. It has to be Joe Little's number. Slipping my cell from my pocket, I type in the digits and dial the number.

The ringing is loud in my ears. My eyes are glued to the doors of the office, hoping that Dad doesn't catch me.

"Who is this?" I recognize Joe Little's voice instantly.

"Harlow-Rose."

"Guess your daddy took me seriously and called in reinforcements," Joe says, with a crass chuckle.

"I'll get you the rest of the money," I say, trying to disguise the trembling of my voice. I'm taking a significant risk doing this, but it's what I must do to help Dad. He'd never let me, otherwise.

"That's what I want to hear."

"Once I do this, I need you to disappear for good. Is that clear?"

"I'll vanish without a trace. It's what I want to do anyway. No one will see or hear from me again."

A new idea sparks in my mind. "I'm glad we agree. Before I make the transfer, there's one last thing I need you to do."

CHAPTER 22

SANTOS

Before I have a chance to swallow my first sip of coffee, the door of my office on the third floor at the Kimbell Fire Station opens. Gary Logan leads Eric Watson, a forensic accountant on staff with Lasso County, into the small office. The presence of the two additional men ratchets up the temperature in the tight space. From the looks on their faces, I know we finally have a break in the case.

So much for spending the morning continuing my internal debate on whether or not to call Harlow back. With each hour of the past day, my anger at her has waned, and I wonder why she's suddenly gone silent on me. I want to know that she's okay and not in some ditch hurt. Irrational, but that's where my mind takes me.

If I wasn't stubborn, I'd call her back.

Give her a chance to explain why she treated me like a piece of gum on the bottom of her shoe. Did I expect her to whisk me inside to enjoy the celebration with her? Hadn't I practically pushed her away, telling her that we didn't have a future? What did I expect her to do?

Not what she did.

Dismissing me without a goodbye to fall into the folds of her rich, society friends is the last thing I expected. A quick glance back, eye contact, or something would've made that pill easier to swallow.

She gave me nothing.

Maybe that's why waking up to see the missed texts and calls from her yesterday morning had changed things. Even if I was too angry to admit it to myself until now. My heart isn't ready to truly let her go. The visceral yearning to see her after days with no contact is torture.

But what's worse is what her surprise party made crystal clear to me. Seeing her surrounded by the uber-rich, an echelon that she firmly fits in, had reminded me of how broke I am. How much I have nothing to offer her. At the heart of it all was pure embarrassment, plain and simple. Never in my life had I wanted to be part of that pompous world until I saw Harlow with them.

I wanted to be the one leading her into the winery, schmoozing with her friends and by her side the entire night. Truth was, that's exactly where Harlow wanted me to be. She'd told me on the drive to the winery. But what goes along with that reality would be the sneers and stares from her so-called friends. The things they'd say about her scrub of a man with my common occupation and paltry salary compared to all of them.

Knowing what she'd have to endure, I want to at least be on good ground financially before trying to have a relationship with her. Give her something positive to say about me as the rumors of her being my sugar mama swirl around.

I'm years away from being able to do that, though.

And if we try to be together before then, how long would she be content to forgo all those things so I won't feel inadequate? I can't afford to do the things and go the places she's used to. I sure as hell won't let her pay my way.

How long would it take for her to resent me?

To start sneaking off to be with friends she has more in common with?

To find another man who doesn't have the same baggage? To give her the best in life.

That's how I know starting a relationship with Harlow is a bad idea.

Probably the worst.

I need to focus on fixing my life. And that includes reading the letter that Papi left for me. I don't want to set either of us up for guaranteed disappointment.

My fingers itch to grab the phone and call Harlow. I care too much about her to not help her understand why this is really for the best. Life isn't a fairy tale where things work out because we want them. What we'd face is real, hard life. Ignoring that would be a waste of time.

But that conversation would have to wait until after I get the update from Gary and Eric.

"Well, what do you have for me, fellas?" I settle back into my seat as Gary and Eric sit in the two plastic chairs.

Hours later, piles of evidence clutter my usually neat desk, and I look up at both men in shock.

"You're absolutely sure about this? No chance that we got it wrong?" Irritation claws up my spine as I fight back the urge to unleash a string of expletives. With this news, the whole arson investigation has taken a sharp turn toward hell. I shouldn't be surprised, but I am. There's a long history of power, money, and influence circumventing justice in this country. I never thought that would be part of this investigation, though.

Eric looks at me with a grave expression, one likely practiced from years of delivering news about financial fraud and improprieties. "There was a second set of books on the brewery's ERP system that only the owner, Scott Robinson, and the former CFO, Joe Little, had access to. It was erased two weeks before the fire, but we still recovered the files. This second set had dramatically different financial information than the main books. Additional journal entries were recorded to improve the brewery's financial position."

My mouth gapes open. I rub my fingers against my temples, trying to massage away the throbbing in my head. I know what this means, but I still need him to say it aloud. I need Eric to confirm it. Holding up the documents we obtained from the bank, I say, "These financial statements we received matched the more positive statements."

"Yes, those are the ones that were changed to present the brewery in a better light."

"You're telling me the brewery was sending fake financials to the bank. They were trying to make it appear that they were doing good so the loan wouldn't go into default?"

"That's correct, sir." Eric tilts his head slightly in the affirmative. "It's the most common type of fraud. The debt has several covenants that would trigger a default. These manipulated records make it appear that the brewery was in compliance when they actually were not. The evidence is clear."

I wanted to slam my fist against the desk, but it wouldn't do any good. Had Scott Robinson lied to my face when I interviewed him? Did he know that any sign that the brewery was in financial trouble would catapult him to the top of my suspects?

"Both Scott and Joe had access to the second set of books," I stretch to the left, then to the right, trying to relieve the knots in my neck. "Any indication on who changed the records? Were they both involved?"

"That I can't tell you," Eric winces. "The setup was smart. Normally an audit log tracks all activities, but it was turned off for this second set of books. We can't tell who went in and made the changes. But we do know that the access was set to just the executive leadership team."

I turn to Gary. "Did you interview the bank again?"

"Yes, sir. I spoke to the bank president, David Bell, Sr. He told me that even though there is an audit clause in the bank's loan agreements, he rarely exercises it for local businesses. He knows most of the CPAs in Kimbell personally and trusts them. Never had a reason not to."

"Until today," I mutter under my breath.

"Mr. Bell said as long as Joe Little signed off on the financials, he didn't question what was in them. The brewery had hit a rough patch about a year ago but had been steadily improving over the past several months."

Eric chimes in, "Our investigation shows about six months of manipulated financials provided to the bank, all signed off by Joe Little. The improvements were gradual, but when aggregated show a drastic improvement in revenues and cash flow."

"Enough to stop the bank from digging any deeper. But how was the brewery able to make the loan payments if the revenues were faked?" I ask, glancing at the exorbitant quarterly loan payment amount.

"We're still looking into it, but seems like the brewery required prepayments on beer orders. Normally, revenues would never be recorded on the orders until they were actually shipped."

I nod my head as the pieces come together in my head. "They actually booked revenues when the cash came in the door, making it appear like the business was doing better than it was."

"These should be accounted for as deferred revenue," Eric explains. "A type of liability to the company and money owed back to the customers if they don't send the goods."

I ask, "So, the bank has no clue that the cash is for future orders they haven't sent? Scott Robinson is hiding liabilities of the company?"

"That's right." Eric nods his head vigorously. "Production data show that they were years away from being able to fulfill all the prepaid orders. I wouldn't be surprised if calls from frustrated customers waiting on their beer shipments haven't already started."

I glance at Gary. "Schedule repeat interviews with key employees in operations and accounting. I want to know if they've gotten calls like this over the past few months. Be discreet about it. We don't want to tip our hand yet."

Gary seems reinvigorated. "I'm on it. What's next?"

I turn toward my laptop and access the county databases. "I find Joe Little."

CHAPTER 23

H*ARLOW-ROSE*

Raucous cheers and hollers fill the packed restaurant as Aggie college students cram into the tight space after the team's victory. I maneuver through the crowd, blending with the teenagers in a Texas A&M t-shirt and matching maroon sweatpants. In just ten minutes of getting here, I've already had to fight off the advances of a few college guys trying to get my attention. I angle toward the back of the restaurant near the bar, where high tables are set up, with my mug of Elm Beer. Memories of hanging out almost a decade ago in this very place with Zaire and her sorority sisters when I'd come back home for visits from Stanford flood my mind. It wasn't the most popular hangout for

A&M undergrads, but there were more than enough of them to keep the place in business for years.

When Joe Little had told me to meet him here, I'd been shocked. But now I see this is the perfect place. The rowdy crowd of drunk college-goers and alumni old enough to be my grandparents pretty much guarantees that we won't draw any attention. Hiding in plain sight is a good move.

I gaze at the walls filled with memorabilia from decades of A&M events until I spot the one Joe told me to stand under. A picture of the original Miss Rev, the Aggies collie mascot, is near the back corner. A crowd of frat boys is nearby, but there's enough space for me to squeeze behind them and wait for Joe. Picking up my beer, I move again and settle on the bar stool. I have the best vantage of the entire restaurant as I wait for him to arrive.

I'm more than a little nervous, but I need to do this to get to the truth.

My cell phone buzzes in my pocket.

I reach for it, then frown as I read the text from an unknown number.

You set me up. You'll pay for this.

I reread the text, on the verge of hysteria. It's not the same burner phone that I called Joe on days ago, but I know the text is from him. Why does he think I set him up? What is he talking about?

My hands tremble as I try to type a response.

"What are you doing?" His words slam into me, harsh blows to my soul.

The voice unmistakable. I hear it in my dreams as I clutch my pillow tightly, wishing it was him.

Santos.

We haven't seen each other, talked, or texted since the night he dropped me off at the winery before my surprise party. Over the past four days, I've been avoiding him, and for whatever reason, he hasn't tried to reach me either. But now he's here when I don't want him to be. If he finds out I'm here to meet Joe Little, it can ruin everything for Dad. I can't let that happen.

I don't want to look into those gorgeous honey eyes.

I can't help myself.

I lock my cell phone and gaze up at him.

Regret floods through me.

For the first time, I see disappointment, anger, and mistrust where there had usually been a softness and a twinkle reserved only for me.

He's not alone.

A sheriff's deputy and two other men wearing Lasso County Fire Marshal jackets stand next to him.

Santos turns to the other men, "Split up. Search inside and out. He couldn't have gotten far. I'll deal with …" He looks at me as if I'm a stranger. "… this."

"Ms. Robinson, a word outside," Santos says. It's not a request. It's a command. His professional demeanor is cold and abrupt.

I stand on shaking legs and follow him. Santos moves quickly through the thick crowd, his strides lengthening until we get to an empty part of the packed parking lot. I struggle to keep up.

When we are out of earshot of anyone around, he turns to me.

My breath catches in my throat. This is bad. I wait for guilt or regret to consume me. It doesn't come. I did what I needed to do for my family. I wish I had been able to get answers before Santos and the deputies arrived.

"Are you involved in this mess with Joe Little and your father?"

Santos demands. I catch a brief glint of worry in his intense gaze, but it disappears quickly.

"Of course not," I stammer, trying to calm the pounding of my heart. "I don't know if there is a mess between Joe and Dad." I choose my words carefully, painfully aware that I could be arrested for what I tried to do. Meeting up with a critical witness in an ongoing arson investigation is probably a crime. I can't let my feelings for Santos cause me to forget that he can arrest me, too.

"Instead of telling me that you knew how to get in touch with Joe Little, you decide to impede a county arson investigation? Unbelievable." His hands fly toward the sky as he backs away from me.

"I don't know what you're talking about."

"We got an anonymous tip about a cell phone belonging to Joe Little. We've had surveillance on it for weeks. Finally got a hit, and it's a text to another burner telling someone to meet him at this restaurant underneath the picture of that damn Aggie dog!" Santos says, muscles and veins straining in his neck as he struggles to control his anger at me. "We get here, and who do we find but you! Do you know I could arrest you right now for obstruction of justice?"

My heart sinks. I avoid his gaze as my body trembles.

"Look at me, Harlow!"

I slowly raise my eyes to meet his. A flutter settles in my core at the care and concern I see reflected back at me.

"What do you know about your father's involvement with Joe Little and the incidents that led to the fire at the brewery?"

"Nothing. I swear I came here to get the same answers you're looking for."

"What tipped you off? What made you try to find Joe Little, a man your father fired weeks ago and seemed to have it in for your family? The whole town of Kimbell thinks Joe set the fire to get revenge for getting sacked, yet you felt comfortable enough reaching out to him to talk? Why is that?"

I cover my face with my hands. Telling the truth is not an option. I have to do whatever it takes to protect my family. "I grew up with Joe. He's like an uncle to me. He'd never do anything to hurt me. I thought that if anyone could convince him to come back and tell what he knows, then it would be me."

I feel despicable at how easily the lies flow from my mouth. I wanted to meet up with Joe to determine how bad the financial situation is for Dad and the brewery. I wanted to know what evidence he was using to blackmail my father and make sure that it would be destroyed—permanently—before I arranged to pay him off. Send him packing for good. I can't tell Santos any of this. It's the kind of behavior he's experienced and abhors.

"Cut the crap, Harlow. We both know that your father isn't innocent in this. Our forensic accountants uncovered the fraudulent financial statements he's been handing over to the bank. It's the only reason why the brewery didn't default on the loan and have to file for bankruptcy. Burning up the brewery gives your father a chance to start over with a huge chunk of insurance money and dig the company out of the hole it's been in for years."

I feel sucker-punched. Fraudulent financial statements? Dad had been faking the books to make the brewery look profitable? I force my voice to remain calm. "I don't know anything about that. My dad built the brewery from nothing. It's his pride and joy. He would never do anything to destroy it."

"If you really believed that, you wouldn't be sneaking around trying to talk to Joe Little behind your dad's back."

His words sober me. I hate that Santos can always read me, tap into my deepest thoughts and feelings as if they were his own, then force me to see them. To deal with them.

"Fine! You're right. I don't know if Dad got so desperate to save his business that he …" I can't let myself say the words. "He cares so much about the brewery. Everything he has, the man he became, was because of that place. Can you blame him for trying to do whatever it takes to save it?"

"If whatever it takes includes a fire that could've taken the lives of three of his employees and spread to other businesses in downtown Kimbell, then yes, I can blame him. It's selfish and shortsighted, but most importantly, it's a crime."

I wince. "I wanted to help him."

"By letting him get away with arson?"

"I don't know," I hedge. My dad had given me the best of everything that life could offer. All the privilege and success I've had was because of Mom and Dad picking me. There's no way I could ever repay them, but that doesn't mean I won't try. Especially when Dad needs me now. I'm the only one who can get him out of this mess, whether he wants to acknowledge that or not.

Santos scoffs. His face goes from soft to hard. "It's that simple, isn't it? If daddy dear sets his brewery on fire to stop it from going bankrupt, you'll call in a few favors to make the problem go away. Or were you going to bribe Joe Little into taking the fall? What's a few years in prison if he had a million-dollar payday waiting on him when he gets out. Is that your way of trying to help your dad?"

I cringe, knowing that the thought, and a few others, had crossed my mind. Ultimately, helping Joe disappear was my only option … after discovering exactly what he was holding over Dad. Now, because of Santos, I know about the fraud. It had to be the reason why Dad fired Joe Little. Joe had probably found out what Dad was doing and threatened to tell the bank. Dad couldn't let that happen, so he fired Joe and paid him off to keep quiet. As soon as Elm Street Brewery caught fire, I'm sure Joe was on the phone to Dad raising the stakes. He'd want more money to stay quiet, knowing that Dad torched his own business. But was that it? Or did Joe have definitive proof that Dad caused the fire? Is that why Dad was so desperate to keep Joe away?

I stay quiet. Nothing I can say will help Dad or me.

"Well, not on my watch." Santos rakes his hands through his dark curls. A sight that should cause my heart to flutter. Today, it fills me with dread. He's going to go after Dad. Stop at nothing to make sure my father ends up in prison.

Jasmine's warning rings in my ears.

I hate that she was right about Santos, the one man I completely opened my heart up to. As I watch a flurry of conflicting emotions pass across his face, I know without a doubt that I'm in love with him. It's a fact. A part of me that has simmered under the surface of my consciousness and has surfaced at the worst possible time.

I love Santos, and it doesn't matter.

Not anymore.

He points a finger at me. "Having money and privilege doesn't give you an out from being punished for your crimes."

My words are low. "There's no proof that Dad was involved in this. Can't you give him the benefit of the doubt? Why are you so certain that he's the bad guy?"

"Evidence is piling up against him by the hour. It's amazing what rich folks think they can get away with, but the truth will come out. All the money in the world won't be able to buy him out of this, even though I know you wish it could."

Everything Santos tried to explain to me rings true in this one moment.

We come from different worlds, and they are utterly incompatible with each other. Thinking that we could ever overcome them is naive and foolish. Stripped down from our environment, Santos is perfect for me. But it's impossible for us to exist that way. We have to live in the real world like everyone else. The real world, where our differences slowly erode every deep connection we have to each other. This is inevitable.

My heart aches to know that Santos was right all along, and I couldn't see it. A hot, humid breeze rustles through the trees and blazes across my skin. Tension pulses between us in anticipation of the fall out to come. The end of something so beautiful yet so fragile that neither of us could protect it from being destroyed.

Summoning every ounce of courage I can muster, I reach up and place my hands on the sides of his handsome face. He relaxes from my touch. His body slumps, and his eyes gaze down to the ground. I lean forward and place soft kisses over his thick lashes, inhaling the scent of him. Tears spring to my eyes, but I can't let them fall. I pull away slowly, my heart and mind protesting the disconnection with this man. I don't want to walk away from him, from us, but there's no other choice. Even if we tried, we wouldn't be able to survive this.

My love for him would wither and die the minute he arrested my dad for arson.

He looks at me with those honey eyes. The struggle to endure this moment, etched on his face, mirroring everything that I'm feeling. Hurt and misery are what will be left between us, crowding out all the memories of the good times we shared.

A lump forms in my throat as I try to speak. "Do you need to arrest me?"

He shakes his head in my hands. "I'm not going to do that." His words are low and full of emotion. "As much as I want to protect you from any kind of pain, I can't. Not this time. I can't bend the rules. Not even for you, Harlow."

"I understand." I wish I didn't. Knowing how those with privilege have caused him and his family so much pain throughout his life growing up, I get why he's so committed to pursuing justice. Trying to right the wrongs of society one case at a time, doing his part. I hate myself, but I can't help but wish that his convictions didn't have to come at the expense of my family.

And that makes me what Santos hates.

A member of the privileged few, expecting the rules to be different for us. My stomach sours, and I take a step back from him.

He reaches for me. His hand is warm and firm against mine. I look at our fingers intertwined and mourn the end of us.

"For what it's worth, I'll never forget you, Harlow." He strokes my face with his free hand. His eyes are filled with regret and sadness that unleashes the floodgates I'd been holding within. Tears course down my cheeks faster than his fingers can catch. My body shakes as he pulls me into his warm embrace. Hard muscles envelop me for the last time.

"I hate for it to end like this," he says. His face nuzzled against my thick hair.

Pain erupts within me, and I can't take it anymore.

I can't be around him. It's too hard.

"Me too." I pry myself from his arms.

Without a second glance, I turn and walk away from Santos for the last time.

CHAPTER 24

ARLOW-ROSE

THE SUN PEEKS THROUGH THE CLOUDS, STARTING ITS ascent as dawn breaks. I push my feet against the damp grass, catapulting the bench swing back and forth. The repetitive motion that I've done for the past several hours as I struggle to comprehend what's next.

The tears have long since dried on my face after driving from College Station back to Kimbell. The grief from walking away from the man I love has only started to take root. All my hopes and dreams of convincing Santos that we could beat the odds have been crushed.

In one evening, everything in my life took a devastating turn for the worst, and there's nothing I can do about it.

I chose family over justice.

A choice Santos can't condone or understand. We are on opposite sides with no way to bridge the gap between us.

We are over.

He's going to arrest Dad and ruin my family.

The events have left me numb.

My fingers linger on the edge of the bench where a heart is carved into the surface.

HRR + NB 4Ever

My life was simpler back then when Nate and I were together. I trace the outline of the carving.

"Trust me, it's not worth it to go back to simpler days."

I look up to find Nate staring back at me. He looks better than great. Tanned and refreshed as if he's ready to take on the world.

"But we're still together, forever, just in a different way. What brings you out here?" Dressed in jeans and a Kimbell Fire Fighter t-shirt that shows off his toned physique, he pushes through the tall field of wild daisies and sits next to me on the bench.

"Did some silent alarm go off? You came to see who was trespassing on your property?" I ask, lifting my legs from the ground and allowing Nate to take the swinging duties. I was one of only a handful of people who knew the private dirt road that led to the back of the Bell Compound. Acres of lush, manicured woodlands stretched for miles owned by the town's founding family. Beyond the fields of grazing cows and horses is a secret park Nate created to be his own sanctuary. A place he could come to get away from the pressures of being the youngest Bell child and all the expectations that had been laid on him since the day he was born.

He'd shared this place with me when we were kids in high school, giving me complete access to use it whenever I wanted to. I hadn't been here in years. Didn't have a reason to until now.

"I pay Ace Lallo to come out once a week and tend to the area since I'm too busy to do it myself. He was about to do the landscaping when he saw you out here. He said you seemed … lost."

I nod my head. What an accurate description. I'm floundering, adrift in a sea of disappointment with no way to make it back to what was my happy life.

"Is this about Santos?"

Oh God, why is Nate asking me this? It can't be good. "What do you mean? Is he about to arrest …" I swallow hard, then manage to add, "someone?"

"Not that I know of." Nate looks confused, then says. "I meant did y'all get into a lovers' quarrel or something? You two are seeing each other, right?"

My gasp makes him laugh. It was the last thing I expected him to ask me. The last thing I'd expected him or anyone to know.

"What makes you think Santos and I are seeing each other?" I hedge, not ready to admit what we both know is true.

"Willow told me."

My legs flop to the ground, stopping the bench from swaying back and forth. "Your sister told you?"

"She's seen the two of you a few times too many over the past month at Maisie's Table in Dripping Springs."

So much for being discreet. I should've known it was a matter of time before someone connected to Kimbell saw us out together. As much as we tried to resist showing our attraction in public, it had grown nearly impossible in the past couple of weeks. Whenever we were together, it was like some invisible force compelled us to hold hands, lean into each other, touch and caress, regardless of who could be watching.

"It's one of her favorites. She drives down from Austin all the time to take friends there. Said from what she could see, the brewery fire has nothing on the blaze sparking between y'all."

"Ohh," I say, looking away as my melancholy returns from the memories of when I had hope that Santos and I could be together in the future. The days I was counting down until he could solve the case, and we didn't have to hide anymore. I didn't know that the faster I got to that resolution, the faster I would be plunged into gloomy heartbreak. The wind rustles through the brush, caressing my skin with early morning dew.

"What's going on with you and that guy?"

"It's a long story."

"Seeing how I saved y'all from being discovered at your surprise party, I think I deserve more than it's a long story," Nate says, tugging on a strand of my hair as he mimics my voice.

"You recognized him?"

"I've seen that crap piece of junk he's driving around in enough to know it was Santos Estrada," Nate says. "Even with that hat on his head, it wouldn't have taken long for most of the Kimbell residents at the party to recognize him. So I distracted them by grabbing you and pulling you inside."

"Everybody got excited thinking something was going on between us."

"While I bought you time to keep your relationship with the arson investigator a secret for a bit longer." Nate winks at me. "You're welcome."

"Why is it that you don't let this sweet side of yourself out more?"

"Because no one would believe I'm being the real me, except

you," Nate says. "So, how in the hell did you and the arson investigator hook up? You know if this gets out, it could compromise the investigation."

"That's why we had to sneak around," I say, leaning against Nate's shoulder. "His job is vital to him. He's up for a big promotion and raise at the end of the year. A raise he really needs to pay off his debt. His boss assigned him to this case to test him, so he can't ask to be taken off of it."

Nate says, "Byron is such a jerk, forcing Santos to come back here after everything that happened with Dr. Jones's trial. It's hard for him and even tougher for Jasmine. Not that you care much about her."

"Maybe not, but I get no joy out of her being upset. And before you ask, my interest in Santos is in no way related to trying to get back at Jas for anything," I say, turning to face him.

"Trust me, the thought never crossed my mind. You're not built that way. She, on the other hand, is. But that's a whole other story. Back to Santos. Do you need me to get him in line? I'll see him at the station later today. I can be discreet."

"Please, no. That would make things worse than they are."

"Talk to me."

"It's over. There is no Santos and Harlow-Rose anymore."

"Because of his investigation? He had to end things before it got out and ruined his promotion?"

"I wish it was that simple."

Nate leans back on the bench, staring up into the cloudless sky. "He's targeting your dad, isn't he?"

"Yep."

"Darren thought so, but I wasn't convinced. Probably because I knew in the back of my mind that y'all were together. I didn't think he'd risk his relationship with you by going after Scott, but I guess I was wrong." Nate says, then rests a hand on mine. "Look, it's common for arson cases to focus on the business owner as the prime suspect. That's not a reason for you to end things with Santos. Willow said you seemed happier with him than she'd ever seen you before. You sure you want to shut things down for a technicality."

"That's just it." My shoulders slump. "I'm not sure it's a technicality. He's going to dig, and eventually, he will probably find evidence that Dad set or paid someone to set the fire at the brewery."

"No, he's not," Nate says, shaking his head.

"I overheard Dad on the phone with Joe Little last week. He transferred twenty-five thousand dollars into Joe's account in exchange for Joe laying low until the investigation is over," I say, picking a wild daisy from the ground. "Joe wants more money, and I was going to give it to him. But I needed details on exactly what he had on Dad. Turns out the financial reports he sent over to your bank for the debt were fraudulent. I think he changed them to look better, probably after Joe had signed off on them. Joe knows that, which is enough to give Dad a motive for arson. I wasn't sure if there was more. Like, did Joe have evidence that Dad actually started the fire? Before I gave him anything, I needed that answer."

"Why? You could go to jail for that. Your whole future could be ruined if anybody found out."

I flinch at the truth of his words. Santos broke all the rules by not arresting me last night. The last thing he could do to show me how much I meant to him before we parted ways.

"I know, but I wanted to help. Dad must have been desperate to set the fire for the insurance money when he could've come to me. I would've wired him funds or bought into the company or whatever he needed me to do, so he could get the cash infusion he needed. I didn't know what else to do."

"You're not supposed to do anything, Harlow. Don't get involved in things you don't understand." Nate taps the heart on the bench. "We've been friends for a long time. When I promised you I'd be there for you forever, I meant it. Doesn't matter that we stopped wanting to be with each other romantically. It doesn't change anything. I'll do whatever I can to help you. Always. Even if that means telling you what you don't want to hear."

"Which is?"

"Let your Dad fight his own battles. He made this bed. Now he needs to lie in it. And you have to let him."

"Fine."

"I'm not done."

"What else could there be?" I ask, in no mood to endure more scolding by Nate after the lecture I'd gotten from Santos yesterday. I already knew I'd crossed a line that I never thought I would in my life. I didn't just try to bend the rules. I was going to blatantly break them if Santos and the sheriff hadn't shown up and stopped my meeting with Joe Little. I thought I was doing the right thing, putting my family first. Now, in the harsh light of the morning, I'm not so sure.

"First, tell me. Are you in love with Santos?"

I bite my bottom lip and look away. I don't want to say the truth out loud.

"Well, that look says it all. Since the answer is yes, I want you to consider whether he needs to be punished because your dad did a stupid thing. How is that Santos's fault? The man is just doing his job."

"Are you done?" I ask, not ready to see Nate's point. If I did, then everything I'd done for Dad that destroyed my relationship with Santos would've been for nothing. I couldn't bring myself to believe that.

"Yeah, I think so. You hungry?"

"Starving," I admit.

"Good, let's go to Gwen's before it gets too crowded."

CHAPTER 25

S *ANTOS*

~

THE TWINS' RENDITION OF "IF YOU'RE HAPPY AND YOU Know It" is on its fifth go-round as I walk next to Ronan toward Gwen's Country Cafe. Finnegan is riding high on Ronan's shoulders while I have the pleasure of being Declan's mode of transportation. Both boys are having a blast, loving the impromptu breakfast with Daddy and Uncle Santos.

As they sing at the tops of their lungs, the twins took to using our heads as make-shift drums, banging away to the tempo. Declan gives me extra love, yanking on my curls with one hand as he slaps my skull with his other.

Instead of being annoyed, I'm enjoying the distraction.

Anything to forget Harlow and the gaping hole where my heart used to be. We both know that her father is guilty. It's just a matter of time before I have enough evidence to arrest him. When I do, she'll hate me. Probably more than Jasmine Jones does, and that's saying a lot.

It's not right, and it doesn't make sense for me to shoulder the blame for the crimes committed by their fathers, but it's what I've been forced to do. Part of me understands how they feel. Hadn't I done the same for Papi? Doing everything in my power to try to save him from the illness that was stealing his life? If it wasn't an illness but some crime instead, would my actions have been any different?

I know the answer, and it makes it that much harder for me to deal with the loss of Harlow. I would do exactly what she's doing. I understand her more than she'll ever know. Especially now since things are irrevocably over between us.

A slap hits my head as the boys start the song all over again. The little rascals could be a pain to deal with, but I loved them all the same. As did the townfolks. They are a popular duo, with people waving and saying hello to them as we make our way from the daycare center to breakfast.

Ronan still hasn't broken the news to the boys that they won't be going back to daycare ever again. This latest stunt had been pouring glue into the fake shampoo bottles and damaging the hair of two little girls playing beauty shop. That had been the last straw, and Ronan was told to find another place to take his kids in no uncertain terms.

"Have you ever thought about hiring a private nanny?" I ask.

"Isn't that expensive?"

"Can't be much more than paying for two kids in daycare and a lot less risky. You wouldn't need one full-time since you're off a few days every week. Plus, the nanny would take care of them at your house, so anything the boys tear up won't be a problem," I say.

"Not a bad suggestion. I'll have to look into that—"

I hear Ronan's phone beep and look at him with hope. The guy needs a break. He's already late for departmental meetings for shift leaders at the fire station because of this.

Relief floods me when I see a huge grin spread across his face. He holds up his hand, and I slap it with a high-five.

"She's going to do it?" I ask.

"Yes, thank God!" Ronan says. "Her shift ends at ten, which is around the time we should be done with breakfast. She told me to drop them off at the hospital, and she'd take them home with her."

"Did you hear that, guys? You get to hang out with Granny today," I say, halting the boys' song.

They break out in a chorus of yeahs. They didn't get to spend much time with Nikki's family, so this is definitely a special treat for them.

"But I promise you, if they tell me they fell asleep after breakfast with as amped up as they are now, there will be hell to pay," Ronan says, reaching for the door to the restaurant.

"What do you think she's doing to them?"

"I don't know. She's a nurse. Probably crushing up Benadryl or some other drowsy medicine in their juice to knock them out," Ronan says, then waves at Gwen Paul, the owner of Kimbell's most popular breakfast spot. "I know they're a handful, but I don't want her drugging my kids so she can take a nap."

"Hey Gwen," I say.

A bright smile spreads across her chubby face. "Good morning, fellas. Looks like you brought two of my favorite people with you."

"Hi Miss Gwen," the twins say in unison, just about melting everyone's heart in the place.

"Please tell me the family table is free," Ronan pleads.

"It's not, but I have one better for you," Gwen says, then points to a round table in the back corner near the kitchen. Behind the table, toys are scattered—legos, trucks, action figures, and blocks. Everything to keep the boys content and occupied for breakfast until Ronan can get them to their granny.

"That's perfect," Ronan says. He lifts Finnegan from his shoulders under a fit of protests and places him on the floor. "You gotta walk like a big boy now."

Finnegan whines, "But I don't want to be a big boy. I want to be up there!" He points a little finger back up at Ronan.

I lift Declan from my shoulders and place him on the floor. My shoulder muscles thank me.

"Look, Finn, legos!" Declan says, spotting the toys. Before I can blink, the twins are racing to the corner to play.

"What'll it be?" Gwen asks.

Ronan turns to me. "Have you had the Gwen's special?"

"Don't think so," I say when I know I haven't. Given what most people think of me in this town, most of my meals have been prepared at Crockett Manor by Alma or from some restaurant when I was with … I groan inwardly. The point is to stop thinking about the woman. Will everything remind me of her? Before the brewery fire, I only had five days of fleeting memories with Harlow. Since then, I have had thousands more over the month that we've spent with each other. Things I know about her that she's never told anyone else, not even Nate, or so she said. Thousands of things to haunt me as I try to move on from her.

"Well, it's my number one best-selling breakfast by a long shot," Gwen says, then rattles off everything in the platter. "Four pancakes, three eggs cooked to order, home fries, and a heaping bowl of bacon."

"Sounds perfect," I say, and more than enough food for the four of us.

"Add two coffees and two milks to the order. The twins can eat off of our plates," Ronan says.

Gwen jots it down, gives us another welcoming smile then heads back to the kitchen.

I follow Ronan to the table. He sits with his back to the door, so he can keep a watch on the boys. Despite my better judgment, I sit facing the door with the little rascals playing directly behind me. This puts me in a prime location to get banged over the head with some action figure, but I can take the blow.

What I can't take is who I see sitting in the opposite corner of the restaurant near the front window.

I curse under my breath.

"What is it?" Ronan asks, concern wrinkling his brows.

"Harlow is here," I say, dragging a hand down my face. Not only is she the last person I want to see today, seeing her sitting with her ex, Nate Bell, is like salt being poured into my bleeding heart. It's a flashing, neon sign that things are finished between us before they had a chance to really get going. It hasn't been twenty-four hours since we ended things, and there Nate is, swooping in to be the shoulder she leans on for support. The thought makes me want to cross the restaurant and punch the slacker straight in the face. I hate not being able to control my emotions when it comes to Harlow. Every part of me feels like she still belongs with me, even though I know it's not true. It will never be true.

We won't ever go on a date without worrying about people seeing us. I'll never take her to meet Alma or my extended family living in San Antonio. She'll never have me over to the Robinson house for dinner with her parents. There will be no double dates between her friends and mine. Worst of all, I'll never know what it feels like to be with her in every sense of the word. My gut twists, and I clench my fists under the table.

Ronan turns and sees them, then directs his attention back at me. He doesn't know how close Harlow and I had become over the past month. I kept our entire relationship a secret from everyone but Alma. And she only figured it out because of how nosey she is.

"Is it hard seeing her with Nate?" Ronan asks, studying me.

"Nope."

"Liar," Ronan says, then leans back in his chair. "Look, brother, I know how hard it is to let go of feelings for a woman you shouldn't still be into. Especially with how the two of you were brought back together by the brewery fire. That was completely unexpected."

"Tell me about it."

"But like I told you weeks ago, you need to cut your losses. Things won't work between you and Harlow-Rose. It'll be like carrying a boulder uphill. I'm not sure trying is worth the effort."

"Trust me. I know it's not," I say. I wish I'd listened to Ronan the first time instead of following my misguided heart. As if to confirm my thoughts, I hear Harlow's beautiful laugh tinkling from across the room. Nate sits next to her in a booth on the same bench as they stare out at the window and eat breakfast. I watch as he slyly snakes an arm around her shoulder and pulls her closer to him. The sight makes me want to vomit, but in reality, this is what I'll have to get used to.

Harlow will move on and be with other men.

It'll be a lot easier once this case is over and I'm not in Kimbell.

The first step in moving on for real will be when I don't have a chance to run into Harlow every day.

"Anyway, Gary mentioned that y'all are getting close to an arrest in the arson investigation," Ronan says.

"Not close enough," I say. Joe Little is still the key, but I don't divulge this to Ronan. The latest intel has been good, and I suspect we'll find him in the next couple of days. Which means in less than a week, I could be destroying Harlow's family when I arrest her father. "But yeah, it should be soon."

"Does that mean you'll disappear again from Kimbell? I'll have to make the drive over to Conroe to visit you?" Ronan asks.

I know what he's trying to flesh out. Will I stick around despite his warnings and try to rekindle things with Harlow? Doing so would be pointless, but I can't tell him why. Maybe in a year or so, I'll fill him in on how I jeopardized my job and career, sneaking around while I investigated the brewery blaze. But until then, I'm going to keep quiet. I steal another glance at Harlow.

"Or we can meet somewhere in between," I say, finally. "It's better if I put distance between me and this town."

CHAPTER 26

ARLOW-ROSE

"WHAT? ARE YOU AND NATE TAKING TURNS babysitting me?" I ask, kicking at a rock. I watch it skip along the sidewalk before coming to a rest in the grass. I should be annoyed, but I'm actually relieved to not spend the day alone. I know I should be sitting in a jail cell for what I tried to do yesterday. Obstructing justice. Interfering with a criminal investigation. Santos broke the rules and risked his career by not arresting me. That one act showed me exactly how much I mean to him. It breaks my heart that circumstances are driving us apart. For once, I'm at a loss on how to deal with the emotional upheaval. Misery is only moments away from sucking me under.

I'm not one to allow myself a pity party for very long. I can't help but focus on the positive. Look for a new plan to make lemonade out of lemons. Find a way to get back on track. But how can I put my life back on track when the things wrecking it are completely out of my control?

That's why having Zaire distract me from my problems is the best thing for me.

"Honey, when sexy Nate Bell calls me to say that my bestie is nursing a broken heart, I drop everything to come and check on you," Zaire says, wrapping an arm around my shoulder. "I was already here watching my money at work for the Founder's Day activities, so it wasn't a big deal to swing by Gwen's and get you."

"Thanks," I mumble, then lean into her embrace. I gaze across the area that makes up Kimbell's Town Center as we walk on the sidewalk along Main Street. Bell Park is a bustle of activity as construction crews work to set up the booths for the market. The stores around the park are being spruced up with fresh coats of paint. New signs are everywhere, announcing special Founder's Day sales.

The railroad and the Bell Train museum are behind the park. I scan the spot where the Elm Street Brewery tent would be set up next to the museum. All the employees should be bustling around creating the replica of the beer garden on the grounds, stacking inventory of the various beers, and constructing the stage for the live music groups we'd donate to the festivities each year. Instead, there's no tent and no stage. Just an empty parking lot cluttered with supplies.

As if she could read my thoughts, Zaire says, "The brewery tent and live music will be back next year, for sure."

I nod my head, and I believe it. Deep down, I know that things will work out for the brewery, even if I can't see how. "Did you step up to sponsor to take up the slack?"

"It was the least I could do. Plus, you know I'm not shy about capitalizing on an opportunity to promote my business. This weekend, there will be enough Kincaid Real Estate signs all around this town that everyone will know who to call when they want to buy or sell their next property."

"You're the best."

We stroll past more workers hammering and nailing booths around the perimeter of Bell Park. The buzz of drills and saws fills the air. A low hum of excitement courses through the space. An excitement I'm immune to for the first time. "I really hate we're missing out this year. Founder's Day has always been one of my favorite times in Kimbell."

"Well, of course, it is!" Mrs. Williamson's voice booms from behind us. "It's our own special holiday unique to our wonderful town when our founding mother, Kimberly Bell, settled here over one hundred years ago."

I give Zaire a knowing look as she rolls her eyes. We both turn to face the long-time planner of activities for Founder's Day. Mrs. Williamson looks like she's ready to jump right in with the construction workers and start cutting wood and nailing planks. She's wearing a t-shirt, overalls, and steel-toe boots as she stops in front of us. Her red hair is twisted into a tight bun behind her head. Her face is coated with a sheen of sweat from supervising the activities, probably since the wee morning hours. A clipboard rests in the crook of her arm, full of papers and handwritten notes.

"Mrs. Williamson, how are you this afternoon?" Zaire asks, then gives the woman a hug.

I follow Zaire's lead and greet the woman with a hug. "Good to see you, Mrs. Williamson."

"I'm doing exceptionally well," Mrs. Williamson gives us a haughty smile. "You know, I do believe our founder Kimberly Bell would be immensely proud of you ladies. When her husband died unexpectedly as they trekked across the country from Virginia to find a new home in California, she never expected him to die on her."

Zaire stifles a giggle. We both know that Mrs. Williamson is about to launch into her history of Kimbell speech that she says to everyone and anyone as Founder's Day approaches. I'm always amazed at how she can weave it into any conversation.

"But that didn't stop Kimberly Bell. She decided to stay right here and build a life for herself and her four kids. She was a brilliant entrepreneur like you two ladies, opening Lasso County's first bank and serving as the namesake and first mayor of our town," Mrs. Williamson says, beaming. "I'm very proud that Kincaid Real Estate is a Tier One sponsor this year. Thank you, Zaire, again for your generosity."

"You're welcome, Mrs. Williamson. I'm always happy to give back to the community," Zaire says.

"Now, Harlow-Rose, I'm sorry about the tragedy that your daddy experienced with the brewery burning to the ground. Understandably, we won't have the brewery as a sponsor, but I thought I might see Harlow-Rose Winery as a replacement on the list of sponsors or at least purchasing space in one of our booths."

I cringe inwardly, regretting not thinking of that myself. With everything going on with Dad and Santos, preparing for Founder's Day had slipped off my radar. I'd had plans of co-sponsoring with Elm Street Brewery and sharing space in the beer garden for wine tastings, but that all vanished when Mom called me to tell me about the fire. In hindsight, I suppose I could have easily sponsored everything that the brewery had done in the past if I hadn't been so distracted.

"When I checked this morning, I didn't see your business listed. Was that an oversight?"

Stunned, I stumble over my words. "Well, it's been … I didn't think …"

"Don't worry, dear. I saved a prime location for your winery near the gazebo in Bell Park. All I'll need is the five thousand dollar booth rental fee. We accept cash, check, or credit card," Mrs. Williamson says, her smile growing brighter. She hands me a card. "Call the office and let us know how you'll be paying. Good seeing you, ladies."

I flip the card in my hand and sigh, feeling like I've been hit by a freight train. "What just happened?"

"Vintage Mrs. Williamson in action. But are you up for running a booth this weekend? It's short notice."

I take out my cell phone and send a quick text to Gina. "No, but by the time my manager is done working her magic, you'll have thought we planned this all along," I say as I type the text with a brief description of what we'll need as well as the information on how to pay for the booth.

"So, that means you'll stay here this weekend?" Zaire asks, her eyes full of hope.

"Yes, I'll be here," I say. I'd been looking for an excuse to stick around, and this works perfectly. I can't predict when or if the investigators will find Joe Little, but I want to be close to home and Dad when it happens. He's going to need my support, even if he's in the wrong.

"Honey, you won't regret it. It's going to be big news that you're participating," Zaire says. Now she's the one typing feverishly on her cell phone. "I'm going to get the P.R. team to work up special flyers to pass around town, so people will know they have a chance to taste Kimbell's own Harlow-Rose's award-winning wine this weekend."

"You really think that's going to help bring out more people?" I'm skeptical, but I've learned never to doubt Zaire.

"Of course. You're one of the big names of Kimbell, now. Almost as big as Ciara Thompson, who is going to be the Grand Marshall of the parade."

"Ciara Thompson from Channel 4 News for You Houston is actually going to be in our parade this year? She finally agreed?"

Zaire nods her head. From what I remember, Zaire had been the town's rep to try to convince Ciara for years to participate in Founder's Day. Ciara had gone to A&M with Zaire and was one of her sorority sisters and good friends. Even with those connections, Zaire had never been able to convince her to come back to town.

"I thought she'd vowed never to come back to Kimbell for some reason," I say, trying to remember the vague excuse Zaire had told me about Ciara's perpetual declines.

Her expression turns somber. "Trust me, she has a very good reason for never wanting to come back home."

"I wonder why she changed her mind?"

"Not why. Who," Zaire says with a sneaky grin. "I have my suspicions that Luke Diamond is a big part of the reason she's been spending more time in Kimbell and has finally agreed to be in our parade. Of course, she denies it."

"You think something is going on between those two?" I ask, thinking about Nate's hunky best friend, who had become one of the stars of this year's Annual Firefighters Alliance calendar.

"Verdict is out on that, but I'll be keeping a watch on them this weekend," Zaire says, lowering her voice as a group of Kimbell firefighters pass by carrying ten-foot two-by-fours toward Bell

Park. "But enough with other people's love lives. What is going on with you and … the man formerly known as Napa Guy?"

I groan and walk faster as if I could actually avoid the barrage of questions I know are coming.

"You have to tell me something. How can you be heartbroken over him so soon? I knew waiting for the investigation to be over would be hard. None of us expected it to still be dragging on more than a month after the fire. I can see why you are frustrated. Is that it?" Zaire asks, then grabs my arm to stop me from walking further. "Or is it something worse? Honey, please tell me you didn't find out he has a girlfriend? A wife?"

"Zaire!" I say, throwing my hands up in the air. "I don't want to get into this. It's complicated."

"Matters of the heart are always complicated. You didn't think getting the guy would be easy, did you?"

"Maybe, I did. I thought we'd be so perfect for each other. That us reconnecting was a beautiful silver lining in an otherwise disastrous event that happened to my family. He and I would be the one bright spot in it all. But I was completely and utterly wrong about everything."

"Oh honey, you're not making any sense," Zaire says, steering me to sit on one of the benches lining Main Street. A massive Oak tree bathes us in the shadows, giving a reprieve from the blazing afternoon sun. "Tell me what happened."

"He told me that he doesn't want to start a relationship with me." I'm sticking as close to the truth as possible without giving Zaire information that could put her on the witness stand. "He's not interested."

"I'm sorry. I never expected that to be the issue."

No matter how much time Santos and I spent together, how close we'd become, we can't deny the fundamental deal-breaking differences in what we believe about Dad setting the fire at the brewery.

Thinking about our last conversation drives me closer and closer to anger and shame. I can't erase the memory of the look in his eyes. The disappointment and pity I saw when he realized that I was no different than that family who protected their guilty teenage son from facing charges after causing the wreck that killed his mom and siblings.

I know he thought I was a much better person than that.

I thought I was, too.

But when faced with the idea of Dad going to prison for arson, my instinct was to protect him by any means necessary.

Not to turn him in, which is what I know Santos expected me to do.

"I hear vacation flings rarely work out when you try to extend them into your daily life. Maybe it's better that he didn't string you along," Zaire says, giving my hand a gentle squeeze. "Aren't you glad you know and can put that part of your life behind you?"

I would be if I hadn't fallen in love with Santos.

"No, I'm not glad at all," I say, then cover my face with my hands as the tears start to roll down my cheeks.

CHAPTER 27

S *ANTOS*

~

"I CAN'T BELIEVE THIS." GARY SLAMS HIS CELL PHONE on the dining room table. "What are we going to do now?"

Crockett Manor is full of guests with the upcoming Founder's Day weekend activities, but they had all finished dinner and retired to their rooms when Gary and I got in from work. Another long day of slogging through the arson scene, pouring over the evidence, and piecing together a potential timeline had been brought to a screeching halt.

I stare at the test results on the small screen of my own cell phone, dumbfounded. The email came in as we sat in silence, devouring Alma's chicken mole.

I was sure that this would give us everything I needed to arrest

Scott Robinson. Instead, these results put a bigger question mark on what happened at the brewery on the night it exploded into flames.

I read the conclusion for the tenth time.

Inconclusive.

Unable to accurately identify ignitable liquid residues in soil and debris samples, likely due to microbial degradation, which resulted in significantly metabolized components of the residue.

I drag a hand down my face and mentally retrace every step we'd taken to preserve the integrity of the samples. We hadn't skimped on any of the required protocols.

And I wasn't distracted by Harlow.

These samples are from the hundreds we'd collected when I'd initially arrived in Kimbell.

Before I'd seen her looking gorgeous, standing inside of Elevation Cupcake Shop.

"Santos!" Gary says, his voice raised in frustration.

I glance up at him and try to temper my own annoyance. "The lab is still processing more debris that we sent in from the later samples—"

"You know as well as I do that this was our best chance to find whatever was used to set Joe Little's office on fire," Gary says. "The later samples have a bigger chance of contamination and will probably come back inconclusive, too. We have two viable suspects but still can't catch a break to eliminate one of them."

"It's not all bad news." I swipe the screen to access another page. "Did you check out page thirteen? With this result, we can almost be assured that the fire started in Joe Little's office first and then spread through the air duct, where it ignited grain dust and caused the massive explosion. That's something we'd suspected but didn't know for sure until now."

"Still doesn't tell us if Joe Little came back to get revenge or if Scott burned his own brewery to either hide evidence Joe had in his office or to commit insurance fraud to get out of debt," Gary says, slumping back in his seat.

His impatience is why he misses the critical information needed to close an arson investigation. I know why Byron paired us together, but I'm almost ready to send Gary packing and finish up on my own.

"The forensic accountants could still find something useful on the credit card statements and bank records that we gathered for both men."

"If they were going to find something, they would've by now. Scott and Joe are too smart to leave that kind of trail back to themselves. We're running out of options to solve this case."

"As long as Joe Little is out there, we still have a chance," I say, thinking about Joe being so close to Kimbell after all these weeks. If Joe had set the fire and gotten away with it, why wouldn't he be thousands of miles away by now? And why would he have agreed to meet with Harlow?

The only thing that makes sense to me is that Joe Little didn't set the fire. But he has evidence that Scott Robinson did. Evidence that would be worth a lot to Harlow to make disappear along with Joe Little himself. The HR records from the brewery had shown that Joe made a lot more money than I expected being the CFO, and he loved expensive things. He wouldn't want to disappear and live the life of a pauper. He wants cash for what he knows, so he can recreate himself somewhere with the lifestyle that he is accustomed to.

"At least we finally have a viable lead on a location for Joe after he got away from us in College Station," Gary says.

"I'm guessing we'll be questioning him before the weekend," I say. Joe Little had made a mistake meeting with Harlow. That move gave us insight into his actions and behaviors we didn't have before. Critical information that's helping Lasso County sheriff deputies track him across the state.

Gary stands from the table and stretches. "I really hope so. We need some good news for a change. Need me for anything?"

I shake my head.

"I'm going up to my room, but I'm available if something pops up."

"Get some rest," I say as the grandfather clock in the corner of the dining room strikes ten at night. Gary ambles slowly out of the room, leaving me alone with my thoughts.

This time, I haven't tried to run away from where I know my thoughts will lead by drowning them in vodka. When I'm this close to breaking a case, I need to be alert and sharp. Analyzing the smallest detail about the evidence we've found is critical to success. Keeping my mind clear is necessary, even if that means it opens the door to the intense pain of losing Harlow. Physical pain that has been my companion since the night she turned away from me in that parking lot in College Station.

The constant throbbing in my temples. My muscles tense and coiled. The sharp ache in my heart that longs for her even as my brain continues to be pissed at everything she tried to do.

I should've arrested her.

I know she has information that would help me crack the case wide open, but I couldn't do it. As much as I hate what she was trying to do and know without a doubt that she's wrong, I couldn't haul her in. It would've been all over the news. It would've ruined her name. Her business. Her life.

Everything she did was because she loved her dad and wanted to help him.

If anyone knows what it feels like to be in that situation, it's me.

Still, I'm angry that I can't do what I should be doing—forcing her to tell me exactly why she reached out to Joe Little. What was going to happen if we hadn't busted up their meeting? What does she know?

And why didn't she trust me enough to tell me?

A hand grips the back of my neck, squeezing gently, then pats me softly. The movement is reminiscent of what Papi used to do. A tough, firm touch that exuded so much love. Alma had witnessed Papi doing this more times than either of us could count. Something about the contact soothes me, halting my jumbled, confused thoughts.

"You want dessert?" Alma eases down into the chair next to me.

I glance at my plate, still heaping with food, then over to Gary's discarded plate with only remnants of the mole sauce remaining on the surface. "No, I guess I'm not that hungry tonight."

Alma grabs Gary's plate, then picks mine up and stacks it on top. "I wasn't trying to eavesdrop, but it sounds like you're close to wrapping up the investigation."

"I think so."

"And you'll be arresting someone?"

"That's the plan."

"Then you'll be leaving Kimbell."

A lump forms in my throat. I swallow past it and give Alma my best smile. "You're going to miss me?"

"More than you'll know. I like having you around. It's like a piece of Tito is still with me. I especially love how you treat me," Alma says. She fidgets with the edge of the table cloth. "I never had any kids, and I know I'm no replacement for your Mami, but you make me feel like I'm your family."

"You are," I say, then feel lighter from the realization. "We'll always be family, Alma. No matter if I'm here in Kimbell or back in Conroe or somewhere else entirely."

"Good. I don't want you to feel alone because you definitely are not."

Alma leans her head onto my shoulder. I wrap my arms around her, hugging her tightly. She pulls back from my embrace. I can see her expression change subtly, and I wonder what's coming next.

She takes a deep breath, then says. "Closing the investigation also means leaving someone else that you've grown close to. Do you want to talk about … her?"

It's a good question.

Alma's a great listener, but I'm not sure I'm ready to dump everything I think and feel about Harlow onto her or anyone.

"Have you talked to her lately?"

"Yeah, and it confirmed everything I already knew."

"I'm sorry."

"But you're not surprised?"

"No," Alma shakes her head, unable to hide her sympathy for me. "It would take a very special, strong … love … for the two of you to withstand what life would throw at you."

Her words are like a gut punch.

I don't respond.

"But I don't want things not working out for you and Harlow to impact your memories of your father."

"What are you talking about?" Irritation creeps into my words.

"I found this in your trash can." Alma takes the crumpled envelope from her pocket and places it in front of me. "I know

Harlow-Rose gave you the courage to face your father's house, and when she found this, it was her presence in your life that made you hold on to it. That made you believe one day you'd be able to read his last words to you. Just because she's gone doesn't mean you can't still do that."

I snatch the envelope from the table and stuff it into the pocket of my jeans.

"One day, when you're in a better place, you'll want to open the letter. I don't want you to regret not having it."

"Thanks," I mumble.

The last thing I want is more regrets.

CHAPTER 28

ARLOW-ROSE

Having money and privilege doesn't give you an out from being punished for your crimes.

Deep in my heart, I know Santos is right. But that doesn't stop me from standing outside Dad's home office to warn him of what's to come. After drowning my sorrows with Nate and Zaire yesterday, I'm done feeling sorry for myself.

I can't think about what could've been with Santos.

I absolutely can't think about being in love with him.

My father's freedom is on the line.

After crashing in Zaire's spare bedroom last night, I got up early and headed back to my parent's house.

Entering through the front door, the house is quiet.

The calm before the storm.

I need to talk to Dad alone, without Mom around. She's a notorious late sleeper while he's usually up at dawn working in his office.

I breeze through the library and knock on the French door, but don't wait for him to answer. I can't lose my nerve or talk myself out of this, even though it feels wrong. Pushing the double doors open, I step into the cavernous space and look around.

The room is empty.

Disappointment snakes through me as I walk around my father's desk. I lift the papers resting on his desk, flipping through them. I scanned the contents, searching for some evidence of his crimes.

There's none.

I return the papers to the neat piles and turn my attention to the computer. The screensaver of pictures of our family float across at varying angles. Happier times than the ones we're going through at the moment.

"There you are."

Mom's voice jolts me. I shriek and stumble back into Dad's chair with a thud. I keep my head down, hoping she doesn't notice how upset I am.

"I was looking for Dad," I say through shaky breaths. Twisting the end of my shirt between my fingers, I'm afraid to look up. "Do you know where he is?"

"He's not here." Mom's voice is low. There's an unmistakable hint of worry in her tone that sends alarm bells through me. Am I too late?

She continues, "David called early this morning and told him that the sheriffs have found Joe Little. He's being brought to

Kimbell for questioning. David thought it was a good idea for your dad to be there when Joe arrived, so he left."

I thought there was more time, but it seems as if time has run out.

The truth of the litany of crimes that Dad likely committed could be a few short hours away from coming out—the financial statement fraud, making blackmail payments to Joe Little, and arson.

My body trembles, and a sob catches in my throat.

Mom rushes to my side, her arms wrapping around me. "I know. I'm worried, too. We need to stay positive and not jump to the wrong conclusion."

"You don't understand, Mom. It's worse than you think."

"Harlow-Rose," Mom leans back against the desk to look at me. "What are you talking about?"

"Dad set the brewery on fire."

Mom's face goes rigid. All the color in her cheeks drains away as her eyes stare into mine.

"I overheard him on the phone with Joe Little. He paid him twenty-five thousand dollars to stay away. That's why the investigators haven't been able to find him. There's only one reason why Dad would bribe Joe. It's because he knows that Dad set the fire himself. The brewery is in financial trouble, and Dad must have seen the insurance proceeds as a way to start over."

"I was afraid of this," Mom says. She grabs my hands and gives them a gentle squeeze. Her eyes grow bleary and unfocused, staring into the distance, away from me.

"You knew?" I ask, but she doesn't respond. I need to know the truth. "Mom, did Dad admit to you that he started the fire at the brewery?"

She snaps out of her trance and looks back at me. "He told me he didn't, but I can't be certain that he was telling me the truth or trying to protect me from another one of his horrible mistakes."

"Another horrible mistake?" I wonder how much Mom knows about the fraudulent financial statements that were sent to the bank, giving the impression that the company was solvent when it was really hanging on by a thread. I'm not sure how much I want to reveal before finding out what my mom knows first.

"I believed him years ago when he told me he'd stopped gambling and again when he said the brewery financial situation had improved, but both times he lied. He could be lying about this, too."

"Gambling?" For as long as I can remember, Dad took trips to Vegas a couple of times a year to play in poker tournaments. It all seemed like harmless fun.

"He wasn't addicted, just arrogant. Too foolish to know when he'd gotten in over his head. By the time I found out, he'd wiped out the brewery's reserves to pay off the debt he had in Vegas."

"Mom! Why didn't you tell me about this?"

"Because there was no way I was letting my daughter bail her father out of a mess of his own making. Scott got himself into trouble, and he's going to get himself out." She runs a soft hand along my face. "I know how much you want to help, but it wouldn't be good for you or for your father."

"Why not? Everything I have is because of what the two of you gave to me."

"That is not true," Mom says. "We gave you a start, but what you did with it is one hundred percent you, Harlow-Rose. From the moment you were a little girl, I knew you'd be brilliant. Your dad saw it, too. He knew you were destined to create and build something much bigger and grander than his small-town brewery.

That's why he forced you to go and find your own path. Your accomplishments and successes were because of your intelligence, your drive, and your commitment. Don't let anyone tell you differently."

"None of that matters if Dad ends up in prison for arson."

"If … your dad did this, it's on him. He created the brewery on his own, and he ruined it on his own. You will not suffer because of that, and neither will I."

Her blunt words stun me. "Don't you want to help him?"

"I love your father unconditionally, and nothing will ever change that. But no amount of help will shield him from being accountable for his actions. It's the right thing. Any interference by either of us wouldn't truly help your father."

I grow still, shocked by Mom's perspective. The mindset that aligns with everything Santos had said to me days ago. The views I hadn't shared that drove a permanent chasm between us. I turned away from perhaps the most monumental love of my life. Now I'm wondering if that was my biggest mistake. Trying to support my dad in all the wrong ways, pushing away Santos instead of taking the approach my mom had embraced.

Mom says, "We will know the outcomes soon enough. Joe Little will probably tell the investigators that your father paid him twenty-five thousand dollars to leave town and why. The investigators will want to talk to your father again, and they will sort out the truth."

"The truth," A mirthless laugh escapes my lips. "I was going to meet with Joe Little a couple of days ago to get the truth before the investigators found him."

"Harlow-Rose! Why would you do that?"

"Because I thought I could help Dad by making Joe disappear. I knew twenty-five thousand wasn't nearly enough. I could offer him so much more. But I didn't get the chance to. He didn't show up because the sheriffs found out about our meeting."

"I'm glad he didn't. You never should have done anything like that. You need to be focused on your own future, not your father! That man has always been a risk-taker. It has profited him with good results on so many occasions, like the success of his brewery. But other times, the results have been bad and sometimes disastrous."

"Why did you keep this from me?"

"What were you supposed to do about it? You were a little girl. Then when you were older, I vowed to do everything to protect you from his bad decisions. I would never allow your future to be sacrificed for him. Trust me, he wouldn't either. But it doesn't change how I feel about him. I vowed to stand by him for better or worse, and that's exactly what I'm going to do. But *you* don't need to."

"I don't know that I could turn my back on him."

"You're not," Mom says, patting my hand. "The kind of support your father needs from you has nothing to do with money or committing a crime to help him. When the truth comes out, he needs to know that you still love him. That's what will get him through. Robinsons are fighters. We will find a way through this difficulty and come out better because of it. Sometimes, you have to hit rock bottom before you can pull yourself out and see better days."

"Guess there's nothing left for me to do but wait."

"Especially since Santos is going to be very busy today. I can't imagine what kind of strain this has put on your relationship with him."

My mouth drops open. I feel like my eyes are about to pop out of my head. "What … how?"

"Dad and I spent a couple of days trying to figure out who Napa Guy could be after you told him that you'd run into him here in Kimbell. It didn't take long for us to figure out it was probably the arson investigator. Then, I was talking to Cindy."

"Nate's mom knows?" I almost screech.

"Willow saw you and Santos having dinner a couple of times in a small restaurant in Dripping Springs. Cindy was so disappointed that you've moved on. I was, too. But you know your Dad was over the moon."

"I can't believe what I'm hearing."

"It took everything in us to not say something when he dropped you off for the surprise party. We understood why the two of you needed to keep things secret, with the investigation going on."

"Mom!"

"Are the two of you in love?" Her eyes twinkle with happiness for me.

A happiness that I don't feel. I can't feel it. The infatuation I felt for him after those five days in Napa pales in comparison to my current feelings. Now that I've had the chance to know the real Santos, his hopes and dreams, his disappointments and flaws, it's like we were made for each other. He's perfectly imperfect and just right for me. But, I never got the chance to find out if Santos had fallen in love with me like I have with him.

I threw away any hope of knowing the minute I tried to obstruct justice by helping Dad pay off Joe Little.

"Yes, I love him very much."

"I'm happy for you, Harlow-Rose. Santos seems like a great man."

"He is," I say, then brush a hand angrily across my cheek as the tears begin to flow.

Concern creases Mom's face as she grabs my hands. "What's wrong?"

"We're not … seeing each other anymore. It's over."

As Mom pulls me into her arms, a rush of tears that I thought had dried up are unleashed, and I cry like I never have before.

CHAPTER 29

S ANTOS

GARY IS AT MY SIDE, CASTING CURIOUS GLANCES MY way. He's likely wondering what I'm waiting on.

If I'm being honest, a small part of me wants to help Harlow's scumbag father out of this mess. Anything to bring a smile back to that gorgeous face. But doing so goes against everything that I believe in. I can't use my position to help those who've always had law enforcement treat them better, while men who look like me are never given the benefit of the doubt. Ever.

I wonder how far she would have gone to cover up what must be going on between her dad and Joe Little. Would she have rationalized that behavior? Found a way to tell herself that what she'd done was okay and not circumventing justice. Or would a part of her have regretted the actions, thought of me, and wanted to do things differently?

I'll never know.

I shake my head to force the wayward thoughts away and turn my attention to Joe Little. A thin man with sallow cheeks, intense eyes, and a wispy gray comb-over on his balding head, he doesn't wear the essence of privilege and wealth like Scott Robinson. I imagine he's always worked for those much richer than him but could never get to their level. Still, he's had a comfortable life and isn't handling being in the hot seat well.

He squirms under my scrutiny, which is what I want.

I glance at Gary and motion for him to take the lead in questioning Joe. Gary's a great 'good cop' interviewer, which I need right now. I want Joe to feel at ease and open up. With my emotions all over the place, I know I'll come on too strong, and he'll clam up. But if I sense that Joe needs to be shook up, I can always interject with a bit of 'bad cop' so he knows what's really on the line for him.

Gary does introductions and launches into a series of foundational questions. Before he can navigate to the harder ones, Joe interrupts.

"I know what's going on here and that it's in my best interest to come clean. I'm going to tell you what happened and what didn't. I'm not going down for that fire. I didn't set it. I swear," Joe Little says.

I pipe in, "Why don't you start from the beginning?"

"Scott Robinson has a gambling problem."

I raise an eyebrow and glance at Gary.

"The brewery was a huge success almost from day one. Scott has the magic touch when it comes to beer. He rode the early wave of breweries in the nineties and cashed in, becoming an overnight millionaire. Problem was that it happened too easily. The challenge was gone, and he needed something to replace it," Joe said, sucking in a deep breath. "He started making gambling trips years ago and was content with winning five figures, sometimes six. Then he got the attention of some real high rollers. Invitations to million-dollar poker games came next. He was killing it at first, but then he hit a losing streak. That's when he started to 'borrow' money from the brewery."

"Mr. Robinson is embezzling funds from his own company?" Gary asks.

"The brewery is privately owned, and there's no crime in Scott taking cash out whenever he wants."

"So he's taking more money from the company than what it's been earning?" I ask.

"Not anymore. His wife got wind of it about a year ago and put a stop to it. By that time, the damage was done. He'd neglected the operations, bled the reserves, and the brewery was a shadow of the success it had once been," Joe explains. "And that was the challenge Scott needed to get him going again. He turned all his attention to revitalizing the brewery, but it was too little too late."

I lean my elbows on the desk between us and glare at Joe. "What was your part in all of this?"

Joe shifts forward, mirroring my move. His eyes grow more intense. "I didn't have anything to do with this. My job was to run the accounting department, certify the financial statements and perform financial analysis. That's all I did."

"We found out about the second set of books. The changes that were made to the financial records that were submitted to the bank," I say and watch as Joe starts to nod his head.

"Me too. I was stunned." A flash of anger crosses Joe's face. "It took me three months of secretly going through all the records to figure out that Scott had been changing the financial reports before submitting them to the bank for around six months. Financial reports that had my name on them. My reputation was on the line because he wanted to fudge the accounting and make it look like prepayments and orders were revenues months in advance of when they would be shipped."

"Did you confront him?"

"Of course, I did, and he fired me on the spot. So much for our friendship, but a real friend never would have put me in that situation."

"Why didn't you tell anybody? The bank. The cops."

"Because as Scott so eloquently told me, there's no proof that I wasn't involved. That I wasn't the mastermind behind the changes. It was his word against mine. Me coming forward wouldn't just hurt him. It would ruin me. I could lose my CPA license. No one in the county would want to hire me again. I'm too old to start my career over. So, I walked away."

Gary whistles. "That's ruthless."

"Tell me about it," Joe agrees. "There was nothing left for me in Kimbell, so I left town. After the fire, I wake up and find twenty-five thousand dollars in my bank account sent to me by Scott."

"Out of the blue? That's odd."

"That's what I thought, so I called him."

Gary asks, "Why did he give you the money?"

"He's worried about this interview. He knows that the primary suspects are the owners when a business burns. He couldn't take a chance that something could happen to prevent the insurance proceeds from being paid out. He thought everything I knew about the fake financial statements would complicate things and wanted me to stay away."

I slam a hand on the desk. "Why would you agree to that?"

Joe shrugs. "Because I needed the money. Who's going to hire me when the only employer I've had for the past twenty-five years fired me? My entire professional reputation was tied up and controlled by one man—Scott Robinson."

The hairs on the back of my neck stand on end. Something about the vehemence in his tone strikes me. "Did you do it?" I ask more forcefully than I intend. "I have several witnesses who saw you entering Elm Street Brewery when the entire staff was away on their corporate retreat at Lake Lasso."

"I went back to see if there was any proof that I wasn't the one changing those financial records. Something that would clear my name if the truth came out, but everything had been erased. Scott made sure that there would be no way I could prove I was innocent," Joe insists. "Despite what the whole town thinks, I did not set that fire. But I know exactly who did."

"Who?" Gary asks.

I don't need to hear the answer. I know who Joe will point the finger at, and it's setting off alarm bells in my head.

"Scott Robinson." Joe Little leans back in his chair, barely able to contain the smug expression on his face.

I ponder this new information. A part of me wants to believe Joe Little, use this information, and shut down the case so I can get away from Kimbell for good. I can tell from the look on Gary's face that he believes Joe.

But I can't ignore the nagging suspicion that something's not right.

Why would Joe Little agree to meet with Harlow? He had to

know that would put him right on our radar after he'd successfully vanished for weeks. Maybe that's what he wanted. A chance to get the ultimate revenge on Scott Robinson. Make him look guilty of arson like Scott made him look guilty of financial statement fraud.

Or am I fooling myself?

Maybe I'm looking for a way to make Harlow's pain go away.

CHAPTER 30

~

"ARE YOU EVEN LISTENING ANYMORE?" GARY'S VOICE rises in the conference room, his face perspiring and red from frustration.

"I'm leading this investigation, and I say we wait."

Gary glares at me from the opposite side of the table. We're facing off like two prized boxers ready to go to blows over this. While he doesn't have as much experience as an investigator as I do, Gary isn't one to back down when he thinks we're slipping on something. It's the one trait I usually appreciate in him. Now I'm regretting it as his tenacity has turned on me.

"Let me lay it out for you again," Gary punches a finger against the table with each word. He doesn't have to. I know exactly what

255

he's going to say. It's the same debate we've been having for the past three hours, without either of us budging on our position.

"We have multiple employee statements that all indicate Scott Robinson was the last to leave the office on the day of the fire," Gary starts, backing up to point at the list of key information and evidence we have pinned to a large bulletin board on the wall. "He arrived at the venue at Lake Lasso an hour after everyone else, giving him plenty of time to have set plans in motion to torch his own company." Gary references the timeline we erected across the top of the board. "Now we have Joe Little's statement that the brewery was on the verge of bankruptcy. Scott changed the financial statements to trick the bank so the brewery wouldn't default on the loan. He made it look like Joe had certified them. Joe went back to get proof and caught Scott in his old office spraying a substance on the walls and up toward the air duct."

I drag a hand down my face. "We don't know that we can trust Joe! He has an ax to grind against Scott. The man fired him two weeks before the fire. Joe could've easily sprayed the walls and set the fire himself. We only have his word that he was trespassing on the property to find evidence to clear his name. He can't prove that. What if he's using us to get revenge? For all we know, Scott could have discovered that Joe changed the financial statements without him knowing and fired him because of it."

A look of incredulous skepticism settles on Gary's face.

I'm saying the words, but I don't even believe myself. Yet here I am arguing to give Scott the benefit of the doubt. To buy more time to get definitive proof before we haul him back in here and demand to know the truth.

"I can't believe this," Gary shakes his head, slouching into the chair behind him.

"Do I need to remind you that we're still waiting on a few

dozen test results to come back? We don't have a positive result on whether an accelerant was found in Joe's old office," I say, trying to convince my colleague that I haven't lost my mind. "Joe wants us to believe Scott set the fire when we don't know what was used to do it. Until we know that, it's going to be impossible to piece together how Scott would've had the means to set it."

"We don't need that to bring him in. There's enough suspicious evidence that points to arson, or nobody would've dragged us down here." Gary counters.

"I'm not saying that we don't bring Scott back in for questioning. But I think we need to do more to check out the statement that Joe gave to us. The man's been hiding out for weeks!"

"Because Scott paid him to do that," Gary says. "That's one more data point in a growing list of information that all seem to point to Robinson being behind his brewery's fire. We finally have a motive and proof that he lied to us when we initially interviewed him. So what's gotten into you? Why can't you see we need to arrest him now?"

Not what.

Who.

Harlow.

I'm fighting this hard because I don't want to blow up Harlow's family. I know what I told her days ago when my brain was in control. Now, my brain is weary and losing the war to my heart. Every part of me wants to protect her and help her family. But how can I do that and still do my job?

I can't pretend that the evidence doesn't implicate Scott.

Yet, I can't bring myself to do what needs to be done.

"All I'm saying is that most of this is circumstantial."

"Most arson convictions have to rely on circumstantial

evidence. We investigate the hardest crimes to nail the bad guys. We have to take every break we can get," Gary says. I've never seen him this riled up before. But we've never been on opposite sides of what to do in the past either.

The door of the conference room opens. I glance up and curse under my breath. Byron Magee, the deputy chief, stomps over to the table and drops a single sheet of paper in front of me. I watch it float down to the surface, my eyes skimming the words.

"Judge didn't hesitate to sign off on that warrant," Byron says, then taps Scott Robinson's name listed on the document. "Question is, why did Gary have to call me to get this done? Why didn't you do your job?"

I squirm under his scrutiny.

Byron jerks the paper from the table and extends it to Gary. "Go get him."

Gary gives me a pitiful look, shakes his head, then grabs the paper. "Yes, sir."

Stewing in my seat, I can't believe Gary went behind my back and over my head to Byron. How was I going to explain my way out of this one?

Arms crossed over his chest, Byron studies me for a long minute. The air in the room has grown stale and hot. Every instinct urges me to get out of here, but I can't run out on my job or my responsibilities.

And I can't deny that I've made a colossal mistake.

"Talk to me," Byron says, his face softening a fraction. He's tough but fair and cares about everyone on the team. It's killing me to think I'll disappoint him and Gary with my actions, but for once in my life, I get what Harlow was trying to tell me. There are times when a sacrifice is worth protecting those you love.

I inhale deeply with the realization that I'm in love with Harlow.

It's foolish of me to keep denying what I know is true in my heart.

I love her.

Maybe I have from the moment I got the tattoo on my bicep. Maybe it happened since we reconnected a few weeks ago. The late-night marathon phone calls. The soothing sound of her voice in my ear as I stared at the ceiling wishing she was lying in bed next to me. Her laugh that sent a flutter through my chest and made me smile. The ease in which I could talk to her and feel not only heard but understood. Harlow is everything to me.

We never became an official couple, but she's my new family in my heart. The ache and hole left when Papi died slowly got filled up by her. I can't imagine doing anything that would hurt her. Not now. Not ever.

Yanking the chair closer, Byron sits and rests his elbows on the table. "I get your hesitation. Joe Little is a wild card. He could be the savior we need to blow this case wide open or the joker that tricked us. Right now, that doesn't matter. What matters is Scott Robinson lied to your face. If we had known weeks ago that the brewery was in dire financial trouble, the whole scope of this investigation would've taken a different angle, and you know it. That's a crime."

"I know all that."

"Well, smart guy, if you know all that, why didn't you pull the trigger on getting the arrest warrant?"

"Because I ..." I stop and rub a hand along my left bicep, resting it on the tattoo of Harlow's winery logo. "I should've told you a long time ago that I couldn't lead this investigation."

A wave of concern settles on Byron's face. "Why not?"

"Conflict of interest."

"Come on, Santos. You really think your history with this town would influence your investigation? That's bull, and you know it."

"No," I shake my head. "Not my history with the town. My history with Harlow."

Byron's eyes grow wide as saucers. "What kind of history could you have with Harlow-Rose Robinson?"

Even he knows we are from opposite sides of the tracks and are an unlikely match, but nothing about Harlow's life has ever been conventional, and that includes her attraction and connection to me.

"I'm in love with her."

"Since when?" Byron chuckles, but the sound dies as he realizes I'm serious. "You're in love with Harlow-Rose Robinson at the same time that you're investigating the fire at her family's brewery?"

"Yes, sir," I say, not bothering to go into more details. Nothing I can say would make this situation any better for me.

"Have the two of you been seeing each other? Were y'all together while the investigation was ongoing?"

"Yes, sir."

Byron slams a fist against the table. "Pack up your things. You're suspended effective immediately."

"Yes, sir," I say, standing. It only takes fifteen minutes for me to remove all signs that I was ever part of the investigation from the Kimbell Fire Station, and I'm behind the wheel of my Ford, heading west.

I don't think. I just drive.

Until the Ford runs out of gas a couple of miles from my destination.

I reach over and grab the bottle from the seat next to me, jump out of the truck then slam the door. Stuffing one hand in my pocket, I stroll along the county road.

My head is clear, and I'm surprised to feel no panic or regret for coming clean to my boss. I'm not worried about money, my career, or the mountain of debt that I still need to pay off. Instead, it feels like a weight has lifted, and I'm free. I didn't expect to be following my heart today, but that's exactly what I'm doing.

I glance down at the bottle of Harlow-Rose wine swinging in my hand.

Because of her, I grew to love red wine. In one week, she taught me everything I needed to know about evaluating the quality of the wine, identifying the underlying flavors, and detecting the differences between the various types.

I never forgot because it was one more way to keep her with me after leaving Napa. But these past several weeks prove to me that having Harlow present with me is infinitely better than all my memories. I thought I could walk away from her and do the right thing for my career. For justice.

I was so wrong.

Trudging along the gravel and dust-covered grass lining the county road, I see the last workers leaving. A tall man with a burly beard and dirty overalls jumps out of his small compact car to press a code into the keypad. The gates close, and he drives off. Dirt kicks up from the ground, peppering me in the face as he doesn't give me a second glance.

As soon as his car is out of sight, I walk straight up to the gate and rest a hand against the fence. Classic and elegant, the black wrought iron is still too new to have lost its shine. Maybe it never will. The gold-plated logo rests in the center, sparkling in the late afternoon sun. I use the logo as a step and hoist myself over the fence.

I don't know how long I'll have to wait for her, but it doesn't matter. I walk across the empty parking lot and settle onto one of the oakwood picnic benches. Soft yellow lights cast a warm glow onto my skin as I sit underneath the portico.

Fate brought Harlow and me back together under the most complicated of circumstances.

Part of me thinks being here is foolish.

But what do I have to lose?

I've already blown up my life for her.

I need her to know what I've done, and I need her to know why.

CHAPTER 31

ARLOW-ROSE

I GRIP THE STEERING WHEEL TIGHTER, TRYING TO CALM
the chaotic thoughts running amuck in my mind. The onyx sky
bathes the county road in darkness. I drive along, going well under
the speed limit, with no fear that I'm slowing anyone down.

For the past hour, I've been the only car on the backroads. My
mind has raced through a myriad of thoughts as I try to figure out
what to do next. I should be focused only on Dad. He was arrested
this afternoon for arson, returning from Houston with a high-
powered criminal attorney. It's as if he knew this was going to
happen. The attorney quickly negotiated bail, and I helped Mom
cover the costs. I can't forget the look in Dad's eyes when he

pulled me to the side in the courthouse. The sheer earnest and pleading for me to believe him.

"Rosie, I swear to you that I didn't do this. I didn't set the brewery on fire. Yes, I got in over my head with debt on the place and fudged the financial statements. I fired Joe Little and paid him off so he wouldn't tell anyone and all of that was wrong. I know it. I know I disappointed you. But I did not commit arson. I will prove my innocence. Please tell me you believe me."

As I wrapped my arms around him, hugging him close, I told him what he wanted to hear. "Of course, I believe you. I love you, Dad." Those words seemed to strengthen him, and he walked out of the courtroom with his head held high.

But deep inside, I'm not sure I do believe him. Ever since I left the courthouse, I've been fighting a tug-of-war of anger toward him for putting himself in this situation. He had other options, including letting me help him, but he chose to make bad decision after bad decision.

It took hearing Santos's words coming from my own mother's lips to jolt me to the truth. Dad is the one who needs to own up to all his mistakes and accept the consequences of his actions. As his daughter, nothing will stop me from loving him unconditionally. I can support him and stand by his side, but I should never have tried to interfere with justice.

And I should never have ended things with Santos in my misguided loyalty to Dad. My parents knew all along that Santos was Napa Guy and were on our side, rooting for us to become a couple. They think he's a great man and didn't expect him to give any special favors to us in the investigation.

So why had I?

I shudder with disappointment.

What must he think of me now?

He got a chance to see the real Harlow-Rose, and I know I'm far from what he hoped. The Harlow-Rose who defaults to her money, influence, and power to protect her family, even if they shouldn't be protected. It was the behavior that Santos abhorred. The actions he thought I was above ever doing, and I did them.

I slow the car at a stop sign, check for deer in the dark, and turn left onto the road leading to the winery. All I want is to lose myself in a bottle of wine and soak my aching muscles.

I want to erase every minute of this day and pretend none of it happened.

But mostly, I want to erase all memories of Santos and obliterate the hold he has on my heart.

The best thing I can do for myself is forget how much I love him.

On queue, my mind betrays me and floods my thoughts with visions of Santos, replaying the moments we've shared—from the first moment I laid eyes on him in the courtyard at the Mondavi winery in Napa to seeing him standing outside Elevation Cupcakes to staying up all night talking under the moonlight at my lake house. Every secret shared, every touch, every kiss. I feel it all as if it's happening to me in real-time. I yearn to have more of those moments, but I know in my heart that I won't.

Loneliness infects me and weighs me down with a sadness more profound than any I've ever felt before. I don't just miss that gorgeous face, the dark unruly curls, and the amazing honey eyes. I miss the man who was my safe space. The one I felt so at ease talking to about anything and everything, knowing that some kind of way he'd understand because he just got me.

I'd never felt that way with any other man.

Deep down, I know that I don't want to find it again with someone else.

My heart wants what it can't have.

Santos.

I slow the Range Rover to a stop outside the wrought iron gate. The headlights shine bright on the logo. I choke back a sob as I press the remote. The gate slides open.

I'm not sure how I will ever get over him.

We never got a chance to truly see where things could lead between us because of me. I ruined any possibility that we could have a real relationship. The truth stings.

I drive through the gate then close it behind me before going to the front of the parking lot. The moon overhead shines bright, illuminating the property in a crisp white glow. Stepping out of the SUV, I inhale deeply. The faint scent of grapes clings to the air. A calmness wraps around me, and for the first time today, I sense that everything will be okay.

I will be okay.

Grabbing my purse from the back seat, I take the stone steps two at a time, walk across the portico to the doors, and then stop.

My eyes are drawn to the left as the bag slips from my grasp and lands with a thud onto the ground. I'm frozen, unable to move from the spot.

"I was starting to think you weren't coming." The deep baritone caresses my ears.

"Santos …" I whisper, not sure if he's really here or if my brain is playing some kind of cruel trick on me.

He eases off the bench and stretches his arms over his head, giving me a tantalizing view of his sculpted abs from underneath the wrinkled button-down white shirt. My throat is dry, but I force myself to swallow as he takes a step toward me.

I hold my breath.

"Harlow …"

He comes closer until he's within inches of me. I look down and try to calm my pounding heart. The heady, intoxicating scent of his cologne wafts around me. He places a finger underneath my chin and tilts my head to face him.

Dark circles ring his eyes, but there is a sparkle in his gaze as he watches me. The honey eyes caress my face as if he's trying to memorize every contour.

"You're so beautiful, you know that?" Santos asks.

I shake my head. "Why are you here?"

"Oh, come on," Santos gives a sly smile. An adorable expression that melts my heart. "You're not the slightest bit happy to see me?"

I don't allow myself to hope. Not until I understand what's going on.

"Shouldn't you be back in Kimbell?"

"I'm exactly where I *should* be." He moves closer, resting his forehead against mine as his hands stroke up and down my back. Everything about Santos being here with me is right, even though I don't understand how it's possible.

I place my hands on his chest, forcing distance between us. "What's going on?"

"I've been suspended from my job."

"Oh God, no. Did they find out about …?" I can't finish the sentence because there is no us anymore. My mind races as I remember that Santos wasn't around when Dad was arrested or at the courthouse for the bail hearing. Officer Gary Logan was there, and other members of the Fire Marshal's Office, but Santos wasn't. At the time, I thought he stayed away to make it easier for me.

"Yes, my boss found out about our relationship. That we were together while I was leading the investigation, and he suspended me. Your Dad will be arrested if he hasn't been already—"

"Why didn't you explain that we're … over. Make them understand that things ended between us."

"Because in my heart," he presses my hand over his chest. The strong thumps of his heart tickle my palm. "We're not over. We'll never be over."

My body floods with the most exquisite warmth. "Santos."

"Byron didn't find out. I told him. I chose love over justice. I chose you."

My hands slide along his forearms and rest on his biceps. "Love?"

"I'm in love with you," Santos says.

His words ricochet through my body, and I'm not sure I heard him correctly. I force myself to focus as he continues to speak.

"I want a relationship with you." His hands cradle my face. "I want that more than I need to be the one to solve the arson investigation at the brewery. The evidence will be what it is, but I can't be the one to hurt you or your family that way. Not when every part of me wants to be by your side, supporting you through this difficult time."

His thumb swipes at a tear rolling down my cheek.

"You're not upset with me for what I was going to do?" I ask.

"No," Santos shakes his head. "You were trying to do everything in your power to help your dad. I did the same thing with Papi when he was sick. Maybe not exactly the same situation. But if Papi had gotten in trouble with the law, I know my actions wouldn't have been any different from yours. I would've fought just as hard to help him."

"But I wish I hadn't. I shouldn't have put you in that position. I don't want you to have to choose between your job and me."

"It's too late. My choice is already made."

"Won't you regret it?"

"Harlow, we've always gotten each other. That kind of connection doesn't break just because we don't see eye-to-eye on a situation. It took me days to realize that. To realize that I love you. Now that I know, I don't want to lose a chance to be with you," he says, a slight frown creasing his forehead. "But is it already too late? I'm not involved in the investigation anymore, but the evidence I've been gathering for weeks is a huge part of the case being built against your dad. Does that change the way you feel about … me?"

I laugh as tears flow down my face. "Never. Mom helped me to see that you were right. I can't try to stand in the way of Dad being held accountable for his actions. She told me that if Dad really did this, he has to come clean and take his punishment. We can't try to stop that."

"Smart lady," Santos says, smirking. "I'd like to meet her, you know, when you take me home to meet your folks."

I stare at him, my mouth slightly open. "Are you serious right now?"

"Serious enough to risk losing my job and my livelihood to ask you to give me another chance."

"Because you love me."

"With every cell in my body, I love you, Harlow-Rose."

I love the way the sound of my full name tumbles from his tongue.

He takes a step back, dropping his arms to his sides. I instantly miss the warmth of his touch and the closeness of him. "I'm not expecting that your feelings have progressed as fast as mine, but I can look in your eyes and tell that—"

"I love you, too," I say. I tremble from relief, finally able to tell him exactly how I feel. Saying the words that I didn't think I'd ever get a chance to speak. The truth was out, and knowing that my feelings were reciprocated had me floating.

"You sure about that?" His eyes narrow, a playful glint in them.

I nod my head quickly.

"Even if I'm broke and unemployed?"

Laughing, I say, "I'm pretty sure I could find something around here for you to do."

"You'd be my lady and my boss," Santos says, raising an eyebrow. "Why do I love the sound of that?"

I slip my arms around his neck and press my body against his. "Why do I have the feeling you'd love anything I said right about now?"

"Because it's true. So what else do you want to say to me?"

"Kiss me."

"Absolutely love that. Yes, boss," Santos gives me a huge grin, then devours my lips with the most passionate and intense kiss of my life.

CHAPTER 32

Santos

I HEAR HER SOFT FOOTSTEPS DESCENDING DOWN THE stairs behind me, but I don't turn around. Leaning onto the bar, my fingers squeeze the edges of the yellowed and frayed envelope. My name is written in scrawling, jagged block letters. Papi's last words to me are inside.

After everything that happened with Harlow and me over the past few hours, I'm ready to close this chapter of my life. Let go of the past, the pain, and the guilt I've been holding onto for two years. Those burdens have no place in the perfect future I want to build with Harlow. But the first step is finding out what is inside this envelope. What had my father wanted me to know in the last hours of his life?

Her soft fingers caress the nape of my neck, then lace through my hair, stroking my scalp. I lean back into her touch and exhale.

"It's no fun waking up without you by my side," Harlow whispers into my ear, then peppers the side of my face with sizzling kisses. "Why are you down here so early? The sun hasn't even come up yet."

"Couldn't sleep."

She wraps her arms around my neck and peers over my shoulder. The weight of her body against mine is like heaven. I stretch my free hand to stroke the side of her face.

"Is that what I think it is?"

"Yeah," I turn slightly and maneuver her in front of me. Wrapping my arms around her, I rest my chin on her shoulder and hold the envelope where we can both see it. "I'm ready to see what's inside. But I don't want to do it without you."

She kisses me on the cheek. "I'm right here and ready whenever you are."

I inhale a sharp breath, then blow it out quickly. Flipping the envelope over, I hesitate. My heart pounds in my chest so hard I know Harlow can feel it. I can't turn back now. I need to go through with this, even if the contents will shatter everything I believed about Papi's death. Yet, I can't bring myself to open it.

"Do you want me to?"

I drop the envelope and wrap my arms around her. "Would you?"

She nods and picks it up from the counter. Her delicate, manicured nail slides underneath the flap, easing it open. Folded pages bulge from the top as she slides them out and lays them flat on the surface of the bar.

"What in the world?" I mutter, reaching for the documents. It's not at all what I expected.

"Looks like a deed to some property," Harlow says.

I scan the document. Tito Estrada is listed as the owner of the house and the five acres of lakefront land that the house rests on. I flip the page and see that Mrs. Crockett transferred ownership to Papi in exchange for one dollar.

I shake my head. "He owned the house and the land. He owned it for years and kept helping Mrs. Crockett all that time when he didn't need to." I point to the date the transfer of deed was signed. "Papi had been living in Kimbell for only two or three years at that time. I thought he worked for her in exchange for living in the house, but this deed proves that wasn't true. Why would he put up with her if she'd already sold him the house and the land?"

"From what you told me about him, that's the kind of man he was. Mrs. Crockett was devastated and lonely after her husband died, and she was horrible at making friends. Your dad could've seen that and worked for her to give her friendship over the years."

"So, she thanked him by selling him property that's worth a few hundred thousand dollars for a measly buck."

"That's what it's worth now, but it wasn't back then. That's way before the explosion of property values and houses along Lake Lasso."

I pause, letting this all sink in.

The deed in this envelope means I own land worth more than all the debt I racked up trying to save Papi from that wretched illness. It's my ticket to getting out from a mountain of bills and starting with a clean slate, even if I lose my job as an arson investigator. There might be money left over for me to forge a new path, although I don't have the slightest idea of what that could be.

"Santos."

"Yeah," I say, snapping out of my thoughts.

"There's no way of knowing when your dad put this deed in the envelope for you. He could've done it years ago, knowing how you felt about the way Mrs. Crockett treated him," Harlow says.

"Which means I still don't have any answers about why Papi's life ended. If it was truly what he wanted or if he was manipulated into giving up. No last letter. No suicide note."

"How do you feel about that?"

With Harlow in my arms, it's too hard to have any negative emotions. She brings happiness and joy to my life that outweighs and outshines everything else.

Turning Harlow to face me, I lean in and say, "I feel ready to let it go."

"Just like that?"

"Wasn't it you that told me I might not ever get the answers I'm looking for? I need to figure out how to live the rest of my life without them because that's what Papi would want for me."

"I might have said something profound like that. Surprised you listened that closely."

"I listen to everything you've ever said to me," I say, brushing my lips across her forehead. "And I know how to live without having those answers. It's by embracing what Papi always wanted for me—the better life he worked so hard to ensure I have. Life doesn't get any better than sharing it with you, Harlow."

She laughs, a sweet sound that delights my ears. "Are you trying to make me fall more in love with you?"

"Is it working?" I wink at her.

"Absolutely," she says, then silences all the guilt and worry that I've lived with over the past two years with a sensual kiss.

EPILOGUE

ARLOW-ROSE

~

"WHAT DO YOU THINK THIS IS ABOUT?" DAD ASKS AS HE looks at Santos.

Santos lays down the hammer and nails he'd been using to construct a display shelf for my wines inside the booth for Founder's Day. "It's unusual, to say the least. I've never done something like this after an arrest."

I lean into Santos, needing to feel his strength and support. Dad's lawyer called minutes ago saying that the arson investigator wants to meet with him now. His lawyer is at the Fire Station, and we should all walk over.

Santos and I have been working alongside Mom and Dad all

morning as we put the finishing touches on my booth for the Founder's Day market in two days. The distraction was good for all of us, and it gave me a chance to introduce Santos as my new man in a less stressful environment. I shouldn't have been worried, though. His charismatic personality won them over within minutes, and it feels like he's always been part of our family. The mood had been playful and festive until Dad got the call from his lawyer.

"Scott, what's the point in standing here speculating," Mom says, slipping her hand in Dad's. "Let's go over there and find out what's going on."

"Your lawyer said it was okay for all of us to come with you?" I ask.

"Yes, he said all of us should come," Dad says, then gives Santos a warm smile. "You, too, Santos. I have a feeling it won't be long before you're officially family."

"Dad!" I say, stunned at his ability to joke at a time like this. "Please don't put any pressure on him."

"Trust me, it's no pressure at all," Santos says, then leans in to give me a quick kiss on the lips. "Who are we meeting with?"

"Officer Strom is who requested the meeting," Dad says.

"He's the lead investigator they brought in to take my place."

"I still don't think you should've been suspended because you fell in love with my beautiful daughter. Seems harsh," Mom says.

"It's protocol," Santos says, flashing Mom his devastating smile. "I know Strom. He's from Montgomery County and a real good guy. I can't imagine he found an issue with anything we did while I was leading the case, but who knows."

"Guess there's only one way to find out," Dad says, then leads the way down the sidewalk next to Bell Park. We walk in silence behind my parents until we reach the Fire Station.

Walking into the conference room on the third floor, I stare at the three men sitting next to Dad's lawyer. The demeanor is relaxed and almost pleasant as we take our seats opposite them. Dad's lawyer gives him a smile and a nod.

I steal a quick glance at Santos, and he looks as confused as I feel.

After a round of introductions, Strom clears his throat, then says, "We are officially dropping the charges against Scott Robinson in the matter of the arson at Elm Street Brewery."

My heart leaps as Mom gasps.

"New evidence has been identified that exonerates Mr. Robinson in this case."

"Do you know who did it?" Dad asks.

"Yes, we have arrested Joe Little," Officer Strom says. "We received results from the lab on several other soil, and debris samples collected from Joe Little's office and identified the accelerant used to set the blaze."

"Samples collected when I was leading the investigation?" Santos asks.

"Yes, but I've gone through your work Estrada, and it was top notch as usual. No signs that any steps or protocols were broken or that you unduly influenced the evidence because of your relationship with Ms. Robinson," Strom says. "In subsequent interviews conducted by my team, Mr. Little revealed details that could only have been known by the person who set the fire, although he tried to convince us that he saw you doing these things, Mr. Robinson. Ultimately, the case was broken wide open when we obtained security footage from a small Farm & Feed shop in El Paso showing Joe Little purchasing the accelerant used to start the fire."

"I can't believe he did this to us," Mom says, shaking her head.

"He's in custody now, but I wanted to inform you before it hit the media," Strom explains.

I turn to Santos with a bright smile on my face. "It's over!"

I fling myself into his arms as Mom hugs Dad just as fiercely.

Hours later, we're back at my parent's home for an impromptu celebration of Dad being exonerated. Just about every Kimbell resident is crowded inside. Gwen brought over a mountain of food from her cafe, and Dad brought out his last few cases of Elm Beer for everyone to enjoy.

I manage to steal Santos away from Alma and pull him outside.

"I thought we were done sneaking around," Santos says, wrapping his arms around my waist as I lead him to the rose garden.

"We need a little bit of time out of the spotlight," I say. "People seemed to forget that this party is to celebrate Dad being cleared of the charges and not to introduce us as the new couple of Kimbell."

"The new, hottest couple of Kimbell," Santos says with a wink.

"You don't even live in Kimbell."

"Neither do you."

"My lake house is almost ready. I'll be living here soon enough," I remind him, slapping a hand against his muscular bicep. I pause to stare at my logo on his arm, then rub my fingers across it. "And technically, you own property here in Kimbell. Have you thought about what you're going to do with it?"

"I have a meeting with Zaire booked for next week to see what kind of deal I can get. The property value is higher than I thought," Santos says, a smile playing at the corners of his lips. "I'm still stunned that Papi is going to be the one to pay off all my debt and help me get back on solid footing, financially. It's amazing."

"I'm happy for you. I know what a strain that was on you."

"And on … us."

"It was one of the reasons you didn't want to start a relationship with me."

"How dumb was that?" Santos says, pulling me into his arms. "How could I have ever thought I could be without you?"

"I don't know, but I'm really glad you came to your senses." I wrap my arms around his neck. "I'm glad I came to mine, too."

"Now about me not living in Kimbell," Santos says, a playful glint in his eyes. "I talked to Alma earlier, and she can give me a great monthly rate on a room at Crockett Manor. But, I told her I needed to think about it."

"You would move to Kimbell for me?" My heart flutters, knowing what a big deal this would be for Santos. Not only does he battle the painful memories of watching his father's illness here, but he also made a lot of enemies when he pursued charges against Dr. Jones and had him sent to prison. There were still a lot of people in town who didn't want him here at all because of that. Picking up his life to live here to be close to me was a huge sacrifice. "It won't be easy for you living here."

Santos trails a finger down my cheek. "Don't you know by now that I would do anything for you?"

My knees go weak as I stare into his gorgeous face. The tenderness and love I see reflected in his honey eyes bring tears to my own.

"I'll face the wrath of Jasmine Jones and anyone else to live in this town if it'll make you happy."

"Having you here with me would most definitely make me the happiest woman in the world."

"Then that settles it."

I squeal with joy and jump into his arms. Santos spins me

around and around as I pepper his face with light kisses. Dizzy from the turns and brimming with excitement as he puts me back on solid ground, I gaze at him and say, "I love you so much, Santos."

"Not more than I love you, Harlow-Rose."

~

I hope you enjoyed Harlow-Rose and Santos's love story.

Next up to find love in Kimbell, Texas is Santos's best friend Ronan O'Reilly. Ronan is a single dad with bad luck in love and a desperate need for a nanny to take care of his precocious twin sons. But his luck is about to change when Emma Young blows into town.

Check out the next book in the Kimbell Texas Sweet Romances …
TRUSTING LUCK!

To keep up with me and the latest about my books and new releases, join my mailing list here.

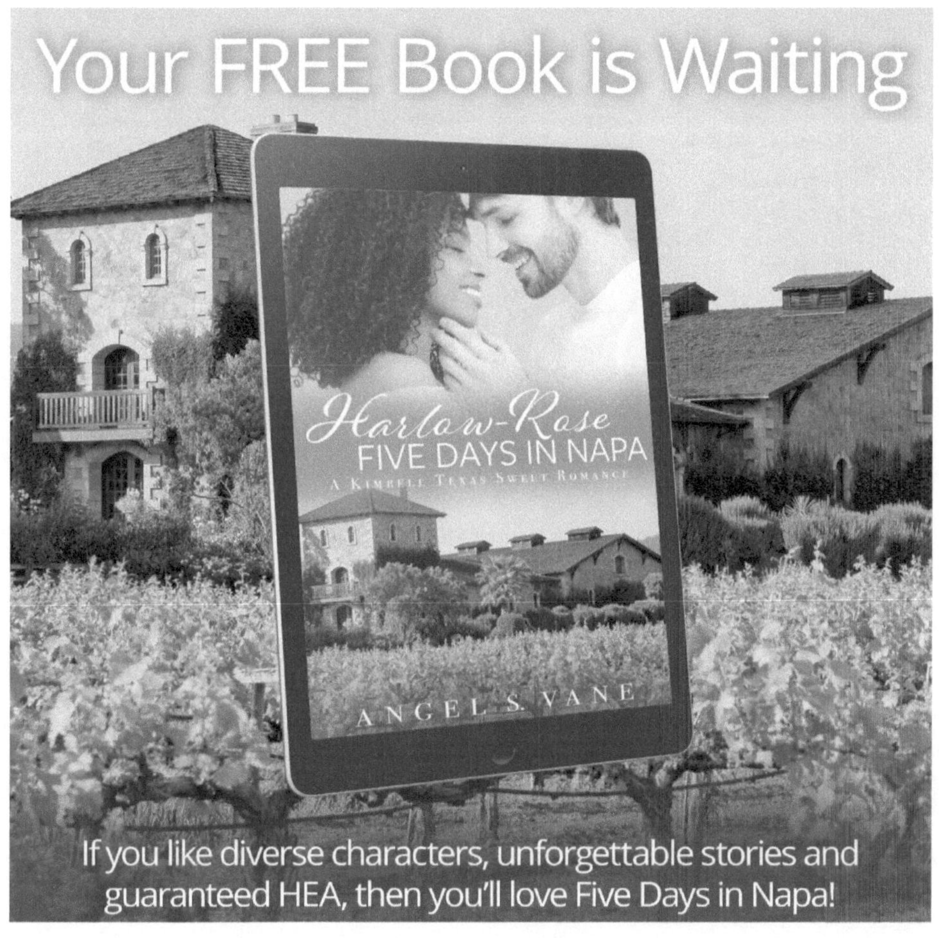

Want to know what happened in Napa Valley when Harlow-Rose and Santos first met? Read all the details in the novella, *Harlow-Rose Five Days in Napa* for FREE.

GET MY FREE BOOK NOW

https://BookHip.com/PLWQZRK

Also by Angel S. Vane

KIMBELL TEXAS SWEET ROMANCES

A series of stand-alone novels that celebrate diverse characters, explore
unforgettable challenges, and guarantee a satisfying happily-ever-after.

Tempting Fate

Trusting Luck

About the Author

Angel S. Vane never imagined she'd stumble into becoming an author. An avid fan of books her whole life combined with an active imagination were the right ingredients to embark on a single goal of completing one book.

Now she's written several books and has tapped into her love of Jane Austen novels by writing her own brand of satisfyingly sweet romances. Learn more at Angel's website.

About the Publisher

BONZAIMOON BOOKS

BonzaiMoon Books is a family-run, artisanal publishing company created in the summer of 2014. We publish works of fiction in various genres. Our passion and focus is working with authors who write the books you want to read, and giving those authors the opportunity to have more direct input in the publishing of their work.

For more information:
www.bonzaimoonbooks.com
info@bonzaimoonbooks.com

facebook.com/BonzaiMoonBooks

About the Author

Claire Boston fell in love with romance and romantic suspense at eleven when she discovered her mother's stash of Nora Roberts novels. Like Nora, she writes series set around families or groups of friends with a guaranteed happy ending.

She loves travelling and learning about new cultures and interesting vocations which she then weaves into her writing.

When Claire's not at the computer typing her stories she can be found creating her own handmade journals, swinging on a sidecar, or in the garden attempting to grow something other than weeds.

Claire lives in Western Australia with her husband, who loves even her most annoying quirks and is currently learning how to knit. You can find her complete book list on her website www.claireboston.com/books. You can connect with Claire through Facebook and Twitter, or join her reader group

(http://www.claireboston.com/reader-group/).

Also by Claire Boston

Romance

The Texan Quartet
What Goes on Tour
All that Sparkles
Under the Covers
Into the Fire

The Flanagan Sisters
Break the Rules
Change of Heart
Blaze a Trail
Place to Belong

Romantic Suspense

The Blackbridge Series
Nothing to Fear
Nothing to Gain
Nothing to Hide
Nothing to Lose
Shelter
Shield
Harbour
Protect

Aussie Heroes: Retribution Bay
Return to Retribution Bay
Trapped in Retribution Bay
Escape to Retribution Bay
Secrets in Retribution Bay

Non-fiction

The Beginner Writer's Toolkit
Self-Editing